THE AQUILA PROJECT

By the same author

The Dried-Up Man
The Dark Kingdom
The Devereaux Inheritance
The Haunted Governess
The Advocate's Wife
The Hansa Protocol
The Ancaster Demons
Web of Discord
Evil Holds the Key
The Gold Masters
The Unquiet Sleeper

THE AQUILA
PROJECT

Norman Russell

ROBERT HALE · LONDON

© Norman Russell 2007
First published in Great Britain 2007

ISBN 978-0-7090-8437-2

Robert Hale Limited
Clerkenwell House
Clerkenwell Green
London EC1R 0HT

www.halebooks.com

The right of Norman Russell
to be identified as author of this work has been
asserted by him in accordance with the
Copyright, Designs and Patents Act 1988

2 4 6 8 10 9 7 5 3 1

Typeset in 11/15pt Sabon
Printed and bound in Great Britain by
Biddles Limited, King's Lynn

Contents

Wet Day in Berlin

Thursday 17 May 1894

S IR CHARLES NAPIER, Her Majesty's Permanent Under-Secretary
of State for Foreign Affairs, was no stranger to the Imperial
German Foreign Office in Berlin. He had contrived, over a period
of six or seven years, to attach himself to various missions from
Great Britain sent to soothe suspicions about the British
Government's European policy, and to hear plausible explanations
of the expansionist ambitions of the German Empire.

Six years earlier, in the June of 1888, the young William II had
succeeded his amiable father Frederick as King of Prussia and
Emperor of Germany. A zealous patriot and unstable hothead, he
had needed a lot of managing, especially after his dramatic
dismissal of the wily old chancellor, Bismarck, in 1890.

Was 'managing' the right word? Certainly, these missions were
a valuable part of Britain's attempt at curbing some of the more
tiresome excesses of the young German Emperor; with respect to
his German advisers, the word 'manipulation' was probably more
apposite.

There must be fifty people here, at least, thought Napier. These
lunch-time diplomatic receptions are proving popular, not only
here in Berlin, but also in Paris and Vienna. Perhaps we could do
something similar in London?

Ah! Here was Paul Claus now, standing uncertainly at the door, and looking round the magnificent salon as though searching for someone. How insignificant he looked! 'Mousy' was the word that came to mind. It was a good disguise for a secret agent. He was supposedly a government clerk, a staunch German citizen, who had been appointed a courier of the Prussian Court of Requests – hence his presence here today, in the Wilhelmstrasse. But he was more than that.

What wretched weather! Napier stood at one of the long windows, half-hidden by green velvet curtains, and looked out at the heavy summer rain falling vertically on to the gardens of the Imperial Chancellery, and the green expanse of the Tiergarten beyond. It was a fine city, at once grand and gracious, but everywhere on earth looked miserable in the rain.

'My dear Napier, you're moping! Why do you not mix? We don't see enough of you in Berlin. You should come more often. Let me get you something to drink.'

'Count von Donath! How kind of you to notice me. How are you? I've not seen you since '92. Not to speak to, at any rate.'

'I'm very well, Napier. You know I had pneumonia last winter? Touch and go, apparently. The Kaiser sent his personal physician to tend me. He's very kind, you know; for a man scarce past thirty, he's very considerate of others.'

Napier regarded his companion with interest. It was well-nigh impossible to tell from his well-studied public demeanour whether the man was a friend or an enemy. That long, cadaverous face, that clipped black moustache – they gave the count a sinister appearance, but the man's voice was soft and purring, and his blue eyes were bold and seemingly without guile. But a man of Napier's experience knew that von Donath was one of the most dangerous men in Europe.

Count von Donath was President of the Prussian Court of Requests, and so Paul Claus's superior. (Where was Claus now? There he was, talking to one of the Rumanian attachés. He was moving nearer, waiting for Count von Donath to go.)

The count snapped his fingers, and a liveried waiter approached with a trayful of tall, fluted glasses of champagne. It was very good champagne, thought Napier. Probably Krug. He sipped his glass with a connoisseur's appreciation.

Count von Donath thought to himself: Napier's a handsome, distinguished fellow, but his air of friendly innocence doesn't deceive me. He's come to Berlin far too often over the last few years for his visits to be nothing more dangerous than mere diplomatic courtesy. Well, Napier, I've got your measure. I know quite well why you're here today, and what to do about it.

'I thought the Chancellor might have been here,' said Napier. 'In England there would be someone weighty at functions of this nature to add *gravitas* to the proceedings. Someone like Salisbury, or Aberdeen.'

Count von Donath laughed, and drained his glass.

'The Chancellor? No, he sent a message to the Marshal of the Diplomatic Corps to say that he was very much occupied with official duties this morning. But the Kaiser sends warm greetings, which is very much appreciated.'

Napier thought: Is von Donath playing cat and mouse with me, or is the man simply being civil? He'll know as well as I do that the Kaiser and the Chancellor will have left the gathering to its own devices, so that rumours and hints could be exchanged, and verbal agreements made between the representatives of potentially warring countries. From such hints and rumours arose the foundations of much of the secret diplomacy aimed at reconciling the self-interest of nations with the stability of the European balance of power.

Paul Claus was only feet away, now. If von Donath remained talking much longer, the opportunity of hearing what Claus had to say would be lost.

'Napier,' said Count von Donath, 'I must leave you. I can see the French Ambassador beckoning to me. I wonder what he wants? You're returning to England tomorrow, aren't you? Early next week, you'll find that a new Second Secretary will have arrived at Prussia House – Doctor Franz Kessler. He leaves for London on Saturday. He'll be anxious to present himself to you, I've no doubt. I *must* go. Let me wish you God speed!'

As soon as the count had gone, Sir Charles Napier turned to the nondescript man who was now standing at his side. Herr Paul Claus had a habit of looking away from you when he was talking, which sometimes made it difficult to catch what he was saying. He dressed soberly in unrelieved black, which allowed him to blend inconspicuously with the assembled company, but Napier had always considered him to be a fish out of water.

Paul Claus claimed Alsatian ancestry to account for his willingness to spy on his native Prussia, but Napier thought that it was love of secrecy, and an equal love of money, that motivated him. There were rumours that Claus was a double agent. Such rumours were enough to make Napier privately determine that this would be Paul Claus's last assignment for the British Foreign Office.

'Well?' asked Sir Charles Napier.

'You were right, Sir Charles,' said Claus, looking across the crowded salon as he spoke. 'It looks like yet another Polish secret society, formed with malignant designs against Tsar Alexander. I spoke to a man in Königsberg who told me that they were dedicated to terror as a means of effecting change. We've heard it all before, but that doesn't mean that it isn't a threat.'

'Can you tell me any names?'

'None, but the man in Königsberg thought that some of the old Polish nobility would be involved.'

'Very likely,' said Napier drily. 'It's the nobility who foment these romantic fantasies of Polish independence. The peasantry are too busy trying to survive to take much interest in the matter. Anything else?'

'Two phrases, sir. I've heard them whispered in various places that I visit. One is "The Aquila Project". I've no idea what it means, but it's a name bandied about in the sub-world of discontents. The other is "The Thirty". Thirty men, perhaps – or thirty pieces of silver, for all I know. There's something else, too. They have a token, a sort of badge of membership. I've secured one of them, and have it here in my pocket—'

'Not here, Claus,' said Napier. 'I've no doubt that a number of curious eyes are watching us at this very moment. Here's the French military attaché making a beeline for me. I suppose I must be civil to him. You'd better circulate a bit. I'll send a man to your lodgings in Landsbergerstrasse this afternoon. You can give him this token then.'

'Very well, sir. Do you want me to probe further?'

'No. No, thank you. I'll take those snippets of information back with me to London, and work on them from there. Thank you, Herr Claus. Call at the British Embassy when you find it convenient – after I've left Berlin tomorrow. You'll find a very pleasing remuneration waiting there for you.'

Just after two o'clock the crowd of guests poured out of the Imperial Foreign Office building and into the Wilhelmstrasse. The rain had slackened, but the wide granite pavements glistened, and in the sky above them the sullen black clouds had been rent here and there to reveal patches of weak, cold blue.

Count von Donath stood on the steps for a moment, watching Sir Charles Napier as he hurried away towards the nearby British Embassy, and then joined the throng and press of umbrella-wielding Berliners moving in a typically ordered phalanx towards Unter den Linden.

A man in the crowd uttered a muffled cry, stumbled, and fell to the ground. The procession of citizens came to a sudden halt, and a number of people bent down to assist the unfortunate man. What was it? A fit? Was he, perhaps an epileptic? A man carrying a black bag pushed his way through the crowd.

'Stand back, please!' he cried. 'I am a doctor.'

Count von Donath stooped down, and quietly retrieved something that must have fallen from the stricken man's pocket, or perhaps from his hand. He quickly slipped it into his right-hand glove. The doctor looked up at his companions, his face stern, almost accusing.

'This man is dead. He has been stabbed in the back. Does anyone know who he is?'

Yes, several people knew him. He was a government courier, with rooms in the Landsbergerstrasse, a man called Claus. Herr Paul Claus. Look! Here was a policeman. He'd know what steps to take.

Count von Donath continued on his way. He had business at the Reichs Bank, and this particular walk was a favourite of his. Besides, it had become hot and oppressive at the reception, and the cold air of the wet Berlin day would clear his mind.

What had Claus been saying to Sir Charles Napier? And how had he obtained that token? Well, whatever he'd said to Napier, it was of no import now. Thanks to the ruthless vigilance of Franz Kessler, Herr Claus's days of gossiping treachery were over.

As Count von Donath passed the new cathedral and crossed over the Kaiser Wilhelm Bridge, he took a blood-caked knife from his pocket, and dropped it into the swirling waters of the River Spree.

1

Tower Bridge Day

30 June 1894

DETECTIVE INSPECTOR ARNOLD BOX hurried out of Whitehall Place and crossed the cobbled square fronting the complex of old, smoke-blackened buildings known as King James's Rents. For a fleeting moment his mind conjured up a vision of the magnificent buildings of New Scotland Yard, rising in all their glory of red brick and Portland stone at the Whitehall end of the Embankment.

Norman Shaw's triumph of modern design had been opened three years earlier, and the Metropolitan Police had migrated there from their dingy headquarters in Great Scotland Yard, taking Sir Edward Bradford, the Chief Commissioner, and his 15,000 officers, with them.

Sir Edward had 598 inspectors, and Arnold Box was proud to be one of them, but it had not been his good fortune to move into New Scotland Yard. There was still a goodly number of officers remaining in Whitehall Place, and also here, in the sooty, mildewed obscurity of the Rents, fifty yards on across the cobbles.

As Inspector Box hurried up the worn steps of 2 King James's Rents, a neighbouring clock struck the quarter after eight. So that was it. He was late, and no doubt Old Growler would have something to say about it. Well, he'd make up the lost fifteen minutes at the end of the shift.

He began to divest himself of his smart fawn overcoat as he crossed the vestibule towards the glazed swing doors of his ground-floor office. He could glimpse the small fire burning in the grate, and the massive figure of his sergeant, Jack Knollys, peering at one of the many notices stuck to the big fly-blown mirror. Would he reach the sanctuary of his office before his lateness was detected?

'Is that you, Box?' called a voice from above. 'I thought you weren't coming in, today! Up here, if you please. I shan't keep you more than five minutes.'

Superintendent Mackharness stood on the half-landing at the top of the stairs, looking down at Box with what he recognized as his master's air of patient resignation. The Superintendent was a man well over sixty, with a yellowish face adorned with snow-white mutton-chop whiskers. His thin grey hair was neatly brushed and combed. His civilian frock coat was smart and spotless.

Box struggled back into his overcoat, hurried up the steep flight of stairs, and entered his master's dark front office on the first floor. As always, the room smelt strongly of stale gas and mildew. Old Growler had stationed himself behind his massive carved desk, upon which he had arranged a number of papers and folders.

'Sit down in that chair, will you, Box,' said Mackharness, 'and listen to what I have to say. Three minutes ago, I heard the clock in the turret of Craven Street Brewery chime a quarter past eight. Punctuality is something that those in positions of authority should be particularly assiduous in observing. It sets an example to one's inferiors. It inculcates habits of precision and – and, er, regularity—'

'I'm very sorry, sir. If I might explain—'

'Yes, well, never mind all that, Box. Now you're here at last, I can tell you what I want you to do. Tomorrow, as you know, will see the opening of the new Tower Bridge, which, I may say, will be acknowledged by all as one of the greatest engineering triumphs of the age. The thirtieth of June, 1894, Box, will for ever be remembered for the public inauguration of that great – er – achievement. Yes. Now, what was it I wanted to tell you? These constant interruptions of yours make me lose the thread of what I'm saying.'

'About the Tower Bridge, sir.'

'Yes, that's right. When I came in here this morning – at six o'clock – I found a letter waiting for me. It had been delivered by courier an hour earlier. It came from Superintendent Keating of "J" Division at Bethnal Green Road. One of his detective inspectors has apparently uncovered a plot to explode a bomb in the engine room of the new Tower Bridge, on its southern approach, at the very moment when the Royal procession is crossing it, which will be soon after twelve noon tomorrow.'

Arnold Box sighed. Here we go again, he thought. Whenever a time of general rejoicing comes, some fool will want to throw something more lethal than a spanner in the works.

'Does Mr Keating take the threat seriously, sir? We've had one or two crackpots recently threatening to do things to the new bridge.'

'Mr Keating takes the matter very seriously, Box, and he's a man whose judgement in these matters I respect. Besides, the detective officer who uncovered the lair of this man was Inspector Fitzgerald. As you know, he has a knack of unearthing people of that sort.'

Mackharness's eyes met Box's briefly, and then returned to one of the documents on his desk. That glance had made a statement about Inspector Fitzgerald's methods of investigation that neither man would have cared to put into plain words.

'Mr Keating enclosed a photograph of the suspected bomber, or assassin, or whatever he is. He's been under observation for the past three weeks. His name, apparently, is Anders Grunwalski.'

Mackharness rummaged among the papers on his desk and

produced a photograph, which he handed to Box. 'That's the man,' he said. 'I don't know him, but you may have seen him before.'

It was not a portrait study, but a candid image of a man standing at a coffee stall, a man in the process of handing over some money to the stall holder. The photograph had evidently been taken without the man's knowledge. About thirty, thought Box, with a long, narrow face; good features, dark hair, respectably dressed. An artisan of some sort, perhaps. There was something earnest about his deportment.

'No, I've never seen him before, sir. Or heard of him, either. He's a new rogue for the gallery. I know where he is in that photograph, though: he's standing near the opening to Hoxton Square where it turns off Bowling Green Walk in Shoreditch. What do you want me to do, sir?'

'Do? I'm not sure that I want you to do anything, yet,' Mackharness replied. 'I've drafted a little plan of action for you tomorrow – you and Sergeant Knollys, that is – but I don't want to waste your time over what may be a mere flash in the pan. You see, the security of tomorrow's event is entirely in the hands of the City of London Police. It's nothing to do with us in the Metropolitan Force. Lieutenant Colonel Smith, their commissioner, had very kindly furnished us with a complete plan of the route, together with details of his dispositions, and I've already put those out for consultation and information in Room 6 along the passage.'

'So City will be out in force?'

'Yes. There'll be vast numbers of their officers stationed everywhere along the routes and in the immediate vicinity of the bridge. And then, of course, the army will be out in force – the 2nd Norfolk, the 8th Hussars, the good old 3rd Grenadiers, and the 1st and 2nd Life Guards. It's all supposed to be pomp and pageantry, Box, but of course it's really preventive security. Very clever, you know.

'However, City has agreed with our assistant commissioner

that this business of Grunwalski should be left to the Metropolitan Police, and I want Sergeant Knollys to accompany a special detail provided by Southwark Division, who are going to secrete themselves in the first boiler room of the Tower Bridge. The information gathered by "J" reveals that the attempt to blow up the bridge will be made by the placing of an infernal device in the boiler room nearest to the Surrey end of the bridge approach. Knollys will be there to render any assistance necessary. As soon as you've left me this morning, I'll make the necessary arrangements.'

'And me, sir?'

'Well, Box, I want you to take up a position on the roof of Carmody's Wool Depot at the end of Pickled Herring Street, tomorrow, and survey as much of the scene as possible. Take some powerful field-glasses with you. From that height you should be able to see all the southern approaches to the bridge, and a good part of the bridge itself. Keep a watching brief, and stay alert for anything suspicious. You may see this Anders Grunwalski approach the scene, or you may spot an accomplice. Be up there on Carmody's roof by ten o'clock tomorrow morning, and leave as soon as the Royal personages leave. I think that's all, Box. It's not a great affair, but it would be no bad thing if Scotland Yard were involved.'

'If that's all, sir,' said Box, 'I'll go downstairs and tell Sergeant Knollys about it.'

'I've already told him,' Mackharness replied. There was a slight smirk of satisfaction on his face as he added, 'Sergeant Knollys was here on the dot of seven-forty-five.'

Arnold Box rose to go. The guvnor was entitled to his little victory. As he turned towards the door, Mackharness put out a hand to stop him.

'Don't go yet, Box,' he said. 'Sit down there for a while longer. I shall be there tomorrow, you know, as a guest of my friend Lord Maurice Vale Rose. We shall be sitting in the northern pavilion that they've put up, running up from Tower Hill to the north end of the bridge. I'll be there with Lord Maurice at about ten thirty.'

The superintendent stopped speaking, and rested his chin on his hand. Box saw an expression of wistful sadness fall like a shadow across his superior's face. He sat in silence, content to wait for Mackharness to speak. The old floorboards creaked and settled, and Box could hear the muffled footsteps of other police officers treading the many corridors and passageways of King James's Rents.

'I can't help thinking, Box, of ten years ago,' said the superintendent at length. 'The thirtieth of May, 1884, when we had the Fenian dynamite outrage just over the way in Great Scotland Yard. It was a little after nine o'clock in the evening when the bomb exploded, blowing out the front wall of the police station. I was there at the time, calling upon Inspector Robson of the CID. The noise of that explosion reminded me of the cannon in the Crimea....

'There were other explosions and alarms that night, Box, which make the whole outrage stay in my memory. I don't usually reminisce, as you know, but this news of an attempt on the bridge tomorrow – well, it brings it all back to me. These people can only destroy, never create....

'Well, there it is. Get down there tomorrow, Box, and keep a weather eye out for villainy on the bridge. For the rest, we can leave everything to the City of London Police.'

Arnold Box walked thoughtfully down the stairs and pushed open the swing doors of his front office. He was assailed by the smell of stale toast and coffee, which mingled none too subtly with the pervading odour of inefficiently burnt gas from the rickety mantle suspended from the ceiling. The gaslight burned night and day throughout the year in Box's office, because full daylight never penetrated beyond the vestibule of the old building. The office was always cold, which was why a small fire was burning in the grate, even though it was the end of June.

Sergeant Knollys, who had been attacking the fire with a poker, looked up as Box entered, and treated him to a deferentially mocking smile.

'Nice to see you, sir,' said Knollys. 'It was very pleasant weather earlier on!'

'You cheeky man,' Box replied, sinking gratefully into his chair at the cluttered office table. 'I've greeted the rising sun, Sergeant, more times than you've had hot breakfasts. There's a smell of toast in here. Is there anything to eat?'

Jack Knollys, thought Box, was looking even more gigantic than usual that morning. Smartly dressed, as always, with close-cropped yellow hair and an engagingly ugly face, he was an intimidating man at the best of times, his appearance rendered even more fearsome by the livid scar that ran across his face from below the right eye to the left corner of his mouth.

'Didn't you have any breakfast, sir?' asked Knollys.

'No, I didn't. I got up late, by reason of having been out at that raid on the Bolt brothers' den at Highgate. I was there till after three. That's why I got up late. I fair ran all the way up Fleet Street, and stopped for a cup of coffee at a stall on the corner of Lancaster Place. "'Ere, guvnor", said the man, "you'll scald yer stummick if you drink it orf like that!" "There are worse things than a scalded stomach, my man", I replied. Meaning Old Growler, you know. And sure enough, he was lying in wait for me on the landing, as usual.'

Knollys lifted a battered coffee pot from the hob, and poured what coffee remained into a chipped enamel mug. He set it down in front of Box, and pushed a biscuit tin across the table.

'That's the best I can do, sir,' he said. 'Did Mr Mackharness tell you about tomorrow?'

'He did, Jack, so sit down for a minute, and let's talk about this business of the mysterious bomber. Mr Mackharness tells me that you're to go with a detail from Southwark to lie in wait for this madman, Anders Grunwalski.'

Box removed the photograph from his pocket, and put it on the table.

'Unless I'm very much mistaken, Sergeant,' Box continued, 'that picture was taken by Detective Inspector Fitzgerald of "J". He shares my interest in the use of photography in the solution of crimes. It was he who unearthed this Anders Grunwalski.'

Jack Knollys stirred uneasily in his chair, but said nothing.

'Ah, so you've heard about Bobby Fitz,' said Box. 'He's a renowned expert on the doings of the Fenians, with a sideline in anarchists. He doesn't often stir from his patch in Bethnal Green, but he knows all kinds of things. The trouble with Mr Fitzgerald, though, is that he has his own ways of obtaining information, some of which could get him into trouble, to put it mildly.'

'I've heard about that, sir,' Knollys replied. 'Apparently it's something that everybody knows, but that nobody speaks about.'

'That's right, and I'm only mentioning it to you because we're alone here in the office, and there's no one at present next door in the drill hall. But if Bobby Fitz has winkled out this man Grunwalski, then Grunwalski's a genuine menace. I've never heard of him, and neither has the guvnor, but that doesn't mean he's not dangerous. He looks mild enough, doesn't he? But you can't go by looks. So when you're on duty tomorrow in that boiler room under the bridge, watch out for yourself as well as for him. I want you back here in the afternoon, Sergeant, in one piece.'

Saturday, 30 June, 1894, presented the thronging people of London with a cloudless sky and a hot summer sun. Arnold Box left his lodgings in Cardinal Court, Fleet Street, at eight o'clock, having breakfasted on bacon and egg, buttered toast, and generous spoonfuls of Crosse & Blackwell's orange marmalade. Mrs Peach, his motherly landlady, had made sure that there was to be no scalding coffee tossed down at a stall in the street that morning.

As Box walked briskly along Fleet Street in the direction of St Paul's, he recalled the detailed plans that Superintendent

Mackharness had put out for display in Room 6 at the Rents. Really, the guvnor was first-rate at that kind of thing.

The day's great celebratory pageant would begin soon after eleven o'clock, when five semi-State carriages would set out from Marlborough House, just off Pall Mall. Four of the carriages were to contain a whole panoply of equerries, lords-in-waiting, chamberlains, various court ladies, and Princess Maud of Wales. The Prince and Princess of Wales would be in the fifth carriage, with the Duke of York and Princess Victoria of Wales.

Their route would take them along Duncannon Street and so into the Strand, whence they would all progress in stately fashion along Fleet Street, Ludgate Hill, Cheapside, and so to the Mansion House. From there they would journey along King William Street, Eastcheap and Trinity Square, ending up at Tower Hill.

The streets were already crowded with spectators, and the first-floor fronts of many shops and offices were covered in flags, bunting, and coloured heraldic shields. When Box reached the Mansion House, he saw that the vast open space fronting the official residence of the Lord Mayor of London was filled with a cheerfully noisy crowd waiting to see the Lord Mayor and Sheriffs join the Royal procession.

The police were heavily supplemented by detachments of regular soldiers and militia, who were already taking up positions at key points along the route. All this formidable security, presented as so much colourful spectacle, would ensure that there could be no threat to the Royal personages here in the City. No; it would be on the bridge that deadly danger would lurk, if this man Grunwalski was to triumph that day.

Forsaking the crowds and their keepers, Arnold Box made his way down Garlick Hill, negotiated the heavy morning traffic in Upper Thames Street, and crossed to the Surrey side by way of Southwark Bridge.

*

From his vantage point on the roof of Carmody's Wool Depot at the far end of Pickled Herring Street, Box looked down through his field-glasses at the southern abutment of the new Tower Bridge, its steel framework clad in Portland stone, rising, solid and sturdy, towards the clear June sky.

For the last week Box had been combing the popular newspapers for facts and figures about the new bridge. Beneath that stone cladding there were 12,000 tons of steel. Each of the piers carrying the main towers weighed 70,000 tons. Surely no little bomb could bring that massive creation tumbling down into the river?

He scanned the five wide arches containing the doors to the engine rooms. From right to left, they consisted of the first and second boiler rooms, the fuel store, which also housed two of the four hydraulic accumulators in a tower above, and then the two chambers containing the massive steam-driven pumping engines. The malevolent Fenian, or anarchist, or whatever he was, had chosen the first of the two boiler rooms to carry out his act of terrorism.

Those boiler rooms could be seen as the heart of the enterprise. The boilers heated the water, which produced the steam to drive the pumps operating the hydraulic system. A bomb, exploded down there, would empty the system of its power, leaving the two drawbridges that carried the roadway locked together, helpless. But how would the explosion affect the Royal personages crossing the bridge? They'd be shocked and shaken, no doubt, but that would be all. Did this man Grunwalski know that?

Away to the left, Box could see the magnificent baronial Gothic towers of the bridge, and the dual footways, 142 feet above high water level. It was a breath-taking sight, that seemed to be glowing with its own sun-like brilliance. Box felt that he could have stretched out a hand and touched it, it seemed so near.

Box's eyes were suddenly dazzled by a brilliant flash of light from somewhere to his right, in the direction of Queen Elizabeth

Street, one of the tangle of roads and alleys crowding down to the river. Here, rows of stands were packed with children from the local schools, in the charge of their teachers. The flash was gone in an instant, but not before Box identified it as a momentary reflection from a telescope. Had somebody seen him there, standing on the roof of Carmody's Wool Depot? Well, two could play at the game of I-spy.

Box was careful not to let the sun glance from his own powerful binoculars as he trained them tentatively in the direction of Queen Elizabeth Street. In seconds he had located the source of the flash. At the point where the road began to merge into Tooley Street, a handsome landau, drawn by a beribboned black horse, had drawn up to the pavement near a public house, which Box, who was no stranger to that part of the Surrey shore, knew to be The Tanner's Arms. A man in capes, evidently the landau's driver, was standing on the pavement, adjusting the horse's bridle.

Sitting in the landau, a telescope across his knees, was a tall gentleman in a fashionable black morning suit and shining silk hat. In startling contrast to his sober attire, the man sported a massive mane of blond hair, which hung down over his collar. His hair was supplemented by a great bushy golden beard. A gaggle of excited children carrying Union flags ran past the carriage, and the man smiled and waved at them.

A little breeze suddenly ruffled both beard and hair, and Box was reminded of a picture he had once seen of a Viking warrior standing at the prow of his ship, a sword raised above his head. The Viking effect of the man in the landau was rather spoiled, Box thought, by the gold-rimmed monocle that he wore in his right eye, its black cord disappearing somewhere in the region of his double-breasted waistcoat.

The Viking suddenly stood up in the carriage, and once again applied his telescope to his monocled eye. Box realized that he was looking intently at the entrance to the boiler room under the southern abutment.

Or so it seemed! Many people would be out that day with fields-glasses and telescopes to get closer views of the Royal processions. It was a prime error to jump to facile conclusions. But it was an odd vantage point to choose, a bleak street some way from the bridge, on the faded skirts of Bermondsey....

Box swung his field glasses away from the Viking, and focused on the approach to the boiler rooms. Four men in stoker's uniforms, each carrying a wide shovel, were walking rapidly down the slope to the boiler room. One of them had something wrapped in canvas under his arm. Yes! It was the man in the photograph, Anders Grunwalski. It was almost twelve. The man had aimed at planting his bomb just minutes before the arrival of the Royal party.

The door of the boiler room was opened from inside, and the four men passed from view. Down there, Box mused, hidden in various points of vantage, was a special police detail provided by 'M', Superintendent Neylan's stalwarts from Blackman Street, Southwark, and with them, as a representative of Scotland Yard, was Sergeant Knollys. They would let Grunwalski position his bomb, in order to establish his guilt beyond doubt, and then they would quietly arrest him.

Box trained his binoculars once more on the Viking man in his landau. The world as glimpsed through binoculars was a silent world, but Box saw that the gentleman had just said something to his coachman, who leapt up on to the seat, and turned the horse's head in the direction of Artillery Street. He's going to cross the river by way of London Bridge, thought Box. Why hadn't he stayed to watch the arrival of their Royal Highnesses? Or had he been there to witness the appearance of Grunwalski and his infernal machine? Mere supposition....

As Box turned his glasses back on to the southern abutment of the bridge, he saw a police constable emerge discreetly from a doorway some distance away from the boiler room. The man looked up at him, and waved his arm in a gesture that said, 'All's well.'

Before Box had turned away from the parapet, the door of the boiler room burst open, and Grunwalski, apparently running for his life, emerged on to the slip road, a pistol in his hand. He was followed by four policemen, two of whom staggered as they ran, blood pouring from head wounds. There was no sign of Knollys. At the same time, a tremendous cheer, sounding high into the air and across to the South Bank, told Box that the Royal carriage had started its progress across Tower Bridge.

2

The Deadly Stoker

AT NINE O'CLOCK that same morning, Detective Sergeant Jack Knollys left his lodgings at Syria Wharf and made his way on foot down to Swan Lane Pier, where one of Thames Division's steam launches conveyed him under London Bridge and out across the river to a landing-stage below the Anchor Brewery at Shad Thames. By ten o'clock, he was walking rapidly down the slip road that would take him to the Number 1 engine room of Tower Bridge.

He gave a low knock on a stout door set in a stone arch below the southern approach to the bridge, and it was opened immediately by a man dressed in the dark blue overalls and glazed peak cap of a naval stoker. Knollys recalled having read somewhere that, in the peculiar way of English institutions, the new bridge had been registered as a ship.

'Sergeant Knollys?' said the man in the peaked cap. 'Come in, and close the door behind you. I'm Inspector Hare, of "M". The powers-that-be thought it right that this little posse should be made up of officers from Southwark Division, rather than asking City to do the honours. It's a fine point of etiquette, Sergeant, which we'll leave others to debate.'

Knollys glanced at Inspector Hare's lined face, which bore the more or less permanent half smile of a born cynic. This man, he thought, is not taking our anarchist seriously. He probably thinks the whole affair is a pathetic stunt by a washed-out Fenian.

'Is there any special reason, sir, why you're dressed as a stoker?' asked Knollys.

'It was a whim of Superintendent Neylan's, Sergeant. It's supposed to be a disguise. I was obliged to comply. But I've got six properly dressed constables here, and there's a man from the Home Office as well – a man who knows how to defuse bombs and suchlike. Come through into the boiler room.'

There was nothing of the damp crypt about the white-tiled chamber, well lit by glazed half-moon-shaped windows high on the walls. The centre of the room was dominated by two massive cylindrical Lancashire boilers, each thirty feet long, which hissed and bubbled, filling the chamber with an overpowering heat.

An archway to the left of the boilers led into the second boiler room, which, like the first, housed two gigantic Lancashire boilers, and here, Inspector Hare had assembled his posse of constables. They were all in uniform, and stood, tense and expectant, against the inner wall. Just feet away from them a team of stokers continued to fuel the twin fire-boxes of each boiler as though nothing untoward was going to happen.

'Those men, Sergeant,' said Hare, 'must stay at their work, because the boilers have to be stoked constantly if the bridge mechanism is to work properly – which it must, on this day of all days. They work in both rooms, moving from boiler to boiler as the need arises.'

'They look very experienced, sir.'

'They are. They're all ex-Royal Navy stokers. Now, when the shift changes, which will be at a quarter to twelve, one of the relieving stokers will be our anarchist. Apparently, it's known that he'll try to gain entrance by attaching himself to the relieving men. They've already been warned to accept him as one of their number as they walk down the slip road.'

'Somebody, somewhere, sir, knows an awful lot about what's going to happen.'

'Somebody does, Sergeant Knollys. It makes you think, doesn't it? Still, ours not to reason why. We'll do the job, and then fade into the background.'

Inspector Hare turned briefly to look at the sweating stokers, who seemed oblivious of the police presence. Their efforts were concentrated solely on keeping the fire-boxes supplied with coal. They had closed the furnace doors for a while, and were resting on their spades.

'You men,' said Hare, 'mustn't make any attempt to assist the police if this anarchist turns violent. When your relief party arrives, this dangerous man will be part of it. You must leave him to us. Climb up into the accumulator shaft, and stay on the platform there, until I give the all clear.'

The men nodded their understanding, threw open the doors of the fire-boxes once more, and replenished the glowing fires with vast quantities of fine furnace coal.

Mr Hare pulled a large turnip watch out of a pocket in his naval jacket.

'It's just gone half past ten, Officers,' he said. 'You'd better make yourselves as comfortable as you can on those benches against the wall. It's going to be over an hour's wait. Sergeant Knollys, the Home Office man wants to see you. He's in a little tiled storeroom at the rear of Number 1 Boiler Room. He says he knows you.'

Knollys left the seven police officers to wait in nervous anticipation for the arrival of the destroyer, and went back into the first of the chambers. The boilers hissed and rumbled. The fingers on the gauges flickered behind their glass covers. Water ran fiercely through mysterious pipes.

The clean, modern room seemed tinder-dry, magnifying tenfold the heat of the June day. Knollys imagined the black smoke rising vertically from the tall chimney sited between the two boiler rooms.

In a small tiled room behind the boilers Jack Knollys found a morose, elderly man with a long drooping moustache. He was sitting on a metal tool box, reading a backless book which looked as though it was regularly gnawed by mice. Beside him, on the toolbox reposed a black bowler hat and a claw-hammer. Despite the overwhelming heat, the man wore a thick black serge suit, and had wound a green muffler round his neck.

'Hello, Mr Mack,' said Knollys, 'I thought it might be you.'

'It's nice to see you again, Mr Knollys,' said Mr Mack. 'I was hoping that you'd give me a hand here, if the worst comes to the worst, and this madman actually turns up. It sounds very peculiar to me. Some crazed individual with a grudge wants to rush in here with a little time-bomb, hoping it will blow Tower Bridge to pieces. Most unlikely, you know. It may have naval stokers, but it isn't a ship. And it won't sink. Still, the Home Secretary thought it was a matter for Home Office Explosions, which is why I'm here. Colonel Majendie's in Cardiff this week, so it had to be me. I demurred, of course, but there's no arguing with Mr Asquith. So we'll all contain ourselves in patience until a quarter to twelve.'

It was at just twenty minutes to the hour that Sergeant Knollys, who had stationed himself behind the outer door of No 1 Boiler Room, heard the clatter of boots on the slip road which heralded the arrival of the relief stokers. He alerted Inspector Hare with an urgent whisper, and then rejoined Mr Mack in the tiled storeroom. The retiring stokers moved swiftly to the iron staircase rising up to the accumulator platform, and in seconds they had disappeared from sight. The police officers drew their truncheons and stood silently in the shelter of the inner wall.

At a quarter to twelve the door was opened, and four men came into the room. Three of them passed through the arch into the second boiler room, apparently intent on their work. Knollys saw the fourth man, who was dressed like the others in the uniform of a naval stoker, dart across the floor to the rear of the first boiler, and wedge a canvas-covered parcel underneath two of its supporting struts.

The man had taken no more than a couple of steps backwards when Jack Knollys, with a mighty bellow of rage, hurled himself on to the would-be destroyer and brought him crashing to the floor. At the same time, the posse of Bermondsey police rushed through the arch, truncheons drawn. In a moment, they had hauled the man to his feet.

Mr Mack had left his shelter in the storeroom, dragged the parcel from its hiding place, and unwrapped it from its concealing cloth. Knollys saw him raise his hammer, and smash a small glass dial let into the front of the device. Knollys had seen the old explosives expert perform that crude but effective remedy for timing-clocks before. For the moment at least, they were all safe.

Outside, beneath the blazing June sky, the Prince of Wales's carriage passed on to the bridge. There came a sustained bout of cheering, and the band of the Coldstream Guards struck up 'God save the Queen'.

Beneath the southern approach road, in the hidden boiler room, Inspector Hare confronted the man who had tried unsuccessfully to plant a lethal device beneath the first boiler. He saw a man of about thirty, with a long, narrow face, good features, dark hair, and cold blue eyes. His arms had been pinioned by two of the constables. His head hung down upon his chest in what looked like total despair.

Knollys, who had rejoined Mr Mack, turned round to look at the man, who raised his head and caught his glance, and there was something in the bomber's expression that intrigued Knollys. He had expected anger, or even wild hatred. But this man regarded him with what seemed like reproach. *Reproach?*

'You are Anders Grunwalski,' said Inspector Hare, 'and I arrest you—'

Grunwalski suddenly sprang back to life. With a shrill cry of rage he wrenched himself free from his captors, seized one of the constables' truncheons, and used it as a deadly flail to cut a way of escape towards the exit. To the accompaniment of shouts and curses from the dazed and bleeding officers, who had fallen to the floor, he threw the door open and dashed into the slip road.

Oh, no, my beauty, thought Jack Knollys, you're not going to escape so lightly. He leapt over the injured men and darted out in pursuit. There he was, sprinting with an athlete's effortless speed up the approach road. What was that sudden burst of cheering? The Royal carriage must have passed on to the bridge. All eyes would be on them: no one would take any notice of one single running man....

What's he doing now? He's pulled a pistol from his pocket! If I don't catch up with him, thought Knollys, someone will be killed. He could hear the harsh panting of his own breath, and the faltering steps of the injured constables behind him. He summoned up sufficient breath to shout: 'Stop that man!' but at the same moment there came a wild and uninhibited chorus of steam whistles and church bells rising from the river and the river-side districts on both banks. Nobody would hear him above that din.

Pursuit of the fleet-footed assassin was useless. Knollys knew that he was built too heavily to catch Grunwalski before he gained the entrance to the bridge. Perhaps he had designs on one of the notables sitting in the pavilion at the north end? Had the business in the boiler room been a mere diversion?

It was then that Knollys saw a small detachment of soldiers assembled at the top of the slip road. He remembered Superintendent Mackharness's great map of the day's dispositions, and recalled that these men were a detachment of the 3rd Middlesex Volunteers. As Grunwalski neared the group of men, one of them saw the running terrorist and his deadly weapon. As swift as thought, the artilleryman drew his cutlass, and felled Grunwalski with a single blow from the flat of its blade. In seconds Sergeant Knollys was upon him. A moment later, the unconscious man was secured, manacled and fettered.

No one on the bridge, mused Knollys drily, and no excited spectator in the festive stands surrounding it, could have been aware of the deadly drama that had just taken place.

Arnold Box, still at his post on the roof of Carmody's Wool Depot, watched as Anders Grunwalski was carried unconscious down the slip road and into the boiler room. The frantic cheering of the crowds of spectators continued as the Royal procession reappeared at the end of Tooley Street on its way back over the bridge. The river rang with the hooting of steam whistles, and the deeper vibrant tones of the liners lying at anchor further down-stream. No one had noticed the attempt to blow up Tower Bridge on its inaugural day.

Box trained his binoculars on to the Royal procession. He'd no idea who some of those people were – upper-crust folk crammed into carriages, and dripping with medals and diamonds. Ah! Here were the Prince and Princess of Wales. *She* looked lovely, as always, smiling and gracious. She's wearing a silk dress – blue, it is, with silver threads in it. He'd tell Mrs Peach about that. *He* looked magnificent, as you might expect. Kitted out as a Field Marshal, by the look of it.

The incident at the bridge had disturbed Box. How had the man come to escape from a posse of seven police officers? It had taken a single young soldier to subdue him. Before that had happened, Grunwalski had produced a pistol. Why had they not searched him? The authorities should have let City handle it.

What would Inspector Hare do now? If he stuck to the plan pinned up in Room 6 at the Rents, he'd take his prisoner and the whole posse in a Black Maria to Weavers' Lane Police Station in Bermondsey, where he'd lock Grunwalski up for the night. The whole business looked like the pathetic attempt of one disgruntled man to make his mark on history. Well, he'd failed.

It had been a heady morning for Superintendent Mackharness. Freed from the thrall of his dark office in King James's Rents, he had arrived at the long pavilion running up from Tower Hill to the northern end of the new bridge at half past ten. He was accompanied by his old friend from Crimea days, Lord Maurice Vale Rose, who had secured him a ticket. It would be an hour before the Royal personages arrived, but there was plenty to see. Aldermen and sheriffs, mayors wearing their gold chains of office, exotic foreigners in peculiar clothing – all these, and more, arrived in a steady stream.

Box would be stationed on the roof of Carmody's Wool Depot by now. If there was anything untoward to see, then Box would see it. Sergeant Knollys would be under the southern approach road, adding his very considerable weight to the posse of police provided for the day by Denis Neylan. Surely nothing could go amiss? This Grunwalski was almost certainly acting alone. And in any case, what possible effect could a single bomb in the boiler room have upon the massive triumph of engineering rising giddily above them to the sky? The man was a lunatic....

The next hour passed swiftly, and the assembled audience amused themselves by watching notables as they arrived, importantly late, in order to create a stir. Here was Mr Asquith, the Home Secretary. There was the Bishop of London.

At last the Royal Procession arrived. (Had they seized Grunwalski yet? Was the bridge safe?) The carriages crossed the bridge, and passed out of sight. It seemed an age before they returned, the train of vehicles halting at the dais prepared for the Prince and his suite. At last, the formal opening of the new bridge was about to begin.

The Prince of Wales took up a position in front of the mechanism that would operate the bridge machinery. It had been fancifully disguised as a loving-cup standing on an ornate pedestal. The Recorder of London began to read an interminable and inaudible speech, its words carried away on the breeze, and drowned very effectively by the continual cheering of the crowds. The Prince of Wales read an equally inaudible reply, and then slowly turned the valve that would operate the hydraulic mechanism.

Immediately the two massive leaves of the carriageway, each 115 feet in length, began to move upwards. There came a blast of trumpets, a wild crescendo of steam whistles from the boats thronging the river, and, behind all the popular clamour, the booming of guns from the Tower of London.

Mackharness, and the others occupying the seats in the pavilion fell silent as the divided roadway rose majestically and noiselessly into the air until each section blocked the archway of its respective tower. A thunder of cheering rose into the summer sky, and almost immediately a triumphant procession of flag-draped vessels began to pass under Tower Bridge.

There was an hour to spare before Box was due back at King James's Rents for a prearranged meeting with Sergeant Knollys, ample time for him to take a cab and visit his old father at his premises in Oxford Street. Toby Box had joined the Metropolitan Police in 1840, at the age of twenty-one, and had risen to the rank of sergeant. He'd always been a uniformed man, a divisional man, not a detective, like his son.

In 1875, Toby Box had been shot in the leg by a villain called Joseph Edward Spargo, a man who was later hanged for murder. There had followed eighteen years of suffering and the threat of total immobility, and towards the end of '92 the possibility of gangrene had been mooted. Toby Box's leg had been amputated at the Royal Free Hospital in Grey's Inn Road early in January 1893.

And now, after eighteen months' convalescence, old Mr Box had come home to Oxford Street. He had learnt to walk with his new leg, and was determined to assume his normal life as proprietor of Box's Cigar Divan and Hair-Cutting Rooms, a tall and narrow shop a few yards further on from the Eagle public house, just before you came to the turn into New Bond Street.

As Box came into Oxford Street, he saw the Viking's landau,

with the beribboned black horse between the shafts, draw away from the pavement and join the stream of traffic moving slowly up the busy thoroughfare. He stopped underneath the awnings of Marshall and Snelgrove's, which stretched low over the hot flags.

What had the Viking been doing in that particular stretch of Oxford Street? His behaviour at the bridge had been odd, to say the least. It would do no harm to make a few enquiries about him. He was obviously a gentleman of sorts; maybe Superintendent Mackharness would recognize his description. Had he stopped at that particular spot, just by the Eagle, in order to get his hair cut at Pa's salon? He'd ask Sam, if he remembered.

The street was crowded with tall, rumbling omnibuses, lorries and vans, and a procession of hansom cabs crawling head to tail towards Oxford Circus. Box darted nimbly through the traffic, and made his way to Box's Cigar Divan and Hair-Cutting Rooms.

It was pleasantly cool and shady in his father's shop, which was perfumed with the many subtle aromas of exposed tobacco. A middle-aged, balding man wearing an alpaca jacket lifted the counter-flap and came forward to greet him.

'Inspector Box, sir,' said the man, 'I'm glad you could come this afternoon. All the building work was finished by Thursday night, and Mr Box took up his new quarters yesterday morning.'

'And how is he, Sam?' asked Box. 'Is he coping with the leg?'

'He's fine, Inspector. I think he's more mobile than he's been for years, and he'll want to do his bit around the shop, I expect. But he'll not be able to cope with stairs anymore.'

Arnold Box glanced at the narrow staircase that led up to the cigar divan. It had also given access to Toby Box's snug quarters on the first floor, a tiny sitting-room with a bedroom beyond, looking out on to a tangle of yards. Pa wouldn't ever go up those stairs again, unless he was carried up in a chair.

Sam opened a door in a dim recess beyond the counter, and

motioned Box to enter a long, newly decorated room, which had been furnished in the heavy, ornate style of earlier in the century. There was a narrow window at the far end, and a gas bracket on either side of a tall mirror above the fireplace.

'Inspector Box to see you, Mr Box,' said Sam. He closed the door after Arnold Box, and returned to the shop.

A stout, elderly man in his seventies was sitting in a chair near the fireplace. His bald head was framed by a halo of scanty white hair. As Box entered the room, the old man rose stiffly from his chair to greet him.

'How are you, Pa?' asked Box. 'Have you settled in, yet?'

'I have, boy,' said Toby Box. 'They've done a marvellous job down here, and it suits me fine. It'll be like a new start for me after all those years marooned upstairs. They brought all my furniture down here, as you can see, and converted my upstairs place into a kind of guest apartment. Very handy, if someone wanted to stay.'

'And is the extension finished? They said it would be done by last Monday.'

'It's all finished now, Arnold. Through that door beside the window there's a snug bedroom and a little washing-place beyond that, built on part of the back yard.'

'It's very nice, Pa,' said Box. 'I'm sorry I couldn't get here to see it all earlier. It's been hectic this last two weeks at the Rents.'

Arnold Box looked at his old father, who had resumed his seat. He was wearing a new black suit, with trousers reaching down to his ankles. For years he had worn old-fashioned knee breeches, because of the thick bandages that he'd had to wear on his infected leg. He may be old, thought Box, in fact, seventy-five this year, but his eyes are as keen and bright as they'd been in the days when he'd worked with some of the legendary detectives of Great Scotland Yard, people like Mr Thornton and Mr Aggs.

'You'd best be on your way, Arnold,' said Toby Box. 'I'll just smoke a pipe, and then I'll take a nap.'

'Are you sure you're all right, Pa?'

'What? Of course I'm all right. Off with you, now, boy. Duty calls!'

Box left his father to fill his long clay pipe with strong tobacco, and returned to the shop, where Sam had resumed his station behind the counter. The busy clashing of scissors came to Box's ears from behind the beaded curtain separating the tobacco shop from the haircutting rooms. He parted the curtain with his hand, and saw that the two barbers were preoccupied with hirsute customers, draped anonymously in white sheets, like pieces of stored furniture. In one corner, hemmed in by a floor brush, Box saw a pile of blond hair, the relic of a previous customer. He suddenly remembered his Viking.

'Sam,' he asked, 'did you have a big blond fellow in here just now, a sort of Viking, with a mane of fair hair and a big golden beard?'

'Why, yes, Mr Box. How did you know that? He was a very striking gentleman, very tall and commanding. A well-dressed man with a rose in his buttonhole. He came in a very fancy carriage, with a man up on the box. A landau, it was. You must have just missed him.'

The beaded curtain parted, and a customer emerged into the hair-cutting saloon, dabbing his neck with a handkerchief. He nodded briefly to the two men, and left the shop, setting the little bell behind the door jingling. One of the two barbers came into the space behind the counter, drying his hands on a towel.

'Frank,' asked Sam, 'was it you who cut that big blond gentleman's hair? Inspector Box has been asking about him.'

'Yes, I saw to him,' said Frank. ' "Give me a good trim, my man", he said, "but don't scalp me. And you can trim the beard to make it more spade-like". So I did. He seemed very satisfied. Gave me a shilling, which was very handsome, considering it's only fourpence for a trim.'

'What kind of a man was he, Frank?' asked Box. 'I'm asking because I fancy I saw him near the new bridge this morning. He was watching the proceedings through a telescope.'

'Well, Mr Box, he was a big, jolly kind of man, who spoke with what I'd call a laughing voice. He wore a monocle in his right eye, and had the sense to stow it away in a pocket before I threw the sheet over him. And he *had* been near the new bridge, because he told me about it. Quite chatty, he was. He described all the flags waving, and the people cheering. He was a foreigner.'

'Was he, now? What kind of a foreigner?'

'Well, *I* don't know, Mr Box. He was just a foreigner. He spoke perfect English, though. And now I come to think of it, he did say something about being foreign. Leastways, he mentioned a foreign town. Now, what was it?'

'Paris? Berlin? Come on, Frank – think!'

'It was – yes, Warsaw. "We've some fine bridges in Warsaw, my man". That's what he said. Warsaw's in Poland, isn't it? So I suppose he must be a Pole.'

A Pole.... That man Grunwalski was a Pole. How did he know that? Because Grunwalski was a Polish name. And, if Frank was right, the Viking with the telescope was also a Pole. The general feeling back at the Rents was that Grunwalski was acting alone, perhaps at the urging of some festering grievance to do with his native land. If that was so, then the business of Grunwalski was a divisional affair, something that had come to light in Bethnal Green, which was Mr Keating's patch, and would be terminated across the river with 'M' Division in Southwark.

But what if those two men were part of a conspiracy? Had the Viking been there to witness Grunwalski's success or failure, and then to report to someone else? It was certainly possible. Meanwhile, it has surely been a quirk of fate that the Viking had stopped for a haircut at Box's Cigar Divan and Hair-Cutting Rooms.

3

Outrage in Weavers' Lane

'So WHAT DO you think, Jack? About this Anders Grunwalski, I mean. Was he acting alone, or is he part of something bigger, and more sinister?'

It was just after four o'clock. Box and Knollys were sitting at the long cluttered table in Box's office at 2 King James's Rents.

'I'm not sure, sir,' Jack Knollys replied. 'He seemed quite desperate when we finally got the darbies on him. It may have been that he was frantic at letting down some confederates – so yes, he could well be part of a gang. He refused to speak at all, or to answer any of the charges made against him. He was in very good shape physically, as though he'd been in training for the escapade. Lithe and strong, he is, with a steady, cool eye.'

'Hm.... Did they find anything in his pockets? Or needn't I ask?'

'There was nothing at all in his pockets, sir, and no labels in his clothes. There was nothing there to interest us. The only item he was carrying in a pocket was that pistol.'

Arnold Box lit a thin cheroot, and threw the spent wax vesta into the fireplace. He sighed, and shook his head in dissatisfaction.

'I don't like the smell of it, Sergeant,' he said. 'That pistol.... I saw him produce it myself from my perch on the roof of Carmody's warehouse. What was he supposed to be? A bomber, or an assassin? And what about my Viking?'

'Your Viking, sir? I didn't know you had a Viking.'

Box told his sergeant about the mysterious man in the landau.

'I had a strong impression, Sergeant, that he was watching to see what was happening at the entrance to that boiler room. He was in the wrong location to see the ceremonies. In fact, from where he was positioned, I don't think he could see the carriageway of the bridge at all—'

Box broke off as a constable came through the swing doors.

'A note for you, sir,' he said, 'brought by messenger from the Home Office.'

'It's from Mr Mack,' said Box, when he had torn open the small buff envelope. 'He wants us to go and see him any time after five o'clock. He says he's puzzled. Come on, Jack, let's take a walk up Whitehall, and hear what Mr Mack's got to tell us.'

Box and Knollys had not visited Mr Mack's spacious domain in the Home Office since the affair of the Hansa Protocol. Nothing had changed. The premises still resembled a kind of roofed scrapyard. The twisted, fire-damaged remains of an iron spiral staircase had been bolted into the wall and part of the ceiling, awaiting expert examination. A number of burnt and shattered strongroom doors, their smart paint charred and peeling, were propped against the far wall.

Mr Mack, his pale eyes watering, shuffled out of an adjoining room which had been fitted up as a workshop.

'Come in, Inspector,' he said, 'and you, Sergeant Knollys. Sit down there, by the lathe, while I tell you what I've discovered.'

The old Home Office expert lit a short clay pipe, and sank into a chair behind his desk. In front of him lay the component parts of the fiendish device that he had seized and rendered harmless earlier that day. Mr Mack waved his pipe vaguely at it and then launched into speech.

'This is a very interesting piece of mechanism, gents,' he said, 'and a very curious one, as well. The detonator – that green iron box, there – consisted of a little charge of fulminate of mercury packed into a copper cylinder. An ingenious mechanism, controlled by the time-clock that you, Sergeant Knollys, saw me smash with my hammer. It shoots a percussive bolt into the end of the cylinder, thus exploding the fulminate charge.'

'And that would have blown up the boiler?' asked Box. The old expert sighed, and then laughed throatily.

'Well, hardly that, Mr Box. If you'd let me finish what I was saying, all will be revealed. The point about sensitive explosives like fulminate of mercury, or lead azide, is that they can communicate detonation to any high explosive in the vicinity. In this case, the high explosive was dynamite, which you can see there, on the table. There were eight sticks, all enclosed in the usual parchment cases, but I've opened them all, and extracted the contents.'

'It's nitroglycerine, isn't it? Dynamite, I mean.'

'Yes, it is, but it's absorbed in a stuff called kieselguhr, for safety reasons. That bomb would have blown the boiler to smithereens, and would have killed anyone within five yards of the explosion. But it would have had no visible effect on Tower Bridge itself.'

'So even if we had known nothing about the affair, our terrorist – this man Grunwalski – would have failed in his mission?'

'It's not as simple as that, Mr Box.'

Mr Mack felt in the pockets of his rusty old jacket and produced a hand lens.

'Look at the smashed time-clock,' he said, 'and tell me what you see.'

Box peered through the lens at the shattered clock face still visible beyond the splintered glass of the dial. He gave an exclamation of surprise.

'It was set to go off at one o'clock!' he cried. 'Long after the Royal party had returned to Marlborough House. I don't understand—'

'And here's something else that will interest you,' Mr Mack continued. 'All that dynamite was damp. I don't mean damp through bad storage: it had been deliberately soaked with water.

My view, for what it's worth, was that your man Grunwalski never intended his bomb to work. And that makes me ask, why not? Somebody told me he drew a pistol, and began to run up the slope towards the bridge. Maybe the bomb was a diversion, and he was in reality an assassin. I don't know, but I'm sure you'll give the matter some thought.'

Box was silent for a moment. There was something here that he didn't understand, something of monumental importance that he was simply unable to grasp.

'Sergeant,' he said, 'as soon as we leave here, go back to Weavers' Lane Police Station, and ask Inspector Hare to show you that pistol – the one that Grunwalski produced as he ran up to the bridge. Then come straight back to the Rents.'

He turned to look at the old explosives expert, who was still puffing away at his pipe. The air of the little workshop was thick with smoke.

'You've given us both food for thought, Mr Mack,' said Box. 'You're a shining ornament, if I may say so. Is there anything else?'

'Well, not really, Mr Box. The clock mechanism in the detonator was manufactured by Larousse & Cie of Toulouse, and the detonator itself, by which I mean the copper cylinder and its contents, come from the Minnesota Mining Company. You can buy them readily in England, and I can give you a list of all the suppliers in the United Kingdom, if you want it. The dynamite was produced by the Dunfermline Powder Works. It's the ordinary kind of stuff, used for blasting in mines and quarries.'

Arnold Box looked at old Mr Mack in awe. 'A shining ornament,' he repeated, half to himself. The old expert smiled beneath his straggly moustache.

When Box returned to King James's Rents, the duty sergeant in the front reception room stepped out into the vestibule. Sergeant Driscoll was an elderly, heavily bearded man who walked with a limp. He regarded Box through little round wire-framed spectacles.

'Sir,' he said, 'Inspector Fitzgerald from Bethnal Green's waiting to see you. He wanted to stay with me at the door, but I settled him in your office.'

'Thanks, Pat. Is Mr Mackharness back yet?'

'No, sir. I think he's out junketing somewhere with Lord Maurice Vale Rose, celebrating the opening of the new bridge. I don't think we'll see him till Monday morning.'

Sergeant Driscoll returned to his cramped room leading off the vestibule, and Box pushed open the swing doors of his office.

Inspector Fitzgerald of 'J' Division was standing near the fireplace, reading an early evening copy of the *Globe*. He held the newspaper wide open, using its rustling pages as a kind of shield for his body. A tall man in his fifties, with sharp blue eyes peering out from beneath riotous eyebrows, he held a cigarette steady in the dead centre of his mouth, occasionally sending strong streams of smoke down his nostrils. The front of his dark-brown suit was covered in fallen ash.

'Hello, Mr Fitz,' said Box, sitting down in his favourite chair at the long table. 'We don't often see you here at the Rents. What can I do for you?'

'It's more a case of what I can do for *you*, isn't it?' said Mr Fitz. He spoke with a pleasant London voice, with a hint of mockery behind the simplest words.

'You were down there at Tower Bridge today, and saw what happened to Anders Grunwalski. Well, I've come out all this way to Whitehall to tell you all about him. I think you should know.'

The Bethnal Green detective screwed his newspaper into a ball, threw it into the hearth, and sat down opposite Box. The cigarette still stayed where it had been put in the centre of his lips. He had long ago mastered the skill of talking round it.

'This Grunwalski first appeared on our patch just over a month ago. He's a sober-looking kind of a man with dangerous eyes, the type of man who looks mad, but in fact is coldly sane. For the most part he kept himself to himself, but he liked the drink, and when he had had a few whiskies his flaming temper welled up from somewhere, and he'd be looking for fights. That unlovely quality got him into trouble with the law more than once. Are you getting the picture?'

'I am. A surly cur of a man with a grudge against everyone and everything. Quite a nice addition to your rogues' gallery up in Bethnal Green Road.'

Inspector Fitzgerald threw the stub of his cigarette into the fire. He permitted himself a rather amused smile.

'You know what it's like on our patch, Arnold. We've got street vendors, vagrants, dog fanciers and dog stealers; there are pickpockets, card sharpers, shoplifters – and now, for our sins, a full-blown anarchist with a bomb in his pocket. He's been up for street brawling and smashing windows in pubs, so, as you say, he fits in well on our patch.'

'Where did he come from?'

'Well, that's the question, isn't it? Usually, whenever a new villain moves into our parish, he's got a kind of crooked pedigree. He's someone's friend or relative, or he's worked on cracking a crib with one of our resident beauties. But this Grunwalski just appeared from nowhere a month ago, primed with a set of stories. It makes you think. It certainly made *me* think. He's not a Fenian, that's for sure. I don't know what he's supposed to be.'

'Where does this Anders Grunwalski live?'

'He holes up in one of the blind courts off Half Nichol Street. When he's not there, he's in the Woodville Arms in Navarre Passage. I chose a few occasions when Grunwalski was in the Woodville Arms to send one or two of my light fantastic boys into his den to turn the place over. It was they who found his written arrangements for doing today's bridge job – notes, maps, diagrams. There was even a pencil drawing of his bomb!'

'And that's how Mr Mackharness, and everybody in that posse from Bermondsey, knew what was going to happen?'

'It was, Arnold. I was able to hand your guvnor the whole operation on a plate – if you'll pardon the mixed metaphor.'

The two men eyed each other in silence for a moment. It was growing dark, and the light from the hissing gas mantle was beginning to exert itself in the dim office. A coal settled in the grate. It was time for Box to make his thoughts known.

'Those "light fantastic boys" of yours will get you into serious trouble one of these days, Mr Fitz. Everybody knows about them. They're sneak-thieves and so-called reformed characters out to make a few shillings by breaking the law for you. Those searches of private premises that you tell them to make are incidents of breaking and entering.'

Much to Box's relief, Inspector Fitzgerald seemed to take no offence at his frank remarks.

'I take your point, Arnold, and, of course, you're right from the law's point of view. But I've always hated villains, ever since my father was beaten senseless and his barrow stolen in Crooked Billet Yard in '52. I was only twelve then, but I never forgot it. He lost his barrow, his stock, and seven shillings and fourpence, his takings for a whole day – oh, why am I telling you all this? Let's get back to the matter in hand.'

Inspector Fitzgerald stooped down, and retrieved a Gladstone bag from under the table. He opened it, and pulled out a bundle of papers and a sealed brown envelope, which he laid before Box.

'As soon as I heard that Grunwalski had been arrested this morning,' he said, 'I went to his lodgings off Half Nichol Street, and brought these things away for you to see. And yes, I went armed with a search warrant this time. I've seen all those things before – my light fantastic boys brought them out to me one night, and I read them by the light of a dark lantern in a hansom cab. Then they put them all back where they'd found them. Very nifty fellows, my boys. I'd hoped that Grunwalski had received some letters that might have told us more about him, but we were disappointed. Any letters he might have received he burned, and to my knowledge he never posted any.'

'You don't much care about the rule book when it comes to catching villains, do you, Mr Fitz?'

'I don't. I've only two years to go before retirement, and I'm getting too old to bother about the book. I hate villains, Arnold, and I hate all enemies of our Queen and Country. It's because of me, and my peculiar way of looking at things, that Tower Bridge is still standing this evening.'

Inspector Fitzgerald stretched himself, and got up from his chair.

'I'll take a cab back to Bethnal Green, Arnold. You can keep all those things if you like. There's something very odd about that man Grunwalski, as I think you'll realize when you've looked through those papers.'

'Thanks very much, Mr Fitz. It was very good of you to come all this way out. I was very sorry to hear that tale about your poor father. Did he get a new barrow?'

'He didn't. He died of bleeding of the brain three days after the attack. There was only me left to look after Mother. I'm still looking after her, at my lodgings in Bethnal Green Road. Good night, Arnold.'

As soon as Inspector Fitzgerald had left the room, Box spread out the contents of the bundle of papers that had been retrieved from Anders Grunwalski's lodgings.

What was this? A beautifully drafted plan of the internal structures of the Tower Bridge, expertly traced in blacklead pencil from an architect's original drawing. Who could have made such a plan for a man like Grunwalski? And this other paper – a careful plan of the three interiors of the three boiler rooms on the south side. They looked as though they had been prepared for Grunwalski's convenience by the chief engineer himself. Had these papers been passed to the anarchist by hidden accomplices? There were rotten apples to be found in every barrel.

And here was a professionally drawn picture of the detonator with its accompanying dynamite attached. A carefully written label bore the legend: 'Use the inserted keys to set the time-clock. Remove and discard once time is set.' The words had the typical terseness of a manufacturer's instructions to the user of one of his patent appliances: 'Depress handle sharply to flush the bowl'. That kind of thing.

Did a professional bomber like Grunwalski need such elementary instructions? Or was he simply a lone wolf, driven by his own fevered grudges against society?

Box picked up the sealed envelope. Inspector Fitzgerald had scrawled a rough message on it, signed with his initials. *Object retrieved from Grunwalski's lodgings. May be of interest in investigating his antecedents.*

The envelope contained a heavy copper coin, bearing on one side the image of a double-headed eagle with a crown above it, and seven heraldic shields arrayed across its wings and body. The eagle clasped an orb and sceptre in its claws. One of the claws had been depicted as a human hand.

Box sighed, and put the coin down on the desk. Over the last two years he had developed a wary dislike of eagles on coinage. Europe seemed to be awash with eagles, some with two heads, some with one, all symbolizing one or other imperial state and its satellites straddling the continent of Europe and, to Box's way of thinking, threatening its peace and stability. Here was another such coin, found among Grunwalski's possessions. Which eagle-state would it be? Russia? Prussia? Dozy old Austria?

He turned the coin over, and saw an inscription that he knew to be in the Cyrillic or Russian alphabet. Mr Mackharness knew Russian from his Crimea days, and would be able to interpret those words. There was a big number 30, presumably the value of the coin, and then a figure 2, followed by a word in the ordinary Latin alphabet. *Zlote.* There was a curly line through the letter L. The coin was dated 1836.

Box rose from his chair and threw a scuttleful of coal on to the dying fire. He poked the coal vigorously in order to bring the unwilling flames to life. June or not, it got cold in the Rents at night.

He caught his reflection in the big fly-blown mirror above the mantelpiece, and considered it critically. He looked tired and strained, which wasn't surprising, considering the long working-day, but no one could say that he wasn't a personable sort of fellow. That neatly trimmed moustache suited a man of thirty-six. He'd always tried to be smart and well turned out. Would he look as presentable as this in ten years' time?

To the right of the mirror he had pinned up a photograph of the Duke of York, to join that of his wife, the former Princess Victoria Mary of Teck. Just a week ago, Her Royal Highness had given birth to a baby boy, who was to be called Prince Edward. No doubt the Duke had been given an extra cheer or two when he'd appeared that morning at the opening of Tower Bridge.

The foreign coin still lay where Box had placed it on the table. Somehow, it made him uneasy. Those eagles again.... Grunwalski was a Pole. Perhaps that was a Polish coin? He wouldn't bother Mr Mackharness about it. There was a man he knew living near Maiden Lane who'd know all about Polish coins – if it *was* a Polish coin.

A sudden commotion in the vestibule recalled Box to the present. He could see a knot of uniformed policemen talking excitedly to Pat Driscoll, who had come out of the reception room to see what was the matter. Box saw Sergeant Driscoll point towards Box's office, and in a moment a uniformed sergeant all but burst into the room. Box could see the shining Ms on his collar, telling him that the officer was one of Inspector Hare's men from Southwark.

'Inspector Box? Sir, there's been a bomb outrage at Weavers' Lane Police Station. The outer wall of the cell block has been blown apart, and the prisoner Grunwalski has escaped. Mr Hare wants you to come straight away.'

'Any casualties?' Box was struggling into his overcoat as he spoke.

'Two constables wounded, sir, and one detainee badly injured. No deaths.'

The eagle coin lay where Box had left it on the long office table, glinting in the firelight. He scooped it up, thrust it into one of his waistcoat pockets, and was out through the office door before the sergeant had finished speaking. In less than a minute he was in a police cab, and clattering out of Whitehall towards London Bridge.

Box stood beside Inspector Hare in the alley behind Weavers' Lane Police Station, where the back wall of the cell block had been blown inward to a height of some thirty feet. By the light of the gas flares standing in the alley, he could see the exposed floor of the upper storey, which was sagging downward dangerously. The ground was littered with bricks and shattered timber. There was a smell of gunpowder and scorched plaster in the air.

'It's a mercy that no one was killed,' said Inspector Hare. His voice no longer held the weary cynicism of that morning, when he had received Sergeant Knollys into the boiler room. He sounded not only shocked but affronted. He nodded towards an ambulance standing at the entrance to the alley, two uneasy horses between the shafts.

'Two of my constables are in there, waiting to be taken to Guy's Hospital. One of them has a broken arm, and the other one's received internal injuries.'

'And this was done to spring Anders Grunwalski from custody?'

'It was. We all thought he was some kind of wild amateur with a grudge against society. Other folk thought him worth exploding a bomb to get him out. In God's name, Mr Box, who can be behind this wretched man?'

Hare's uniform was covered in plaster-dust, and his right hand was roughly bandaged. He looked bewildered, and suddenly out of his depth.

'What happened exactly, Mr Hare?' asked Box.

Hare led the way out of the alley and into Weavers' Lane, where the front of the police station was a blaze of light. The roadway was crowded with excited onlookers, who simply ignored the efforts of the police to move them on.

'It was like this,' said Hare, when the two men were safely ensconced in the inspector's cramped office. 'I've two sergeants and four constables here. One sergeant and two of the constables were out on patrol – it was near on nine o'clock. The others were in here with me, carrying out routine work. I had three prisoners in the cells, Grunwalski and a couple of local drunks. The drunks would have been let out tomorrow morning, with a warning from me. Grunwalski was due to appear before Mr Locke in Tooley Street on Monday morning.

'And then, suddenly, there came an almighty crash and bang, and the whole building shook like a house of cards. We ran out into the street and, as we did so, there came another explosion, and a sound like showers of bricks raining down from the sky. The upshot of all this was, that the cells were breached, and Grunwalski was spirited away into the dark. One of the two drunks was very badly injured, and he's already been taken to Guy's.'

'Did my sergeant, Jack Knollys, ask to see this Grunwalski's pistol?'

'What? Yes, he did. He asked whether he could keep it for a while, as he knew where it must have come from. So I gave it to him.'

Inspector's Hare's eyes suddenly assumed an expression of mute pleading.

'Mr Box,' he said, 'this business is too big for me to handle. Will you agree to be associated with the case of Grunwalski's disappearance?'

'I will indeed, Mr Hare. This is certainly a task for Scotland Yard. I think we all realize now that there's more to this Anders Grunwalski than meets the eye.'

4

A Death in Sherry Wine Court

ARNOLD BOX WAS breakfasting in his first-floor lodgings at Cardinal Court when there came a knocking on the front door below. He heard the cheerful tones of Mrs Peach as she admitted someone to the house. In a moment the door opened, and his landlady ushered Sergeant Knollys into Box's living-room.

'Ah! Jack. Sit down, and pour yourself a cup of tea – there's another cup and saucer there, on top of the bookcase. I'm glad you've called. Tell me what you found out about Grunwalski's pistol. Inspector Hare told me that you'd asked him for it.'

Sergeant Knollys did as he was bid, and filled his cup to the brim from Box's brown glazed teapot. He also helped himself to a piece of toast, which he ate without butter or marmalade. Box continued to attack his plate of sausage, bacon and egg.

'Sir,' said Knollys, 'I've heard all about last night's bombing at Weavers' Lane, so there's no need to brief me about that. Evidently our lone wolf Grunwalski wasn't as lonely as we thought. But let me tell you about that pistol. I recognized it straight away as the one that was stolen last month from Knightsbridge Barracks. You remember the quartermaster reporting the theft to us?'

'Yes, he came in here on 17 May, as I recall. Very intelligent of him to think that it might have been more than a routine theft. Go on.'

'Well, Grunwalski's weapon was obviously a military revolver, a .455, and its identifying number was etched along the underside of the barrel. So whoever stole it, sir, stole it for Grunwalski to use.'

'Well done, Jack! That was a peculiar business, you know. Just that single pistol was removed from the armoury, with no sign of a break-in. Stolen to order.... What did you do then?'

'I went straight away to Knightsbridge, and saw the sergeant armourer. He confirmed that the weapon was indeed the missing revolver. "Can we have it back?" he asked. "No", I said. "It's wanted as evidence". Don't you want that sausage, sir?'

'What? No, I've had enough. A single weapon stolen, and it ends up in Grunwalski's pocket.... I'm getting too old for this job, Jack. I can't make head nor tail of it.'

Sergeant Knollys had retrieved the unwanted sausage from Box's plate, and was busy demolishing it.

'You're right, sir,' said Knollys between mouthfuls, 'there's something missing. We're not seeing the full picture. Grunwalski's a Polish name. Do you think that might be significant?'

'I do, Jack, and that's why I'm going to visit an old man I know who keeps a shop in Sherry Wine Court, just off Maiden Lane. He could enlighten us on matters Polish, and especially on *this* interesting piece of evidence. Mr Fitz found it among Grunwalski's effects.' Box produced the Polish coin from his waistcoat pocket, and showed it to Knollys.

'It's dated 1836 – a bit of an antique, I'd have thought,' said Knollys. 'But of course, you never know what passes for currency in these foreign countries.'

'Maybe it's time we found out,' said Box. 'Have you finished your breakfast? Are you sure you wouldn't like me to ring for another slice of toast? Good. It's just after nine, so let's take a stroll up the Strand in the direction of Maiden Lane.'

'Sir,' said Knollys, 'I'd planned to take Vanessa out to Hampstead Heath this afternoon. There's a good train from Broad Street Station at two o'clock—'

'Yes, I know, Jack. But this business won't take us more than half an hour. It may come to nothing, but I want you to be there just in case.'

Although it was Sunday, Sherry Wine Court was thronged with busy people, all intent on various kinds of business. Each side of the narrow thoroughfare was lined with small shops. Knollys, who had never ventured into the small squares off Maiden Lane, counted two kosher butchers, three working jewellers, and an ancient bookshop, with shelves of battered volumes in obscure foreign languages arranged in open book-cases standing on the pavement. The centre of the court was occupied by a fenced-off vegetable market, which seemed to be doing a thriving trade.

Box pointed to a dim shop front, over which was written, *Peter Rosanski. Provisions.*

'This little court, Sergeant Knollys,' he said, 'is a kind of minia-ture Polish quarter. For over a hundred years Polish exiles and immigrants with special skills to offer have set up business here. Some of these shops have been established since the end of the last century. Poles of every complexion, Jew and Gentile, come here to shop and to browse on Sundays, and the authorities turn a blind eye to the legality or otherwise of Sunday opening.'

'It's a fascinating place, sir,' said Knollys. 'Are we going to pay a visit to any particular shop?'

'We are,' Box replied. 'We're going to call on old Peter Rosanski, in what he rather imaginatively calls his provision shop. In fact, it's a grocery, a little political library, a chess club, and a gathering-place for folk who want to read last week's Polish news-papers. I did Peter Rosanski a favour a couple of years ago, and he's looked on me kindly, as it were, ever since. Let's go in.'

Peter Rosanski's premises smelt of exotic pickles and cheeses, overlaid by a strong aroma of pipe tobacco. It was very dim inside, and it took both officers a little time to make out the row of tables where hunched men in foreign clothes played chess or dominoes. Beyond this smoke-laden area was a sort of reading room, where more hunched men occupied themselves with tattered books and newspapers, which they read by the light of guttering candles fixed into empty bottles. A beaded curtain beyond led into what was presumably Peter Rosanski's private quarters.

The proprietor, who was sitting behind a small counter, looked up and smiled as the two men entered the shop. Before they could say a word, he burst into speech.

'Inspector Box! I wondered, yes, I wondered, after yesterday's drama at the bridge, whether one or other of you Scotland Yarders would come here. How are you? And this hefty young man – your sergeant, no?'

Sergeant Knollys looked at Peter Rosanski with interest. He was a man well over seventy, with a mane of silver hair and a thick drooping moustache. He surveyed the world from hooded grey eyes, and his voice still held the trace of a foreign accent. He looked a benign and harmless man, who might yet have experienced hardships and injustices in earlier years. Knollys knew that there were many such foreign exiles in England.

'This is Sergeant Knollys,' said Box, 'a fellow toiler among the teeming millions. I want to show you something, Monsieur Rosanski, and then listen to what you can tell me about it.'

Box produced the coin that had been found among Grunwalski's effects, and placed it on the counter. Rosanski picked it up, peered at it, and then threw it down. He regarded the handsome coin with undisguised distaste.

'You want to know what this coin is? You have reasons? That, my friends, is a so-called Polish coin. I say "so-called" because there is no such place as Poland! It's a political fiction, if you know what I mean by that. You see the inscription in Cyrillic? "30 Kopeks". That is Russian money. And beneath it, in the Polish alphabet, firmly in second place, its equivalent value in the land calling itself Poland: 2 zlotys.'

'So this is a coin of the Kingdom of Poland—'

'I tell you, there is no such place!'

The old man's voice was raised in anger, and one or two of the men at the tables raised their heads to look at him. He turned the coin over on to its other face, and jabbed a stubby finger at it.

'You see that grand coat of arms? It is the arms of Imperial Russia. Poland is simply part of Russia, and the so-called "King of Poland" is the Tsar, Alexander III. You see the great wings of the Imperial Eagle spread wide? Do you see the little shields of the subject peoples displayed across those wings for all to see, to their eternal shame? Look: Kazan. Astrakhan. Siberia. And here, on the other wing, Poland, the Crimea, Finland. Subject states. All parts of the Russian Empire. Any other view of the thing is mere romantic fantasy.'

One of the chess players came across to the counter, and murmured a few words in Rosanski's ear. The language was unknown to Box and Knollys, but they could see from the man's expression that they were kindly meant.

Monsieur Rosanski made some placatory noises, and the man returned to his game.

'This Grunwalski,' said the old shopkeeper, lowering his voice to a confidential whisper, 'I do not know him, and he has not been in here, thank God! That name, you know, is German in origin, and it means "a man who comes from Grunwald". That is the name of a place where a great battle was fought in the year 1410, in which the Poles – they were real Poles, then – defeated the Teutonic Knights. A famous victory, you see. Grunwalski is a rare name in Poland. Perhaps this hothead with his bomb adopted the name out of misguided patriotism, I don't know. But he's not been in here.'

Had the old man realized that he had shown knowledge of Grunwalski, even though Box had not mentioned the name? Age was a careless warder of secrets.

Rosanski picked up the coin again, and pointed to the words

'30 Kopeks'. He glanced round the shop in a furtive way, which seemed uncharacteristic of the man. He lowered his voice once more.

'This coin – there is more to it than meets the eye, Inspector. I have lived in this country for forty years, and I don't approve of conspirators from abroad coming here and making trouble for people like me, and the good traders you will find in this little court. I close this shop on Sundays at four o'clock. Come back then, you and Sergeant Knollys, and I will tell you what this coin signifies. You found it in Grunwalski's house, I expect? Yes, I thought so. Well, that would suggest that he was a member of The Thirty—'

He stopped short as one of the readers at the back of the shop rose abruptly and disappeared from sight through the beaded curtain.

'Walls have ears, Mr Box,' said Rosanski. 'Come back at half past four this afternoon, and I will tell you what that so-called Polish coin – the coin for thirty kopeks – signifies. Meanwhile, keep it safe.'

As soon as Box and Knollys had left the shop, the beaded curtain parted, and an impressive figure emerged, tall, blue-eyed, with a gold-framed monocle in his right eye. He boasted a luxuriant mane of blond hair, recently trimmed, and a fine golden beard. One or two of the men reading at the tables made as if to stand up as he passed, but he prevented them with a kindly gesture.

'You have a goodly crowd here today, Rosanski,' said the notable, stopping for a moment at the counter. 'And, unless I'm much mistaken, a couple of visitors from Scotland Yard. A little word of advice. Take care, *pan*, whom you speak to, and what you say. There are dangerous folk about.'

Old Monsieur Rosanski frowned. He lived in a free country, and did not like that kind of talk. Was it merely a warning, or a threat?

'As to that, *magnat*,' he replied, 'England is a free country, and I shall say what I like about anything, under the law. But I take your words in a good spirit.'

The notable smiled, and settled his silk hat on his head.

'Well, *pan*, I can but advise. I can hardly coerce you into silence. As you say, England is a free country.'

He opened the door, and swept out into Sherry Wine Court.

There was a wild, irregular beauty about Hampstead Heath that appealed to Jack Knollys. London's parks were without equal, but they were carefully planned and laid out, so that the evidence of man's hand and mind was everywhere. The heath, natural and unspoilt, stood over 400 feet above sea level, and the air was pure and invigorating.

He and his fiancée, Vanessa Drake, had strolled up its hills and descended into its hollows, watching the crowds of people who had flocked there to escape the heat and dust of the hot June day. A gaggle of carefree girls had danced for a while to the accompaniment of a mouth organ played by a young man in a bowler hat, before collapsing on the grass in fits of giggles. Here and there, couples with young children had spread out picnics on the grass, which they had to share perforce with interested wasps.

By four o'clock they were both tired, and made their way to the flagstaff, turning round to look once more at the breathtaking view west, where the dome of St Paul's and the towers of Westminster could be seen dimly to the south in the haze, as though London were a far-off city. Then they made their leisurely way to Jack Straw's Castle for tea and cakes in the garden.

Jack Knollys glanced covertly at his fiancée, and saw the familiar wistful expression come into her blue eyes. She's thinking of my exploits at Tower Bridge yesterday, he thought, and she's envying me the excitement of it all. In a moment she'll ask me all about it, and I'll tell her as much about Anders Grunwalski as is prudent.

How he loved her! Slender, and very feminine, with true blonde hair and lively blue eyes, she was as fearless as a lion – why, she had once rushed down a flight of stairs to rescue him from a ruthless killer! She'd only just turned twenty then. She was over twenty-one now, and legally a woman, but her girlish yearning for adventure was as strong as ever. Whatever changes the years brought about, to him she would always be a girl.

'Jack,' said Vanessa Drake, 'are you going to tell me about yesterday? You know I'll nag you till you do. That's not very lady-like, I know, but nature never intended me to sit demurely behind the tea cups.'

Jack Knollys laughed. 'Come on, Cornflower,' he said, 'time for us to catch our train back to Broad Street. On the way, I'll tell you all about it.'

Later, as they sat together in a third-class compartment of the train, Vanessa thought of how her life had changed after the murder of her former fiancé, and her recruitment into an amorphous band of special State servants operating on the fringes of national security. The tasks that had been assigned to her had brought her dramatically into contact with the giant detective sergeant sitting beside her, a startling man in many ways, badly disfigured in a gang fight, as strong as an ox, but unexpectedly tender in a matter-of-fact sort of way that appealed to her. In the pursuit of their different duties, both of them had come perilously near to death.

Well, now she knew all about this man Anders Grunwalski – or, at least, as much as Jack chose to tell her. She knew about the dramatic attempt to blow up the new bridge on its opening day, and how her splendid fiancé had helped to thwart the bomber's plans.

It had been a lovely, exhilarating afternoon out, the kind of treat that Jack loved to provide for her. But oh! She missed the thrill of adventure, the curious satisfaction of flirting with danger, that elevated above the commonplace her rather dull life as an expert needlewoman at Watts & Co in Westminster. Perhaps one day Colonel Kershaw—? Well, she would wait in patience for the time when, once again, perhaps, she would be called upon to play the part of an unsung heroine!

As Arnold Box turned out of Maiden Lane into Sherry Wine Court he saw a crowd of excited men and women gathered around the door of Peter Rosanski's shop. They spoke in a high-toned chatter, and in a language that he assumed to be Polish, but even at a distance Box could detect the signs of fear and anger in the general cacophony.

At the end of the court two vehicles stood, their horses chafing nervously at the bits. One was a Metropolitan Police ambulance. The other was an empty civilian hearse, looking bleak and mournful without its usual adornment of feathers. A police sergeant and a number of constables were busying themselves around the vehicles. What had happened? Was Peter Rosanski injured, or dead?

Box shouldered his way through the crowd, and crossed the threshold of the shop.

It was a bizarre scene that met his eyes. Peter Rosanski lay on a stretcher which had been placed on the floor in front of the counter and, at the moment of Box's entrance, an undertaker, watched by his silent assistant, had just finished composing the dead man's limbs. A dark patch of blood on Rosanski's waistcoat told Box that the old man had been stabbed under the ribs. His fierce moustache still bristled, seemingly in defiance of his fate, but his open eyes were incurious, as though the events of this world no longer interested him.

Standing patiently beside the body was a tall, strong man clad in a blood-covered butcher's apron. The very air around him smelt of blood. He was a stout man, with a double chin and a shining bald head. In his right hand he held a butcher's cleaver, and in his left, a bloodstained steak knife.

For one chilling moment Box thought that he was looking at the murderer of Peter Rosanski, but then the bead curtain at the back of the shop parted, and a uniformed police inspector came out into the dim room. The inspector peered short-sightedly at Box for a moment, and then greeted him by name.

'Detective Inspector Box? You got here quickly, didn't you? This murder's not half an hour old. You won't remember me, I expect. Inspector Pollard, "E" Division. We worked together once, about four years ago, when we brought in Killer Shelmerdine at Hackney. This is a shocking business, Mr Box. Poor old Peter Rosanski never harmed a soul.'

Box glanced at the counter, where a few jars of sweets and pickles were displayed for sale. Written in chalk across the counter in bold capital letters was a foreign word: ZDRAJCA.

'I wonder what that means, Mr Pollard?' asked Box. Before the inspector could reply, the man in the butcher's apron burst into speech.

'That word is Polish, and it means renegade, traitor. It was written there on the counter by the scum who stabbed him in the ribs – a mean little runt of a man, like a weasel, a rat-faced man.... I tell you, Policeman, Peter Rosanski was no traitor. He was a good man, who loved living here in England. He loved the Queen, and this country that had adopted him – adopted all of us who live in this court. Well, rat-face has my mark upon him, and you will put him where he belongs – on the gallows.'

'You did well, Mr Aaronson,' said Inspector Pollard. 'I'll want to ask you a few questions later, but for the moment you'd better go back to your shop. It's getting a bit crowded in here.'

The big butcher nodded, and turned on his heel. They could all hear the crescendo of voices as he made his way back to his premises across the court. The undertaker, who had been showing signs of restlessness, motioned to the silent figure on the stretcher.

'Is it in order for us to take the deceased away now, Mr

Pollard? Perhaps you'd care to step into the back room until we've placed him in the coffin? Then we'll be on our way to Horseferry Road.'

As Box and Pollard walked towards the beaded curtain at the back of the shop, Box saw the plain black coffin that the undertakers must have brought with them. Only that morning, the man who was destined to occupy it had been in vigorous life. Murder was a foul business.

'We have an arrangement with them,' said Inspector Pollard, as they had entered the sparsely furnished back room. 'The undertakers, I mean. It's more dignified to have people taken away in a hearse than bundled into a closed hand-ambulance or a cart.'

'I saw a police ambulance standing beside the hearse at the top of the court,' said Box. 'Who was the ambulance for? Have you caught the villain already?'

'Yes, we have, so, thank goodness, it's an open and shut case. I'll tell you all about it in a minute. Rosanski was stabbed under the ribs with a steak knife. The police surgeon, who's been and gone, says that his heart was ruptured, and that he died instantly. This murder was the work of a professional assassin, Mr Box. It would have been quick, and very effective. There's not much blood to be seen, because bleeding in this case would have been internal, so the surgeon said.'

'What happened exactly, Mr Pollard?'

'Just before Monsieur Rosanski shut up shop, our butcher friend, Mr Aaronson glanced across the court from his shop, and saw the weasel-faced man running down the steps, bloody steak-knife in hand. Aaronson rushed out and tackled him.'

'That was brave of him. Not many men would tackle an armed killer.'

'No, they wouldn't. But our killer had met his match in Mr Aaronson. The man snarled at him and tried to stab him with the steak-knife. Aaronson chopped him in the arm with his meat cleaver, and that put the man well and truly out of action.

Somebody had already run to fetch us, and we were here within minutes. The killer's under restraint in the police ambulance, which I telegraphed to be sent here from Carter Street. Poor Rosanski will be on his way to Horseferry Road mortuary by now. As I said, it's an open and shut case.'

'Did you establish the identity of the killer? Another Pole, I expect, if he called poor Rosanski a traitor.'

'Well, Mr Box, I recognized him as soon as I saw him lying on the cobbles, bleeding like a pig, with Aaronson standing guard over him with that fearsome cleaver of his. But he's not a Pole; he's a German, Oscar Schumann by name, who's been suspected of more than one killing on our patch over the years. Well, we've got him this time. I don't know what his motive was, but I expect we'll get it out of him.'

'Why did he write that Polish word on the counter?'

'I reckon that was a blind, Mr Box. When we searched him, we found a piece of paper in his pocket with that word printed on it. ZDRAJCA. It beats me how these Poles manage to pronounce some of their words.'

'You think he had that paper to remind him how to spell the word when he came to write it on the counter?'

'I do. He wasn't meant to get caught, you see. If he hadn't been caught, we'd have thought it was some kind of Polish vendetta being worked out. We've had things of that sort happening round here before. Of course, he could have been hired by one or other of the Polish factions to carry out the assassination. We'll see. Do you want to be associated with this case, Mr Box?'

'I don't think so, Mr Pollard. It's obviously a divisional matter, and my business with Monsieur Rosanski was nothing to do with vendettas. It was something arising from an incident that occurred at Tower Bridge yesterday. Perhaps you'd send me a note at the Rents in a couple of days' time, to tell me how you've got on.'

'As you please, Mr Box. I'll just straighten things up here, and make all safe, and then I'll get back to Bow Street. I was supposed to be off at three. Maybe, later, I'll be able to salvage what's left of Sunday, and get back home to my family.'

When Box arrived at King James's Rents just before eight o'clock on Monday morning, the frock-coated figure of Superintendent Mackharness appeared at the top of the stairs. He greeted Box with his usual morning ritual.

'Up here, Box, if you please. I shan't keep you more than a minute.'

Box joined his superior officer in the mildewed office on the first floor. Mackharness picked up a folded letter from his desk, and flicked it open with one of his stubby fingers.

'Now, Box, I found a note from the assistant commissioner waiting for me here this morning. It tells us that a Mr Hugo Lang, assistant secretary of the Geological Society, has definite information about Grunwalski, which he is anxious to impart to us. He has asked for you by name. The society has its premises in Burlington House, on the north side of Piccadilly. This Mr Lang is available this morning, at any time between nine and ten o'clock. Go there, will you, Box, and see what this man can tell us.'

'The Geological Society?'

'Yes, Box, it means having to do with rocks and stones – that kind of thing. Oh, and while you're here, I brought you and Sergeant Knollys a little memento of Saturday's doings. The official doings, I mean.'

Mackharness handed Box two attractively coloured programmes, souvenirs of the opening of Tower Bridge. The covers showed three fine photographs of the new structure, together with portraits of the Prince and Princess of Wales. It was a kindly gesture from a man whose normal mien was stiff, rigorously formal, and rather forbidding.

'Well, thank you very much, sir,' said Box. 'That's most kind of you, and most appreciated. Did you have a good day on Saturday, sir?'

'A most gratifying day, thank you, Box. I spent most of it in the company of my friend Lord Maurice Vale Rose, a man who keeps a splendid table, and an even more splendid cellar. Anyway, get down there now, will you? The Geological Society, in Burlington House.'

5

Rumours of Wars

As Arnold Box crossed the dusty carriageway of Piccadilly, an elderly, pink-faced man who had been standing under the grand archway of Burlington House, came down the steps to greet him.

'Inspector Box? I am Hugo Lang. It's very good of you to come to see us at such short notice. Let me conduct you to our offices in the east wing.'

Box followed Lang up a marble staircase and along a carpeted corridor. They passed through a deserted library, and then through a long storeroom, its shelves bulging with sheaves of yellowing papers tied up into bundles.

Box knew by now whom he would find when they reached journey's end. A man would be waiting to talk to him, and they would greet each other by a familiar verbal ritual. The outcome of their interview would be some kind of enlightenment, and almost inevitably an invitation to put himself into danger.

Hugo Lang stopped at a door in the corner of the room, knocked, and motioned Box to enter. He did so and, as the door was closed behind him, he heard a key on the outside turn quietly in the lock.

Yes; there he was, sitting at a plain deal table in the window, looking out at the tranquil gardens beyond the courtyard, a slight, sandy-haired man in his late forties or early fifties, with a mild face and an almost apologetic air about him. He was dressed very formally in a morning coat, complemented by a white waistcoat and dark silk cravat. A tall silk hat, in which he had deposited a pair of black suede gloves, stood on the table beside an ebony walking-cane. The man spoke, and the well-known ritual began.

'Good morning, Mr Box.'

'Good morning, Colonel Kershaw. So it's like that, is it?'

'Yes, Box, it's like that.' His voice, as always on these occasions, held a tone of sardonic weariness.

This would be the fourth time, Box mused, that Lieutenant-Colonel Sir Adrian Kershaw, RA, Knight Commander of the Bath, had begun the process of luring him away from his police work at Scotland Yard and into the perilous subtleties of secret intelligence. Colonel Kershaw was one of the powers behind the Throne. He was rightly feared by his enemies; but it was perhaps more significant that he was feared, too, by his friends.

'Will you smoke a cigar with me, Mr Box?'

'I will, sir.'

Kershaw offered Box his cigar case. Three slim cigars reposed in the case, and beside them a tightly rolled spill of paper tied neatly with twine. Box took a cigar, and with it the spill of paper, which he placed without comment in a pocket. He knew what it was, and there was no call for either man to comment on it.

'The time has come, Mr Box,' said Kershaw, when their cigars were lit, 'for me to tell you some things that you need to know about Saturday's events at Tower Bridge, and what followed them. I should imagine that you've been working in the dark since then.'

'When you say events, sir—'

'When I say events, Mr Box, I mean not only the apparent attempt by Anders Grunwalski to blow up the bridge, but also the murder yesterday of Mr Peter Rosanski in Sherry Wine Court. The two things are linked, as I expect you realize.'

'Anything that you can tell me about Anders Grunwalski will be very welcome, sir,' said Box. 'Is he a lone wolf, seeking vengeance on society for some imaginary slight, or is he part of a conspiracy? And, perhaps of more immediate concern, where is he now? To my way of thinking, those two questions require urgent answers.'

Colonel Kershaw sighed, and his eyes narrowed.

'I don't know *where* he is, Box,' he said. 'I wish I did. We'll talk about that aspect of the affair in a minute. As for Anders Grunwalski himself – well, he is neither a conspirator nor a lone wolf. Anders Grunwalski is one of *my* people.'

Box searched for something pertinent to say. Kershaw remained as still as ever. He was looking slightly shamefaced and abashed, as though he had just owned up to a lapse of taste. He drew on his cigar, waiting for Box to speak.

'One of *your* people?' said Box, finding his voice at last. 'Did you—'

Colonel Kershaw held up a hand to stem Box's projected flow of speech.

'No, Box, I did *not* dynamite a police station in order to set Grunwalski free! I could have easily arranged for his release from custody by less spectacular means. I've no idea *who* blew up the police station in Weavers' Lane in order to get Grunwalski out. And I've no idea where they've taken him. Do you want to hear more?'

'Yes, sir,' Box replied. 'I very much want to hear more.'

Box's daily work was fraught with dangers, but there was something especially thrilling about Colonel Kershaw's invitations to co-operate with him. This man, the head of secret intelligence, often held the whole safety of the nation in his hands. He was answerable only to the Queen, who would place the great organs of the State at his command when the need arose. And it was this man who, on certain occasions, had sought the help of Box, a mere Scotland Yard detective inspector, to be his companion on adventures that could affect the very peace and prosperity of Europe.

'Well done, Box,' said Kershaw. 'I knew that I could rely upon you. If you and I have to follow the chase wherever it takes us, you can rest assured that your way will be smoothed for you at Scotland Yard. But first, let me tell you about Grunwalski.

'Anders Grunwalski is a former officer in the Rifle Brigade, or the City of London Regiment, as it's often called. He's a champion shot with pistol and rifle, and with many trophies to prove it.'

'And he's one of your people?'

'He is. I lured him away from Hounslow Barracks two years ago, and employed him very effectively to quell the French-inspired mutiny aboard HMS *Dagmar* in Portsmouth harbour. You may remember that business? The Fusiliers wanted him back after that, but I wouldn't give him up. I kept him as one of my people.'

'I'd no idea that you were involved in the HMS *Dagmar* affair,' said Box. 'As I recall, the mutiny was fomented by the second mate, a man called Freeman, who had forged links with the European socialist movements. When he realized that his position was hopeless, he shot himself on the bridge of the *Dagmar*, in full view of the mutineers, and that was the end of the mutiny.'

'Well, that's the effect we hoped to achieve, Box. In fact, Freeman was shot dead by Grunwalski, who was posted on the roof of one of the dockside buildings. Now, you're to keep that to yourself, Box, do you hear? You look shocked, but there are times when these things have to be done. There was far more to that affair of the *Dagmar* than a mere mutiny.'

Box said nothing. He knew that preserving the safety of Britain and its peoples required a special type of patriotic duty.

'At the age of twenty,' Kershaw continued, 'Grunwalski distinguished himself in the Afghan War, and was mentioned in despatches. He's thirty-five now. He's of Polish origin, but his family have been British subjects for generations.'

Colonel Kershaw reached into his pocket and produced a small photograph, which he handed to Box. It showed a young, clean-shaven man in military uniform, with the flame-crowned badges of the Royal Fusiliers on the collar. The stern face revealed nothing of the man himself, but Box recognized the likeness: it was the same man as the one in Superintendent Mackharness's photograph – the terrorist on the bridge.

'That's Grunwalski as he really is,' said Kershaw, 'and in a moment I'll tell you what he was doing on Tower Bridge last Saturday, and why he brought with him a carefully doctored and harmless bomb. But first, Box, I must give you a broader picture of what this business is about.'

Colonel Kershaw stubbed out his cigar in a Benares brass vase, and carefully unfolded a great map of Europe, which he spread out across the table.

'Let us look for a moment at this political map of Europe, which I have brought here especially to show you. How would you describe the proportions of that map, Mr Box? Incidentally, it's a German map, and the man who made it sees Europe through German eyes.'

'Well, sir,' said Box, 'I'd say that the map-maker has shown all the major lands of Europe as being crushed up together to the west of the Continent in a dangerous kind of huddle, with Kaiser William's Germany at its centre.... There's France, tinted a nice pale buff, rubbing shoulders with the German Reich; and there's Austria-Hungary, crowding up against Germany's flank. And what's that little country, penning Germany in to the south? Switzerland. Yes, sir, they're all huddled together, and the German Reich in particular looks as though it might explode at any moment to find itself more living-space!'

'Excellent, Box!' cried Kershaw. 'Really, you ought to have been a political strategist. You've read the past history of Europe in those remarks of yours – and, who knows, you may have seen the future as well. Now cast your eyes beyond the eastern borders of Germany and Austria. What do you see?'

The Empire of Russia.... A vast, seemingly boundless land, which the cartographer had tinted a sober greenish grey; a land that stretched down from the Arctic seas to the borders of the Turkish Empire. Far away to the east, at the farthest extent of its Siberian lands, its thriving modern port of Vladivostok extended beyond the landmass of China, and faced the burgeoning islands of the Empire of Japan.

'I can see Russia, sir,' Box replied. 'Rather a large kind of place, isn't it? It's practically falling off the map at the right-hand edge. No lack of living-space there!'

'As you say, Box, it's a large kind of place. And if you look back again to the west, at that part of the vast expanse of green bordering on Germany, you'll see what was once Poland, a mere name on a map – "Polen" in the German language – without boundaries or identity of its own. Poland, at this moment in history, is simply a part of Russia, and the Tsar no longer bothers to call himself King of Poland. The same depressing reality applies to Finland, and Lithuania, and other little Baltic states whose names are now almost forgotten.'

Box recalled the words of Peter Rosanski, spoken on the previous day, hours before his murder: 'There is no such place as Poland! It's a political fiction.... Poland is simply part of Russia, and the so-called "King of Poland" is the Tsar Alexander III. Any other view of the thing is mere romantic fantasy.'

'Poland was a great power, once,' Kershaw continued, 'instrumental in driving the Turk away from the gates of Vienna. But that was centuries in the past. Just on a hundred years ago, in 1794, Prussia and Russia divided Poland between them, awarding part of it to Austria, in order to maintain the balance of power. From that moment Poland ceased to exist.'

'I seem to remember being told at school that Napoleon did something about Poland,' said Box.

'He did. In 1807 Napoleon created the Grand Duchy of Warsaw, but that disappeared in 1815. Despite various abortive risings, and much bravery from the Polish remnant, the country suffered from weak and badly trained armies, which made it an easy candidate for partition. The nation of Poland no longer exists. At the present time, it is merely long-annexed parts of Russia, Prussia, and Austria. A dead land, Box, with no hope of resurrection.'

'Very interesting, sir,' said Box. Almost despite himself, he added, 'Very educational.' Colonel Kershaw smiled.

'Yes, Mr Box,' he said, 'I expect you're wondering what all this history has got to be with the business in hand. Well, let me tell you without more ado. I had a man permanently posted in the town of Memel, a place that just manages to cling on to the German shore facing the Eastern Sea. From there, it's literally five minutes' walk into Russia.

'In March this year, this man of mine reported that an elusive group of Polish nationalists had come into being in Warsaw, a group dedicated to the recreation of a Polish kingdom by means of terror and coercion. They had found willing allies in the German city of Danzig, and in other formerly Polish towns in Russia and Austria. My man informed me that this group was assembling a team of seasoned anarchists to launch some kind of assault on an unnamed head of state that would plunge Europe into war—'

'What would be the good of that, sir? How could a European war benefit the Poles?'

'Well, you see, Mr Box, the "unnamed head of state" in this context could only be the Tsar, because if the Tsar was to be assassinated, and the assassins were seen to be Poles, then the Russians would send a vast punitive expedition to teach its Polish subjects a lesson. But any such massing of Russian troops so near the borders of Germany would send the Kaiser into one of his panic-rages, and very soon there would be what are euphemistically called "military exercises" in the region of Breslau and Posen. It would lead to war between Prussia and Russia – do you want me to go on? You've heard all this kind of thing before, when you and I were involved in the Hansa Protocol affair and its very dramatic aftermath.'

'Please go on, sir,' said Box. 'You have the gift of what I call the larger vision, and it will do no harm to share part of the vision with me.'

'Very well. And I appreciate your remarks about my vision, Box. I need at all times to see the many machinations behind the external scene in Europe, and deal with what I see in the only ways that I know. I value you for your objectivity, and your ability to see details that a man of my stamp lacks. But let me continue.

'I say there would be a war between Russia and Prussia. Now, in 1888, the Grand Duke Nicholas of Russia visited Paris, and began there a process that has led to what they call an *entente cordiale*, which is, in fact, a military and economic alliance. Last year, 1893, there was a secret military convention between France and Russia, in which each country guaranteed the other's borders. If Germany were the aggressor, the French guaranteed 1,300,000 troops to rebuff her, and Russia would throw 700,000 men into the field. So you can see, can't you, what would happen if the Russians sent an aggressive force to the German border as a result of this Polish adventure?'

'Yes, sir, I believe I can. Prussia would invade Russia, and then France would send her huge army to Russia's aid. And then, I suppose—'

'And then, you suppose, Box, that Britain would be drawn into the conflict. Well, you may be right. We've no open alliance with either Germany or Russia, but if it seemed that Prussia was to disappear under a pincer movement, and the balance of power in Europe destroyed, then, I think we would be forced to act.'

'What would we do?'

'Well, some kind of hasty alliance with Austria-Hungary would be botched up, and in we'd go. That's what Sir Charles Napier told me last week when I visited him at the Foreign Office. As a nation, we'd gain nothing from the exercise. There would be thousands of deaths. The usual European story. When it comes to the push, Box, Europe and Britain have nothing in common. Our destiny lies elsewhere.'

'And what would happen when the war ended?'

'There would be a settlement, Box, in which the idea of recreating Poland as a buffer state, its borders guaranteed by the Great Powers, would be a serious possibility. In fact, the idea has been mooted in the chancelleries of Europe for the past five years. Prince Orloff – you remember Prince Orloff, the Russian Ambassador? – Orloff spoke quite enthusiastically of the idea when I saw him last month at the Queen's Drawing-Room.'

'But I thought the Tsar wasn't interested in Poland?' said Box.

'He isn't, but you're forgetting, Box, that he will have been assassinated like his father Alexander II before him: that would be the spark that ignited the power-keg of conflict. There would be a new tsar in St Petersburg, and you can be quite sure that promises of French gold and French arms would make the new tsar see sense. Russia would retain her growing friendship with France, and, to balance that, Britain might at long last forge a military and naval alliance with the Kaiser, in order, as always, to preserve the balance of power. The Kaiser would be delighted.'

'The larger vision,' said Box softly.

'Yes, Box,' said Kershaw. 'It's the way I have to think. Your strength, as you know, is your ability to sift through the minutiae of a situation and bring important facts to the light of day. Now, let me tell you about Grunwalski.

'In February of this year I began to prepare Grunwalski for his mission to infiltrate this amorphous group of hotheads. I didn't know who they were – I still don't – but I knew that they'd be very interested in a man of Polish origin who was rapidly acquiring a reputation as a desperate anarchist. He had been furnished with a history, which included his involvement in a number of unsolved assassinations of minor figures in various regions of the Russian Empire. All fiction, of course, but fiction of a very persuasive kind. My own particular rumour mill spread his fame abroad, and stressed the fact that he was a crack shot, particularly with a pistol.'

'Was your man in Memel part of that rumour mill?'

'No, Box. You see, my man in Memel was stabbed to death in his house, which was then set on fire. No one was brought to book for his murder. One day, I have no doubt, his death will be avenged. Something similar happened to one of Sir Charles Napier's people, a man called Paul Claus.

'When I called on Napier recently, he told me that this Paul Claus, his contact in Berlin, was able to confirm that this Polish conspiracy undoubtedly existed, and that a group of people known as The Thirty were associated with them. Claus also mentioned a plan of theirs, "The Aquila Project". That's all anybody knows about this new threat to the peace and stability of Europe.'

'And what happened to this Paul Claus?'

'He was stabbed to death in Berlin on 17 May last. First my man in Memel, then Sir Charles's man in Berlin. It's all part of a familiar and depressing pattern.'

'What did you do with Grunwalski when you were ready to deploy him?'

'I caused Grunwalski to surface into his particular underworld in the middle of April. He took lodgings in Bethnal Green, and set about acquiring a reputation as a dangerous ruffian. To my intense satisfaction, he was approached almost immediately by agents of this group of potential assassins. He was very discreet, but was able to pass information to me by contacting one or two of my nobodies – you know the kind of people I mean. I knew, by the middle of May, that he was to be used to make an attempt on the Tower Bridge.'

Colonel Kershaw sighed. He looked out of the window, and began drumming on the table with his fingers, his eyes apparently fixed on the Civil Service buildings on the other side of Burlington Gardens.

'And then, on Saturday last, Box, it all began to go wrong. Grunwalski walked into a police trap, and was taken into custody. I think it's your turn now to tell *me* a few things.'

'Sir,' said Box, 'when Grunwalski set up his stall in Bethnal Green, he found himself on the patch of my friend Inspector Fitzgerald of "J" Division. Mr Fitz, we call him. He saw through your man Grunwalski at once, I'm afraid. He knew he wasn't a latter-day Fenian, and he suspected that the man rang false. And so, he—'

Box stopped speaking. Was it in order for him to betray Mr Fitz's peculiar ways of working to Kershaw?

'He what, man? Come, now, tell me what he did!'

'Mr Fitz uses unorthodox ways of working, sir, ways that will get him into serious trouble one of these days. He employs a group of sneak-thieves whom he pays out of his own money to do jobs for him. The "light fantastic boys", he calls them. It was the boys who carried out an illegal search of Grunwalski's premises and uncovered all his written arrangements for the attempt on the bridge – diagrams, maps, notes. Mr Fitz read them, and had them put back where the boys had found them, but after Grunwalski was arrested, he brought them all to me at King James's Rents.'

'And what did you think of all those notes and diagrams, Box?'

'I thought that they were signs that there were accomplices of these anarchists in the bridge engineer's office. Later this week, I would have asked Mr Mackharness to make enquiries. But now I see that the plans must have been provided by the engineers at your request.'

'You're right, Box. Did you see the drawing of the bomb? That was designed with the idea of confusing investigators as to its origin. A very eclectic kind of bomb. Did you like it? It was built at Woolwich Arsenal.'

'Yes, sir, it was very nice. Perhaps I should tell you now exactly what took place at the bridge last Saturday, sir, though of course you already know that the bomb had been deliberately built not to explode. Let me tell you now what happened....'

After Box had finished his account of Saturday's events, Colonel Kershaw sat in silence for what seemed like minutes. His mild face betrayed no emotion, but Box saw how his eyes gleamed with something approaching excitement.

'Mr Fitz, you say?' he asked at last. 'Inspector Fitzgerald? What kind of a man is he, Box?'

'He's a very patriotic man, sir,' Box replied. 'It's his hatred of traitors and the like that first got him to break the law in pursuing his official enquiries. He's an expert on the Fenian outrages.'

'Is he? Is he really? And he's not above bending the law a little to meet his requirements? Well, well. Very interesting. I'll bear Mr Fitz in mind.'

'And what will you do about Grunwalski now, sir? Whatever his showing at Tower Bridge, his masters thought highly enough of him to blow up a police station in order to free him. There was something he did there that pleased them mightily.'

'Do you know what I think happened there, Box? I think the whole attack on the bridge was a *rehearsal*, a rehearsal for something quite different! The bomb was never meant to go off, of course, but Grunwalski *was* meant to sprint like mad up the incline, drawing that pistol which I stole for him, and brandishing it in the air.'

'A rehearsal! Well done, sir!' cried Box. 'And perhaps it was also a test of Grunwalski's courage. So we may be faced with an attempt on the life of the Tsar by a solitary pistol shot—'

'Very possibly dressed up as an intended bomb outrage. But now, you see, I've lost all contact with Grunwalski. I don't know where he is, what he's doing, or who it was that freed him from captivity.'

'I think you'll find, sir,' said Box, with a thrill of pleasure, 'that the people responsible are that very group of conspirators mentioned by Paul Claus – The Thirty. Monsieur Rosanski spoke about them, and he was going to tell me who they were on Sunday afternoon. That's why he was murdered, sir, to keep the identity of The Thirty hidden from the light of day. Some at least of those people are here, in London.'

Arnold Box enjoyed Kershaw's air of bewilderment. It wasn't often that he was able to produce that effect. He reached into his waistcoat pocket, took out the Polish coin, and handed it to Kershaw.

'That coin, sir, a Polish coin for thirty kopeks, is probably used as a kind of passport by the members of this Polish conspiracy. That particular coin was found among Grunwalski's effects.'

Kershaw examined the coin briefly, and handed it back to Box.

'Well, I'm damned!' said Colonel Kershaw, and rose from the table. Evidently it was time for them to go. 'We'll meet again soon, Box,' he said, 'because I think there are more things for us to discuss about this business. You know where to find me. The Thirty.... Well, we must do something about them.'

'And we must do all we can to snatch Grunwalski back—'

'Oh, no, Box. I don't want Grunwalski back: I want him to go on with his anarchist's mission unimpeded. He knows what to do when the moment of crisis arrives. But I don't know where he is, and I don't know how to follow his progress. But if *you* find him, let me know, but leave him to go quietly on his way. Incidentally, I mentioned your name to him as a possible contact in time of emergency, so something might come of that. I hope you don't mind?'

'Not at all, sir.'

So the old fox had known all along that he, Box, would agree to work with him once more!

'Incidentally, sir,' said Box, 'there is a man, another mysterious individual, who has appeared on the periphery of this business. I saw him at the bridge on Saturday, peering through a telescope at the boiler rooms. He's a big, Viking sort of man, with flowing hair, a magnificent beard, and a monocle—'

'Ah! That's a perfect description of a man called Baron Augustyniak, a Polish nobleman who has settled recently in a mansion out at St John's Wood. He's come to England, so it's said, to establish a Polish library and cultural institute, whatever that is. We're very interested in the good baron – me, and the Foreign Office, you know. I know nothing of the man, or whether his mission here is genuine, but I intend to find out very soon. I think I know the ideal person to come up with some interesting information about the baron.'

'Augustyniak.... It's quite a memorable name, sir.'

'Yes, it is. And, as I say, there are ways of keeping a cautious eye and ear on people like him. What was he doing near the bridge on Saturday? Was he waiting to see if Grunwalski was successful? It certainly looks like it. If I find out anything of interest, I'll let you know by word of mouth. As you know, I never write anything to anybody.'

Colonel Kershaw picked up his hat and cane, nodded in friendly fashion to Box, and swiftly left through a door half hidden by a screen at the far end of the room. Box heard the lock of the storeroom door click open, and within the minute he was out in the open again, in the crowded thoroughfare of Piccadilly.

Vanessa Drake sat in a chair at the window of her little sitting-room, and looked out at the pitched roofs and pinnacles of Westminster Abbey. A copy of *The Graphic* lay open across her knees, but her mind was elsewhere. She was thinking of Sunday's outing to Hampstead Heath, and her mistaken conviction that Jack Knollys was going to name the day. He'd come very near to it when they were having tea at Jack Straw's Castle, but had then taken fright, and hurried her back to the train.

Never mind! There was plenty of time yet. Jack had his way to make in the Metropolitan Police, and she was content to live quietly in this former Anglican convent, skilfully adapted as apartments for single young ladies. It was conveniently near to Watts &

Co., where she plied her needle patiently in the embroidery department.

Content? No! She was *not* content. Why had life become so dull and uneventful? There was a time when she had risked danger and death in the service of Colonel Kershaw and his secret intelligence organization. On one of those occasions, she had been within seconds of death. But now....

There came a knock on the door, and a moment later Colonel Kershaw himself walked into the room. He had once told her not to stand up for him in her own home, but she was quite unable to prevent herself from springing up from her chair with an exclamation of delight.

Colonel Kershaw was wearing civilian clothing, and made no attempt to take off his long dark overcoat with the astrakhan collar, because, as she knew, he always liked to create the fiction that he had simply called on her quite fortuitously in passing. He sat down at the table, peeled off his black suede gloves, and deposited them in his silk hat.

'Well, missy,' he said, 'and how are you today?'

'I'm very well, thank you, sir.'

'Excellent. I'm glad to hear it. Your jaunt out to Hampstead evidently did you good. No, I wasn't there myself, Miss Drake, but somebody I know saw you there with Sergeant Knollys. People are always coming to tell me things, you know. Now, if I were to inform you that I have something interesting going forward at the moment, would you care to be associated with it?'

'Oh, yes, sir!'

Vanessa made no attempt to conceal her delight. She saw Kershaw smile with affectionate good humour. He was always amused and gratified, she thought, by her unconcealed enthusiasm.

'What I want you to do, Miss Drake,' said Kershaw, 'is to take up a position as one of two housemaids at the residence of a Polish aristocratic gentleman in St John's Wood. You've no objection, I take it, to turning yourself into a servant for a while? No, I thought not. The gentleman's name is Baron Augustyniak – no, don't write it down, missy, just try to remember it. Augustyniak. We never write down anything in our organization, so there's nothing for our enemies to read.'

'And what am I to do, sir, when I go to work for this gentleman?'

'You're to look and listen – as you were supposed to do when I sent you to the home of Baroness Felssen during our investigation of the Bleibner affair. You remember? You had ideas of your own, which got you into trouble.'

Vanessa had the grace to blush. It was on that occasion that her inquisitiveness had caused her to exceed her orders in such a way as to bring her very near to death, while ensuring the escape of a very dangerous assassin. If Colonel Kershaw saw the blush, he made no sign of the fact. But she had realized that his words had been a warning to do as she was told.

'Keep an ear open, Miss Drake,' Kershaw continued, 'for anything that might be said in conversation about the Tsar of Russia, or about European politics in general. A housemaid, as you may or may not know, cleans bedrooms and reception rooms, looks after the dining-room, and waits at table during dinner. Plenty of opportunities there for you to overhear without seeming to do so. When the time comes, you will be told how to leave Baron Augustyniak's service, and report to me. What do you say to that?'

'When do I start, sir? And what about my employer?'

'Don't worry about Watts & Company, Miss Drake. They know all about me now, and what work I do. As for when you start, well, you must receive a day's training first. You will go to see Mrs Prout at Bagot's Hotel, and she will tell you all about being a housemaid – how to stare straight ahead when waiting at dinner, and not keep looking at the diners. How to curtsy – all that kind of thing.

'After that, you'll go out to White Eagle Lodge, Baron Augustyniak's residence in Cavendish Gardens, St John's Wood. All the staff there have been newly recruited by Thompson's Agency. You will appear on their books as Susan Moore – Vanessa being a decidedly unsuitable name for a housemaid! Mrs Bagot will tell you all you need to know. I'll go now, missy. Do as you're told, and all should be well. And remember: there may be danger, but you will never be more than a breath away from help.'

6

A Half-crown for Kitty Fisher

KITTY FISHER WINCED as a packed train thundered across the railway bridge spanning Ludgate Circus. A great swath of acrid black smoke was blown down on to the pavement, and Kitty coughed, more in protest than discomfort.

Bloomin' cheek! It was no joke standing for hours in bare feet on a hot summer pavement. The trains should have more consideration for the likes of her. This was a favourite spot of hers, in a corner just to the right of Bell & Pritchard's, the tailors. City gents tended to notice a pretty girl of fourteen with a tray round her neck, selling boxes of matches, bootlaces, and packets of pen nibs. When it rained, she'd move under the bridge until it stopped. She could make a shilling or more a day on this patch.

The road was crammed full with heavy Wednesday morning traffic, some pouring in from Fleet Street and Farringdon Street, and some climbing the hill towards St Paul's. The pavements were crowded, too. A close-packed knot of men hurried past her, none of them evidently in need of matches. Oh, well! Perhaps later.

What time was it? She walked to the other side of the bridge, where she could see the clock in St Paul's. Ten past two. In a few minutes' time the barmaid at the King Lud across the road would beckon to her, and she'd be given a cup of mild beer and a piece of bread. God bless her! Janie had a heart of gold. Kitty returned to her pitch near the tailor's shop.

Whatever now? Three men, looking neither to right nor left, had hurried past in yet another throng of busy folk. As they'd passed her, one of them had thrown a little parcel into her tray! Bloomin' cheek!

Ten minutes later, Kitty was sitting in a store room behind the bar of the King Lud tavern, sipping her beer, and devouring her round of bread and jam. When Janie, the barmaid, came in from the front to see how she was, Kitty showed her the little parcel that had landed in her tray.

'It's got writing on it, Janie,' she said, 'but I can't read. What does it say? Maybe it's important.'

Janie, a good-natured girl in her twenties, looked at the thin child in the cut-down black dress and shapeless hat. She'd walked out here barefoot to the Circus early, all the way from Shoreditch. Poor little lass! She was pretty, too, but poverty would soon play havoc with her youthful attractions.

The little parcel had been made from a torn piece of handkerchief, tied firmly with cotton. Around it was a strip of paper – it looked like one of the margins from the page of a newspaper – and on it someone had scrawled a message in pencil, which Janie read out to her young friend.

Take this to Mr Box at 2 King James's Rents, Whitehall. He will give you half-a-crown.

'Mr Box? I know him, Kitty. He comes in here sometimes for a glass of India Pale Ale. He's a famous detective-man. Here, there's something wedged into the end of the packet – it's a shilling! That'll be for you, to make sure that you take the message to Mr Box. Inspector Box, he is, really.'

'Half-a-crown.... Do you think it's true? Will he really give it to me?'

'I'm sure he will. Now, you've got a shilling already, so if I were you I'd go to King James's Rents straight away, and see Mr Box. If he's not there, ask them where he is.'

'Half-a-crown.... Will you come with me, Janie? I don't know where it is.'

Janie considered for a moment. The boss would grumble and growl, but he'd let her go for half an hour. Poor little Kitty! Two-and-six was a fortune to her.

'I tell you what, Kitty,' she said, 'Burton's wagon will be leaving in ten minutes' time. It'll be going down the Strand, so the driver can give us a lift as far as the Whitehall end. Leave your tray here till we get back. Come on, let's go off to see Inspector Box.'

While Kitty Fisher was preparing for her visit to King James's Rents, Arnold Box was sitting at the long table in his office, reading a note that he had just received by messenger. It was from Inspector Pollard at Bow Street Police Station, telling him of some further developments in the matter of the Rosanski murder. It was obviously some kind of Polish vendetta, Pollard thought, and the people behind it had hired Schumann to make away with their imagined enemy. Well, Box knew better than that, but it wouldn't do to disabuse Pollard on that point.

Box turned over the note, and whistled in surprise.

'Now here's something that will surprise you,' Pollard had written. 'Oscar Schumann died last night from natural causes in the Middlesex Hospital. The doctors say it was aneurysm of the aorta. He died without speaking, so we'll never know who employed him.'

Box read on. Pollard had managed to compile a list of everybody who had been present in Rosanski's shop on Sunday morning. He would draw Box's attention to two of these people. One was a certain Baron Augustyniak, of White Eagle Lodge, Cavendish Gardens, St John's Wood. As a nobleman, he would probably be a prominent figure in the Polish fraternity, and so worth questioning. The other man was called Herr Gerdler, and he was another German, like Schumann. Perhaps there was a link there. Gerdler was a gunsmith by profession, with premises in Dover Lane, Covent Garden.

It *was* odd, thought Box. If Rosanski's murder was a Polish affair, why should there be Germans connected with it? What time was it? 2.30. It would be a good idea to act on Mr Pollard's information, and pay a call on this Herr Gerdler in Covent Garden.

Dover Lane was a kind of wide alley near the Russell Street approach to Covent Garden Market. The premises of Herr Alois Gerdler were smart and well kept. A discreetly grilled window displayed an impressive array of hunting guns and pistols. A little bell behind the door jangled as Box entered the shop.

A mousy little man with a stoop looked up from a ledger that he had been studying. His face bore a faintly hostile expression, and when he spoke Box saw that his mouth was cruel and thin-lipped.

'Yes?'

'Mr Gerdler?' said Box. 'I'm Detective Inspector Box, of Scotland Yard. This is just a routine call. Would you please show me your current gun licence? We're checking the validity of all such licences this year.'

Box saw the strands of a beaded curtain behind the counter tremble faintly. He wondered who it was in the back room of the shop, listening so intently to their conversation.

'My licence? Yes, I have it here, in this drawer. You'll see that I've been established here for nearly three years. All my papers are thoroughly in order.'

As Box made a show of examining the licence, the beaded curtain suddenly parted, and a man came down the step from the back room. A greater contrast to Gerdler could not have been imagined. Tall and imposing, the man was dressed expensively in black, and sported an orchid in the button hole of his frock coat. His long face was adorned with the type of fierce moustache, waxed and turned up at the ends, favoured by the Kaiser.

'Inspector Box,' said Gerdler, 'it is my privilege to present an old friend from my German days, Herr Doktor Franz Kessler, who is the new Second Secretary at Prussia House.'

'Pleased to meet you, sir,' said Box. 'Well, I must be on my way. It was just a routine call. Good day to you, gentlemen.'

Box raised his hat, and both Germans clicked their heels in response. They watched him as he turned out of Dover Lane into Covent Garden.

'What did that fellow really want with you?' asked Kessler. 'All that talk of a check on licences was a crude fiction.'

'He was involved in the arrest of Grunwalski last Saturday. He was also involved in the investigation of Rosanski's death. He will know all about Oscar Schumann, I expect. He's pestered me first, and now, no doubt, he'll bother Baron Augustyniak with his little questions. Don't let him disturb you, Fritz.'

'I won't, if you say so. But there have been serious leaks of information, some of which have been stopped at source. Sir Charles Napier was in Berlin last month, and made contact with that money-grubbing Judas, Paul Claus. He wouldn't have spoken to Napier unless he had something to tell him. Well, you know what happened to Claus.'

'Do you think that the British intelligence people have discovered what we intend to do? Is Count von Donath quite certain that it is safe for us to act on the twenty-first?'

'Of course it's safe. What can British intelligence possibly know of the matter? How could they even remotely conceive what we intend to do? I've no doubt that they'll be interested in the sudden arrival of Baron Augustyniak and myself in England. They might even look for links between him and me – and you, for that matter, and of course, they'll find them. But they can't possibly guess what our ultimate purpose is. I ask you, how *could* they? Just think of the elaborate charade that we provided for them – the bridge, the waving pistol, the crowd of notables! As the conjurors, say, the quickness of the hand deceives the eye!'

As Box came into the vestibule of 2 King James's Rents, Sergeant Driscoll came out of the reception room near the door.

'Sir,' he said, 'there's a young girl in the front office who wants to talk to you. Kitty Fisher's her name. A peddler, by the looks of her. Says she's fourteen. She's brought some kind of a message wrapped up in a handkerchief.'

'A peddler?' asked Box. 'Is she by herself?'

'A young woman brought her – one of the barmaids from The King Lud. She says she'll call back for the girl in half an hour's time. Shall I bring this Kitty Fisher in?'

Box had already caught sight of the rather mournful figure standing by herself in the reception room. Even from where he was standing, he could see that the girl was the poorest of the poor. He told Sergeant Driscoll to bring her into the office, and then to leave them alone. The girl might find a uniformed sergeant with a flowing beard rather too intimidating.

Kitty Fisher came into Box's office, and stood for a moment looking about her. Box saw her glance at the soot-blackened ceiling, and then at the fly-blown mirror above the fireplace.

'It's not much of a place, is it?' said Kitty Fisher.

'Well, I'm sorry, miss,' said Box, 'but it's the best we can do, so you'll have to put up with it. What can I do for you? Sit down there, by the fire, and tell me all about it.'

Kitty did as she was told, and then handed Box the little parcel. She hesitated, as though unwilling to part with it.

'He said you'd give me half-a-crown,' she said.

'Did he? How very generous of him. You're right, though. That's what it says on this piece of paper. Tell me how you came by this parcel.'

'Three men walked past me as I stood with my tray near Bell & Pritchard's, at Ludgate Circus. One of the men threw that parcel into the tray. They looked to neither right nor left, but just walked on. It says on that slip of paper that you'll give me half-a-crown.'

'What did this man look like?'

'I don't know. I tell you they just rushed past me, and one of them threw it into the tray. I told Janie about it in The King Lud, and she brought me here.'

Sergeant Driscoll came into the office carrying a mug of tea and a plate with a round of buttered toast on it. He set down mug and plate in front of the girl.

'There you are, Kitty Fisher,' he said, 'get that down you.'

'Thanks, mister,' said Kitty. For the first time since her arrival at the Rents, she managed a smile, which seemed to transform her whole appearance. Box nodded his thanks to Driscoll for his thoughtful kindness, and then carefully opened the small parcel.

It contained a folded wad of notepaper, evidently torn from an old account book. Box unfolded it, and saw that it was covered in tiny writing, carefully produced with a sharpened pencil. He began to read, and immediately he was overwhelmed with a growing excitement. The contents of the parcel were like a revelation from the blue, a sudden ray of light in a darkened sky.

'Are you going to give me the half-a-crown?' Kitty had wolfed down her toast, and had almost finished the mug of tea. The girl's voice held a quaver that warned Box that tears were about to follow. Kitty had evidently convinced herself that the money was not to be forthcoming.

'Yes, I am,' he said. He stood up, delved deep into his trouser pocket, and dredged up a handful of silver and copper. 'I haven't got a half-crown coin,' he said, 'but I can give you a florin and a sixpenny piece, which is the same thing. All right?'

The girl held out her hand and, when Box put the money into it, she closed her fingers tightly over it. The threat of tears receded, and the smile returned.

'Now, Kitty,' said Box, 'I want you to tell me where you live. Just for the record, you see.'

'I live in the Sally Army Refuge in Conduit Street, Shoreditch. I never had no mother nor father. I lived with an old lady called Mrs Morris until she died, and then the Sally Army took me in. Why do you want to know that? I ain't done nothing wrong.'

'I know you haven't, Kitty. I just want to know where you live, that's all. Now, I'm going to give you a note to take to the St Matthew's Clothing Aid Society in Bedford Lane, which is not too far from where you live. Do you know it?'

'Yes, mister.'

Box wrote rapidly on a sheet of paper, folded it, and handed it across the table to the girl.

'You take that to Bedford Lane, and ask for a Mrs Fairhurst. She'll give you a new pair of leather boots and a warm jacket. You'd better go now, and wait in the office by the door until your friend returns.'

Kitty Fisher stood up, and extended a buttery hand to Box, who shook it solemnly.

'You've been very good to me, mister,' said Kitty. 'I'll not forget that it was you what got me some new boots.'

Kitty attempted a little curtsy, and then walked out of Box's office.

Sergeant Driscoll stepped back into the room for a moment, holding the door open.

'Did you give her a docket for boots, Inspector? She'll only pawn them.'

'Maybe she will, Pat,' Box replied, 'but then again, maybe she'll wear them this winter, and not catch pneumonia. You've got to do *something* for people like Kitty Fisher.' The sergeant shook his head doubtfully, and left the office.

Colonel Kershaw needed to see the contents of Kitty's parcel that very day. He felt in the inner pocket of his jacket, and brought out the spill of paper that he had taken unbidden from Colonel Kershaw's cigar case when he had met him at Burlington House. He unrolled it, and read what was written upon it.

The Superintendent's Office, Palace Hill Reservoir

He placed the slip of paper carefully on the glowing coals in the grate, and watched it curl, and then fly up the chimney in a little flurry of sparks.

Palace Hill Reservoir occupied a 400-acre site on high ground a few miles beyond Hampstead. Arnold Box found himself in what appeared to be an immense wilderness of flatland, clothed here and there with plantations of pine and larch, in the midst of which lay a vast artificial lake of water, diverted in channels from the nearby River Mead.

Box presented himself at the door of a fine redbrick pumping station, where he was received by an elderly, bewhiskered man wearing an Afghan Campaign medal on his uniform tunic. Box introduced himself.

'Mr Box?' said the uniformed man, 'You're expected, sir.' He opened a door at the rear of his dim office, and motioned to the inspector to follow him.

They climbed an iron staircase which brought them out on to a railed embankment following the left-hand side of the reservoir. Although it was a hot July day, a stiff breeze blew across the water, sending a thousand ripples scurrying across to the opposite bank.

'Do you see that tall, narrow building down there, Mr Box, rising up from the lip of this embankment?' said the elderly man. 'You'll find him in there. He's waiting for you.'

Without another word, the man turned round and walked slowly back to the main pumping station. Box set off to walk the quarter of a mile along the walkway to Colonel Kershaw's meeting-place.

Box found the colonel in a light and spacious office occupying the first floor of the tower. He was standing at one of a range of tall windows looking out across the reservoir. He turned as Box entered the room, and without preamble asked him a question.

'What news have you brought me?'

For answer, Box produced the little parcel that Kitty Fisher had given to him, adding a few words of explanation as to its provenance.

'Well done, Box!' cried Kershaw, after he had opened the parcel and spread its contents on the office table. 'At last, word from Grunwalski. I told you, didn't I, that I had given him your name? He must be quite desperate to have written to me. He knows our rule about communicating by word of mouth only. Have you read it?'

'Only enough to ascertain what it was, sir. Then I brought it straight to you.'

'Well, sit down there, and the two of us shall read it together. Thank goodness that little girl had the sense to do as she was bid.'

From Anders Grunwalski, the pencilled note began. *I am not a prisoner, and they suspect nothing, but I have not been let out of their sight since they rescued me from Weavers' Lane Police Station. They have not said who they are, and it would be fruitless for me to guess. They are friendly but cautious. They speak at all times in English, but I suspect that they are all foreigners – one, at least, is German. There are six of them, with others visiting.*

Do not try to rescue me. I will stay with them, so that we can see what they intend to do. We move from house to house, in closed vehicles, so I do not know at any time where I am staying.

Later. I have been told today (the 3 July) that we are to embark on the 9th by a devious route to a place in eastern Poland, not far from the territory of the Ukraine. The town is called Polanska Gory. I know nothing of this place, but it seems that my mission is to end there. So far, there has been no talk of bombs. No doubt they will enlighten me once we have arrived in Polanska Gory. We are going out today to

arrange for false papers. I will try to pass this letter to
someone in the street. Let us hope that I am successful. G.

Colonel Kershaw put the note down on the table, and relapsed into thought. Box waited, content to gaze around the room, noting the array of burnished brass valves and dials fixed to the walls. Presently, Kershaw spoke.

'I suppose, Box,' he said, 'that these people are part of The Thirty – the fanatics who have ambitions for an independent Poland. Whatever they intend to do with Grunwalski's aid will be directed against Russia and the Tsar. So, when the time is ripe, we must follow them, isolate them, and render them harmless.'

'Because of the Balance of Power?' Box hazarded.

'Yes, broadly speaking. This is not the time for any deliberate upsetting of the uneasy amity between the great nations of Europe. There are ramifications, Box. If anything happens to the Tsar, and Russia acts as I suggested, rushing troops across the Polish territory towards the borders of Germany, any resultant conflict will wake other sleeping monsters further east.'

'You mean—'

'I'm thinking of threats to India, Box, if we came into any conflict at this time on Prussia's side – as we *would* do. That would be inevitable. India's borders are inviolable and beyond negotiation, but Russia would defy us if we openly sided with Prussia. Yes; I could see more than just the possibility of a massive conflict. There are other factors, too; things that Sir Charles Napier will know more about than I do. And then, again, there's Grunwalski....'

Kershaw shifted restlessly in his chair. He picked up the note, and immediately threw it down again on the table with something like disgust.

' "Do not try to rescue me", he writes. Have you ever encountered a police officer whose devotion to duty was something akin to fanaticism? Well, Grunwalski was always like that. I don't suppose he has any great love for Russia, and he might take it into his head to espouse the cause of his captors. Still, it's too early for me to be making judgements yet about the man.'

'What will you do, sir?'

'I shall communicate with Sir Charles Napier immediately, as this matter of Grunwalski is of direct concern to his Foreign Office intelligence regime. This town – Polanska Gory – is quite unknown to me, Box, but Napier will know about it. I expect he'll be able to see us tomorrow – I take it that you want to come?

'Yes, sir,' Box replied, 'I'll be there.'

Sir Charles Napier chose to receive his visitors sitting behind his vast mahogany desk in his room at the Foreign Office. A number of books and papers lay where his secretary had deposited them half an hour earlier. The books had neat slips of paper inserted to mark various pages. Neat comments in red ink adorned the papers, all of them printed documents in English, German and Russian.

Napier stole a glance at Colonel Kershaw, who was standing at the window, apparently absorbed in the antics of a group of children disporting themselves beside the lake in St James's Park. Wily old fox! He'd lost one of his precious agents, and here he was, asking for professional help in finding him!

'This Grunwalski,' he said, with the suspicion of an amused drawl in his voice, 'is he some kind of mercenary, or one of your own people?'

'He's no mercenary, Napier, I can assure you of that.' Kershaw moved away from the window, and sat down near the Under Secretary's desk. 'I plucked him out of his regiment to perform certain tasks – very dangerous tasks – which he did to my complete satisfaction. Well, maybe not complete, but near enough.'

'And this man Grunwalski will soon be on his way to Polanska Gory? Well, that's something of great significance, don't you think?'

'No, I *don't* think, because I know nothing of Polanska Gory, as you well know! So come now, Napier, tell us all about it. Mr Box and I are all ears.'

'Polanska Gory, Kershaw, is a modest but exclusive spa town, not so very far from Lublin, on the way to Chelm. It was founded by Catherine the Great, who claimed that its mineral springs were beneficial to her health. Very soon, therefore, the boyars found that it was very beneficial to *their* health also, and they paid ritual visits to the place in the summer. That is the origin of Polanska Gory. This book, which I have procured for you, gives a succinct history of the spa, and contains a number of fine engravings.'

Napier pushed one of the volumes across his desk towards Kershaw. 'It's in Russian. You read Russian, I think?'

Colonel Kershaw smiled, but refused to rise to Napier's bait. 'The engravings are very nice,' he said, glancing briefly at the book. 'What else have you got to tell us?'

'Just this. The Tsar's kinsman, the Grand Duke George Constantine, has built a villa at Polanska Gory, and the Tsar has taken to visiting it privately several times a year. Tsar Alexander is not in good health, and he finds the spa waters as beneficial as did his ancestress, Catherine the Great. I say private visits, but this month he is to make a formal visit to the town, scheduled for Saturday, 21 July, in our calendar.'

'How do you know that?' asked Kershaw.

'I asked the Second Secretary at the Russian Embassy to give me sight of the Tsar's engagement book, and he was only too happy to oblige. I gave him the kind of reason for wanting to see it that diplomats can easily concoct, and that other diplomats pretend to believe. And do you know why the Tsar's making a formal visit? It's to open a new bridge across the River Gor.'

It was pleasant to sit back and watch Kershaw's stunned reaction to his statement. In their continuing battle of wits, he, Napier, was to have the upper hand that morning. He picked up one of the documents annotated in red ink, and handed it to Kershaw, at the same time motioning to Box to come over to the table.

'There it is, gentlemen,' said Napier, 'the Catherine Bridge, which the Tsar will formally open on the 21 July. That picture is the architect's engraving. And here, in this folder, I've obtained some photographs of the bridge taken during its construction. As you can see, it's a modest, elegant construction, with fine balustrades bearing cast-iron lamp standards. But look below the bridge. What do you see?'

Box and Kershaw examined the photographs, while Napier, his teasing of Kershaw finished, watched them. Had they seen the stone inclines leading to what looked like store rooms built under the new bridge, and half hidden by vegetation? Tsar Alexander and Empress Dagmar would cross that bridge in an open carriage....

Arnold Box recalled the frantic figure of Anders Grunwalski sprinting up the incline to the Tower Bridge from the boiler rooms, as though all the devils in hell were behind him. At the moment when the Prince of Wales's carriage had crossed on to the bridge, Grunwalski had brandished a pistol. Was he being spirited away from England to this obscure Polish town to do the same thing, but to more deadly effect?

'Well done, Napier,' said Colonel Kershaw quietly. 'You've excelled yourself with this morning's piece of work. Grunwalski's antics on Tower Bridge were merely a rehearsal for what is to take place on the twenty-first at Polanska Gory. He has been hired to assassinate the Tsar by pistol, possibly during the diversionary exploding of a bomb. The twenty-first – that's just over a fortnight away.'

'Exactly,' Napier replied. 'Your man Grunwalski is in the clutches of The Thirty, who have now embarked upon what they guardedly refer to as The Aquila Project, which I believe is nothing less than the assassination of Tsar Alexander III. I have suspected as much since May, when I was in Berlin, and I have already alerted the Russian authorities to the danger.'

'Nevertheless, Napier,' said Kershaw, 'I think I had better go out there myself. Grunwalski is a strange fellow, who might well see it as his duty to himself to go along with these keepers of his! If I were there on the spot, I could persuade him to remain safely in the world of reality. Come, Box. There are things that I have already set in train, and I need to know what information they reveal before I venture abroad.'

When they left the Foreign Office, Colonel Kershaw accompanied Box along Whitehall as far as the opening into Great Scotland Yard. He had been silent since they left Napier, but now he stopped on the pavement, at the same time detaining Box by the simple expedient of tugging him by the sleeve.

'Box,' he said, rather diffidently, 'will you come out there to Poland with me? You would not be pursuing a wanted felon this time, as you were when you and I were in Prussia together, but I'd value your presence – and your ability to see things that I have missed – when I embark upon this adventure in Poland.'

'I'd be delighted, sir,' Box replied. 'But I would need to consult my superintendent—'

'Leave all that to me, Box. I'll see the commissioner myself this afternoon. You'll find that Mr Mackharness will raise no difficulties. I'm so very glad that you've consented to come. We shall meet again soon.'

Colonel Kershaw raised his hat, and in a moment he was lost in the crowd of busy people making their way towards Trafalgar Square.

At nine o'clock the next morning, Vanessa Drake, in her character as Susan Moore, housemaid, stepped on board the Dark Green City Atlas omnibus that would take her out to St John's Wood, and the residence of Baron Augustyniak.

7

White Eagle Lodge

'YOU MAY WONDER,' said Mr Quiller, butler at White Eagle Lodge, 'why I have gathered you all together here in the kitchen on this bright Saturday morning. The reason is, that this is a new establishment, and we are all agency staff – Thompson's Agency, to be exact. It'll take some time before we mould ourselves into a proper household. So let me tell you a few things before you disperse to your duties.'

Vanessa Drake, clad in her long black dress, starched white apron and matching cap, tried to look suitably demure and expressionless in her guise of Susan Moore, one of the two house-maids. Mr Quiller, she thought, was a rather faded kind of man, as though a life in service had quenched his spirits, but he had a kindly, agreeable face, and an honest London voice that held an ever-present edge of wit. Somewhere in his mid-fifties, he had lanky grey hair, which tended to fall across his forehead. Listen! What was he saying?

'First,' said Mr Quiller, 'a little word about the master and mistress, Baron and Baroness Augustyniak. Let me hear you say it, so that you'll always get it right: Augustyniak. Good. They are both Polish nobility, and you'll hear them speaking to each other both in Polish and French, though you'll be relieved to hear that they are both fluent in English.'

'How do we address them, Mr Quiller?' asked a rather haughty young woman wearing the cap and ribbons of a house parlour-maid.

'A good question, Partridge,' Quiller replied. ' "Sir" and "Madam" will do, as they're not English nobility. The baron seems to be a very amiable and friendly gentleman. The baroness, I'm told, is a mite temperamental – fond of the occasional scene. So keep a wary eye out in that direction. They're both great enter-tainers, and hold frequent dinner parties and receptions, so there'll be plenty of work for all of us.

'Now, I want everyone to tell everyone else who they are, and where they've been in service.' Vanessa saw the butler smile to himself as he added, 'Madam, as you know, has her own personal maid, Jeanne, a young French person. She came from Poland with the baroness, and is not part of the household.

'Now, I'll start with myself. I'm Mr Quiller, butler and wine steward, as one or two of you know already, having worked with me before. I've served in some of the best houses, both in Town and out in the sticks, for more than thirty years. Now, let's hear your names, and a bit about you, starting with the lady on my right.'

'Mrs Stafford, cook general,' volunteered a rather forbidding woman in a black dress. 'I was formerly with Sir James and Lady Standish in Eaton Square. And this,' she added, pointing to a shy girl of fourteen or so standing beside her, 'is my kitchen maid, Victoria, late of the Langham Hotel, but now trying her hand at private service.'

One by one, the remaining seven staff introduced themselves. Mary Partridge, house parlour-maid, formerly with Lord and Lady St Pancras. Gladys Jones, chambermaid, various posts in gentlemen's houses. Ellen Saunders, housemaid, formerly with the late Miss Pepper of Pont Street, Chelsea.

'Susan Moore, housemaid, formerly with Colonel Macdonald of the Indian Cavalry.'

Vanessa listened to her own nervous, piping voice. Surely they were all looking at her? Didn't she fit? Could all these genuine servants see that she was an impostor? Who was that gloomy, bewhiskered man standing by the kitchen door? Why was he looking so fixedly at her? Did he—

Albert Smith, footman, formerly with Mr Seaton Hughes of Putney. Alexander Scott, footman, formerly with Mr Adams of Salisbury.

The sour-faced bewhiskered man, his cold eye still fixed on Vanessa Drake, was the last to introduce himself.

'Joseph Doyle, coachman, last employed by Captain Wainwright of India Lodge, Hammersmith. Can I get back to the mews, Mr Quiller? There's a lot to be done since the baron's last coachman suddenly got a fit of the sulks and left without working out his notice.'

Without waiting for a reply, Joseph Doyle slipped out of the kitchen door, muttering to himself. Quiller looked after him with a wry smile, and gave his staff permission to begin the morning's work.

Vanessa had arrived at White Eagle Lodge, a fine, detached three-storey villa standing in its own well-tended gardens, on the previous day. She had found the house in turmoil, as a number of builders and decorators were still putting the finishing touches to various alterations demanded by Baron Augustyniak when he had moved into the house a month previously. It was only now, on the morning of the 7 July, that Mr Quiller had been able to assemble the new household for his little talk. The other servants had arrived during the earlier part of that week.

Vanessa had quickly made friends with her fellow housemaid, Ellen Saunders, whose tiny bedroom was next to hers in the attic storey of the house. Ellen was a pretty, unaffected girl of sixteen, who had worked with Mr Quiller before. She had been in domestic service from the age of thirteen.

'Mr Quiller's had ever such a romantic life, Susan,' Ellen confided, as they left the kitchen to go about their work. 'A couple of years ago he was butler to a gentleman in Warwickshire who turned out to be a murderer! He's not accepted work in the country since then. "London will do me fine, Saunders", he said to me when we were both working for Mr Leopold Grace in Chiswick.'

'Why did he call you Saunders?' asked Vanessa. 'It's not very friendly, is it?'

Ellen looked at her new friend in puzzlement. What a funny question to ask!

'Well, I'm a housemaid, aren't I? What else should he call me? And you're a housemaid too, which means that you'll be called Moore, just as I'm called Saunders. Didn't you know that?'

Vanessa bit her lip in vexation. Her one day's intensive training as a housemaid, under the expert tuition of Mrs Prout at Bagot's Hotel, had taught her a lot, but evidently not enough. She would have to be careful. How rotten it was, to tell lies to this nice, friendly girl!

'Colonel Macdonald always called me Susan,' said Vanessa. 'I believe that was the custom in the Indian Cavalry. What do you think of this Baron Augustyniak?' she asked, hastily changing the subject. 'Have you seen him yet?'

Ellen Saunders giggled. 'The master? Yes, I've see him,' she said. 'I came here on Tuesday, you see. He's ever so handsome, and I'm almost certain he winked at me yesterday when I met him on the upstairs landing. A roving eye, that's what he's got.'

'What did you do when he winked at you?'

'I did what all maids should do when that kind of thing happens: blush and curtsy, then make yourself scarce! My Miss Pepper taught me that. Madam's jealous of him, I think. She's one of those smouldering foreign ladies. But come on, Susan, we've got those grates to do in the reception rooms, and the flowers to change.'

That same evening there were guests to dinner. The dining room at White Eagle Lodge was lofty and well lighted by three long windows looking out on to the rear gardens of the villa. It had been newly furnished, and everything gleamed and glittered in the light of two gas chandeliers, heavy with crystal.

Vanessa and Ellen Saunders took up their positions against the wall opposite the sideboard, waiting to hand round the dishes. Mr Quiller supervised them, while attending to the pouring of the various wines served with the different courses. It was a nerve-racking experience. Vanessa watched everything that Ellen did, and tried to do the same. There were no accidents, though she saw the butler glance at her quizzically from time to time. Serve from the left, remove from the right.... Or was it the other way round? Mrs Prout, Colonel Kershaw's secret colleague at Bagot's Hotel, had taught her all about the different kinds of service: French, Russian, standard silver – but now they all mingled together in her mind in a confusion of panic. Watch Ellen, do as she does, and you'll be all right....

Between courses the two girls stood against the wall, staring neutrally into space. Vanessa contrived to examine the company closely through veiled eyelids.

Baron Augustyniak sat at one end of the long table, dominating the room by the sheer power of his personality. His evening clothes sat easily on his massive frame, their sober black contrasting with his mane of blond hair and his bushy golden beard. The light from the chandeliers glinted off the gold-rimmed monocle that he wore in his right eye. He was inclined to his right, talking in low tones to a little balding man who nodded vigorously at everything that he said. They appeared to be speaking in Polish.

A raised finger from Quiller signalled that it was time to change the plates and serve the next course. Mercifully there were only eight guests that evening, and Vanessa was quick to learn from Ellen's deft and experienced service. Only once did she catch the baron's eye fixed on her, but with a little thrill of pleasure she realized that he was merely admiring her, not suspecting her. Ellen had said that the master had a roving eye. Back to the wall.

At the far end of the table sat Baroness Augustyniak, an impressive woman, with dark hair and flashing eyes. Her extreme haughtiness contrasted with her husband's natural affability, and she scarcely deigned to speak to the guests sitting to her right and left. She wore a black satin dress, its soberness relieved by the brilliance of her magnificent diamond necklace and bracelet. When Vanessa resumed her place by the wall, she saw the baroness glance briefly at her. There were tears standing in her eyes.

The eight guests were all earnest, worthy men of middle age, learned experts in the various branches of Polish culture. They spoke English at the table for most of the time, and their conversation was about the endowment and running costs of the projected Polish Institute. It was a dull, worthy evening. The gentlemen did not linger over their port, and the party broke up soon after coffee had been served in the drawing-room.

Was Colonel Kershaw right in suspecting that Baron Augustyniak was more than he claimed to be? It was early days yet.

After they had carried all the dishes and cutlery into the kitchen for Victoria to wash, Vanessa and Ellen returned to the dining-room, where they busied themselves in polishing the table and the massive sideboard.

'You don't know much about service, do you, Susan?' asked Ellen. 'When you offered the asparagus dish to that little baldy gentleman sitting on the master's right, he almost had to stand up to see what you were giving him!' There was indulgent humour in the girl's voice, but her remark gave Vanessa an unpleasant jolt. How much longer would she be able to keep up the pretence that she was a trained servant?

'Poor Colonel Macdonald was an invalid, you see,' said Vanessa. 'He never entertained at all. That's why I'm a bit clumsy now.'

Ellen Saunders chuckled to herself. She continued to polish the dining table with evident devotion to the task, but she glanced mischievously at Vanessa.

'Colonel Fiddlesticks!' she laughed. 'You made him up, didn't you? Where did you *really* come from, Susan? Did you run away from some man?'

It was an immediate way out of Vanessa's dilemma.

'Promise you won't tell anyone,' she said.

On Sunday morning, Baron and Baroness Augustyniak, accompanied by the French maid, attended Mass at the local Roman Catholic church. Mr Quiller told Ellen and Vanessa to blacklead the grate in the drawing-room, and to lay and light a small fire there.

'This man,' said Vanessa, as she polished the steel fender, 'was ever so charming at first, and said that he wanted to marry me. His mother and father kept a pawn shop in the Mile End Road, so he had expectations. But then he showed himself to be a fiend in human form.'

'What did he do?' asked Ellen, pausing with the blacklead brush in her hand. Her eyes sparkled, and her pretty face was animated by curiosity. Vanessa felt quite encouraged. It wasn't often that she told elaborate lies, and she found that she was quite enjoying it.

'He took me to the Alhambra one night,' Vanessa continued, 'and afterwards we went to five different public houses. First he got tipsy, and then he got drunk, and started to hit me. A man who was passing by saw what he was doing, and knocked him down in the street. And then the brute swore something dreadful – words I'd never heard before in my life – and said that he'd have revenge on both of us. He said he had a razor at home, and that he'd come and find me and cut my throat in the night.'

'Coo...' whispered Ellen, in ecstasy.

'And that's why I fled,' Vanessa concluded. 'I was a seamstress, you know, but a friend managed to get me on the books of Thompson's Agency. A military friend,' she added, thinking of Colonel Kershaw. 'So promise you won't tell on me?'

' 'Course I won't tell on you,' said Ellen. 'All you have to do is watch what I do, and take pattern from me. What was he like, this brute? What was his name?'

'Albert,' Vanessa replied. 'He was a giant of a man, with yellow hair, and a long white scar across his face. I don't know why I fell for him, Ellen. Maybe it was because he was so well-spoken, quite like a gentleman. But there was a demon bottled up inside him, like that Mr Hyde in the story.'

'Coo...' whispered Ellen, as they left the room together. Her friend Cecil never thumped her, or anyone else, for that matter. And he had no long white scar across his face, only spots, which wasn't quite the same.

After lunch, which passed without incident, Quiller told Vanessa to dust and tidy the baron's study, as he wished to work there on his private papers that afternoon.

The study was a spacious room at the back of the house, across the entrance passage from the dining-room. It was panelled entirely in white-painted oak, and a number of family portraits hung on the walls. A large desk stood on a Turkey carpet in the centre of the room, and a tall, very ornate set of shelves held a collection of leather-bound books.

Directly opposite the door there was a finely carved and gilded fireplace, above which had been fixed an heraldic shield showing a crowned white eagle with gold claws and beak, its wings outstretched. The eagle was displayed on a field of bright scarlet. There was a small scroll affixed to the panelling below the shield, and Vanessa stood carefully on the raised fender, steadying herself by her fingertips on the mantelpiece in order to read the single word written on it in black and red: GNIEZNO.

'What are you doing?'

The baron's voice, sharp and imperious, almost made Vanessa stumble as she jumped in shock. She hastily turned to face Baron Augustyniak, who had silently entered the study. She remembered

Ellen's advice, dropped her eyes, and curtsied. When she looked up, she saw that the baron was smiling, but she sensed a dangerous gleam in his eyes, as though he had trained himself to remain always on the alert.

Baron Augustyniak did not wait for her to answer his question. He sat down at his desk, and looked first at her and then at the heraldic shield above the mantelpiece. She had noticed his appreciation of her youthful charms in that brief glance, but was sensible enough to realize that this foreign aristocrat would not let her get beyond his guard.

'It is a dangerous practice, you know,' said the baron, 'to stand tiptoe on a fender. One slip, and you would be in the fire. What is your name? I saw you waiting at dinner last night, but your name has slipped my memory.'

'Moore, sir,' said Vanessa. She stood with her hands clasped in front of her, and her eyes fixed modestly on the carpet.

'Haven't you another name, my dear – something less formal? Most people have, you know.'

'Susan, sir.'

'Susan. Well, Susan, let me tell you about that shield that you were standing on the fender to admire. That is the White Eagle of Poland, the symbol of our nation since the earliest ages. I don't suppose you know the story of the White Eagle?'

'No, sir.'

'Once upon a time, a thousand years ago, there lived three brothers, Lech, Czech, and Rus. They were all warriors, and set out with their followers to find new lands in which to live. They travelled over empty plains and through dense forests, until they came to a mountain peak, where they agreed to part. Czech turned to the west, and discovered the land which is now Bohemia. He was the father of the Czech people, and some say, of the Slovaks, too.'

Vanessa listened in fascination to the baron's tale. He was a natural story-teller, and his English was perfect, well modulated and expressive. For the moment she forgot her role as Susan Moore the housemaid.

'What happened to Rus?' she asked, and then bit her lip in vexation. 'Susan Moore' would never have asked such a direct question. The baron smiled, and the dangerous light leapt once more into his eyes, to be gone in an instant.

'Rus journeyed to the east, and in the vast and boundless lands that he found there he established the peoples who take their name from him: the Russians, the Byelorussians, and the folk of the Ukraine.'

Baron Augustyniak rose from his desk, and crossed to the mantelpiece. Vanessa moved aside respectfully. She was fascinated by the man's dominating personality, reassured by his evident kindness and condescension to servants, but at the same time intimidated by the suggestion of ruthlessness evident in the dangerous gleam of his eyes.

'The third brother, whose name was Lech,' he continued, looking up at the shield, 'journeyed straight ahead, and came upon a land of towering mountains and fertile plains. And it was there that he saw one day a great white eagle circling round its nest, high on a craggy outcrop. Rays of light from the red setting sun tipped the white eagle's wings with gold. It was a sign to Lech that he should settle his people there, and this he did. And there, on that shield, you see the great eagle displayed against the red of that setting sun!'

'And that word, sir, written on the little plaque – what does it mean?'

'GNIEZNO? That is Polish for "the eagle's nest", and it was under that name that Lech founded a city, which was the first capital of Poland. So there it is, Susan Moore,' the baron concluded, gathering up some papers from his desk, and moving to the door. 'You may not be skilled in service at table, but now you know more about the legend of Poland than your friends below-stairs!'

He held the door open, and Vanessa knew that it was a veiled order for her to leave the study. As she made to obey him, Baron Augustyniak suddenly barred her way.

'And remember what I told you, Susan Moore: young ladies who stand tiptoe on fenders are in great danger of falling into the fire.'

8

Twenty Guests to Dinner

ARNOLD BOX LOOKED up from the charge-sheet that he was reading as Jack Knollys burst through the swing doors into the office. It was a few minutes after nine on the morning of the 9 July.

'I wish you'd learn to enter rooms with a little more finesse, Sergeant,' said Box. 'All this crashing about is bad for a fellow's nerves at this time of day. Where have you been, anyway? It's after nine.'

Jack Knollys carefully removed his overcoat, hung it up on the coat-stand, and added his scarf and hat. Then he sat down opposite Box at the big table. He looked thoughtful, and did not reply in kind to Box's banter.

'Sir,' he said, 'as I came into Garlick Hill this morning on my way up from Syria Wharf, an elderly clergyman fell in step with me, and started a conversation. He had a quiet, confiding manner, and he told me that Vanessa had been employed by Colonel Kershaw to keep an eye on things at Baron Augustyniak's villa in St John's Wood.'

Inspector Box removed the little round spectacles that he had been wearing, folded them, and put them into a tin case.

'Did he tell you anything else? This clergyman, I mean.'

'He said that if the colonel had sudden need of my services, which was more than likely, he'd let me know by word of mouth.

Then he tipped his hat politely, and hurried away in the direction of Cannon Street.'

Box was silent for a while. He had told Sergeant Knollys some salient facts about the Polish conspiracy, but had been constrained by his instinct to keep Colonel Kershaw's business secret. But now that a clerical 'nobody' had revealed Vanessa's role in the business, Box judged that the time had come to tell Knollys all.

'That was very decent of the colonel to let you know about Vanessa,' said Box, 'and I'm taking that as a signal to tell you everything that the colonel has told me during the two interviews that I've had with him recently. It's time you knew all about The Aquila Project.'

Box spoke for nearly half an hour, during which time Knollys listened impassively. When Box had finished his story, the giant sergeant stirred, as though from sleep.

'And he wants you to go with him to Poland?'

'He does. All the usual strings will be pulled, Jack, and there'll be no trouble with Mr Mackharness. The colonel says that I see things differently from him, which makes me a valuable ally. I think he's never forgotten how I saw through those hoax bombs in the Hansa Protocol business.'

'So our friend Grunwalski has been primed to assassinate Alexander III at this spa – what did you call it? – Polanska Gory.... You know, sir, I only had a glimpse of the fellow when we seized him on Tower Bridge, but I thought then that he looked a wild kind of individual, with ideas of his own. No wonder the colonel is worried. It would be a bit of a let-down if his own man decided to do the bidding of this group of anarchists out of a misguided sense of honour.'

Arnold Box produced a cigar case, opened it, and offered it to Knollys across the table. When he spoke, his voice, Knollys noted, contained a kind of provisional doubt. Evidently something was worrying the guvnor.

'You know, Jack,' said Box, when they had lit their thin

cheroots, 'there's a peculiar German flavour to all this business. All right, there's a lot of Polish stuff – Grunwalski, Augustyniak, Peter Rosanski, and that Polish coin.' Box produced it from his waistcoat pocket, and held it up for a moment for Knollys to see. 'But there are quite a few Germans in the background, if I may put it like that. For instance, there's Oscar Schumann, who murdered Rosanski; and last Wednesday I visited a certain Alois Gerdler, a German gunsmith, with premises in Dover Lane, Covent Garden.'

'Yes, you told me about him.'

'I did. And there, lurking in the back room of the shop, was another German, a recently appointed diplomat called – what was it now? – Doctor Franz Kessler, the new Second Secretary at Prussia House. It's a Polish or Russian mystery right enough, but there's a slight whiff of Germany in the air. It's just a point, Sergeant.'

'It's a very interesting point, sir,' said Knollys. 'It's well known that some of the citizens of Danzig secretly consider themselves to be Poles. I believe that Danzig was originally called Gdansk, and was part of the old Kingdom of Poland. I wonder—'

Knollys broke off as a young constable came through the doors. He handed an envelope to Box.

'This came for you by hand, sir,' he said. 'It was misdirected to Whitehall Place.'

The constable saluted, and left the office. Box opened the envelope and extracted a single sheet of blue note paper.

'This is from Superintendent Radcliffe, Sergeant,' he said. 'He was my old guvnor years ago, when I was still a sergeant. A chief inspector, he was, in "C". I wonder what he wants? "If you can spare the time, please call upon me at the Home Office this morning". I suppose I'd better go.'

'The Home Office, sir?' said Knollys. 'What's he doing there?'

'He's one of the Royal Protection officers in Special Branch, Sergeant. I meet him occasionally, and he's always very civil. He's very upper-crust these days, very genteel, which comes from mingling with Royalty all the time. I'll go and see him now. You'd better take yourself down to Mr Shale in Beak Street with those unsigned warrants from the weekend. We've both got busy mornings ahead of us, so I'll see you back here at twelve, and we'll slip out for a bite of something and a glass of ale at The Grapes.'

While Box and Knollys were conferring at King James's Rents, Vanessa Drake and the other members of the household at White Eagle Lodge were listening to Mr Quiller, as he announced the arrangements for that day.

'There's to be a big dinner party tonight,' he said, 'when, in addition to the master and mistress, twenty ladies and gentlemen, mainly Polish and Russian diplomats and their wives, but with one or two Germans, will sit down at the table. I've pinned up a list of the guests in the pantry. Mrs Stafford has duly risen to the occasion. In fact, she started preparations on Saturday. There will be five courses, each accompanied by a suitable wine. Contrary to the usual custom, there will be no port left on the table for the gentlemen guests, as a little group of them – six, to be exact – intend to meet Baron Augustyniak for a private conference in the study. Brandy, cigars and coffee will be set out there, and those gentlemen will remain undisturbed.'

'So they'll all rise together, Mr Quiller?' asked Ellen.

'Yes, they will. The baron's party will go to the study, and the other guests, both ladies and gentlemen, will be entertained by Baroness Augustyniak in the drawing-room. She will sing a selection of Polish and Russian songs, accompanying herself on the piano.' He treated them to one of his wry smiles, and added, 'I'm sure a good time will be had by all.'

'When will dinner start?' asked one of the footman. 'It seems to be at a different time every day.'

'They will sit down to table at seven. Carriages will be at tenthirty. Partridge, I'll need you to assist Moore and Saunders at the table. Moore, take a bit more care when handing dishes. You seem nervous of approaching the diners, and that nervousness unsettles them. The ideal server at table should be neither seen nor heard. Albert and Alexander, you'd better come with me now to extend the table and make all ready. Saunders, I want you to help Gladys upstairs this morning. Moore, go and dust the study carpet with pan and brush. That's all.'

The study was deserted, although Vanessa knew that the baron was somewhere about the house. Putting her dustpan and brush down on the carpet, she glanced quickly at the books arranged on their ornate shelves. Most of them boasted quite impenetrable titles, which she took to be Polish. A number of books were in French; they appeared to be gazetteers and political directories. She crossed to the desk, and admired the baron's agate pen tray with its attendant cut-glass bottles of blue and red ink. She opened the flaps of the leather blotter, but saw that the blotting paper was entirely free of tell-tale blotted letters. Perhaps the baron was extra careful about things like that?

In a little glazed case standing on the desk reposed a coin, set off by a red velvet background. A souvenir, perhaps? She could see the big, bold numbers on the face of the coin – a 30, a 2, and the date, 1836, but the letters were in what she knew to be the Russian script. It would be impossible to commit those words to memory, and the colonel had often warned her never to write anything down. Still, she would tell Colonel Kershaw about that coin.

She glanced briefly at the great white eagle on its scarlet shield over the fireplace, and then completed her inspection of the room. To the right of the fireplace a white-panelled door opened outwards to reveal a small chamber, little more than a cupboard, lit by a barred window at the further end. It contained a small safe, and a number of valuable silver trophies and shields, carefully wrapped in chamois leathers. A line of shelving held tied bundles of documents. With a sudden leap of excitement, she saw a possibility of finding out more about the baron's affairs than would be possible from merely waiting at table, and dusting furniture.

After dinner that night, Baron Augustyniak would retire to the study with some kind of inner coterie. If she were to conceal herself here, in this little chamber, she would be able to eavesdrop on their conversation. No one would know that she was there, and when the carriage-bell was rung at twenty-five past ten, they would leave, and she would slip quietly away. Yes! It was a daring but brilliant idea.

Falling to her knees, Vanessa began to sweep the carpet vigorously, moving crab-wise across the floor from door to fireplace. By the time she had finished, the carpets looked as though they had been cleaned properly for the first time.

Later in the morning she met the baron as she was crossing the hall to the green baize door that opened into the servants' wing. He glanced at her with an almost covert look of admiration, in which there was a curious and unsettling suggestion of mockery. She curtsied, and he inclined his head in acknowledgement, before opening the glazed door of a conservatory filled with exotic plants.

Almost immediately Vanessa heard the high, complaining voice of Baroness Augustyniak. She lingered near the door to listen unashamedly to her mistress's words.

'All these girls!' cried the baroness. 'You cannot keep your eyes off them. Why do you wish to break my heart? They are hussies, all of them, English hussies....' The baroness was weeping now, and her words were punctuated by choking sobs.

Baron Augustyniak's voice came low and placatory through the partly open door. 'Don't talk nonsense, Anna. What do you mean? Am I supposed to avert my eyes from my own servants?'

'I saw you ogling that Susan, the housemaid, a mere slip of a girl,' continued Baroness Augustyniak, her voice rising to something like a shriek. 'I saw her mock blushes, the yellow-haired baggage! You will break my heart.... You'll be glad to see me dead....'

Vanessa quietly closed the door of the conservatory, and went into the kitchen wing. She caught sight of her own reflection in a mirror, and smiled in spite of herself. It was rather fun to be admired! Then she watched the smile fade as she recalled that a jealous woman could be a dangerous enemy. She'd already attracted Mr Quiller's attention by her clumsiness and obvious lack of experience. She would have to watch her step.

Box found Superintendent Radcliffe in a very small room on the ground floor of the Home Office, sitting behind a plain deal table covered in books and papers. In addition to the table, the room contained a tall cupboard, a small fire grate, and two upright chairs.

'Ah, Box! You managed to make time to see me. Sit down for a moment, will you? There's something here that I need to finish before I lose track of its details.'

A distinguished man in his early fifties, dressed in impeccable morning clothes, Mr Radcliffe looked as though he were himself a scion of the Royal Family. Box observed him at his work, and remembered the uniformed chief inspector who had been his chief guide and mentor when he was a brand-new sergeant, newly transferred to 'C' Division at Little Vine Street, Piccadilly. Tom Radcliffe had risen in the world, and had long ago been poached by the Home Office, but he and Box shared many stirring memories of their days as uniformed officers.

There were many books and gazetteers on the table, including, Box noticed, the *Almanac de Gotha*, a volume which recorded the pedigrees of European royalty and nobility. Radcliffe was poring over a kind of family tree, underlining some words and phrases in pencil.

A small stack of printed programmes lay beside the *Almanac de Gotha*, and Box could see engraved portraits of a lady and gentleman, underneath which was a page of text, produced in the crabbed Gothic German typeface. More Germans....

'There,' said Superintendent Radcliffe, sitting back in his chair with a little sigh. 'That seems to be it. How are you, Box? It must be nine months since I saw you last.'

'I'm very well, sir,' Box replied. 'Very busy, and very much out-and-about these days. You seem to be groaning under the weight of all this paper. A bit different from your Piccadilly days!'

'Oh, yes, Box, it's very different now.' Radcliffe smiled ruefully, and waved his hand vaguely over the mass of papers on the table. 'My work so far this morning has been to plot a train journey across Europe for later this month in connection with an aristo-cratic marriage in Berlin, on the twenty-first, at which the Marquess of Lorne will represent the Queen. My task will be to accompany him as security officer to Berlin, leave him there, and come straight back. It's a matter of protocol, you see. It's a very minor affair, but the Kaiser, and Empress Augusta Victoria, will both be present, and it would be seen as a snub if no one from our own Royal Family were to attend. The Marquess, as Princess Louise's husband, and a former Governor General of Canada, should go down well enough.'

'And who are the happy couple, Mr Radcliffe?'

'Oh, you won't have heard of either of them, Box. The groom is Prince Adalbert Victor of Savoy, and the bride is Princess Gretchen of Hesse-Darmstadt, a kinswoman of the Kaiser. As is customary with these minor marriages, the ceremony will take place in Die Kapelle an der Brücke, the private Hohenzollern chapel in Berlin, rather than in Berlin Cathedral. The various orders of precedence pose a minor nightmare for security officers.'

'And you think that I can be of some assistance?' asked Box in some bewilderment.

'What? No, of course not. That's not why I wanted to see you.'

Superintendent Radcliffe stared gloomily at the papers on his desk, and toyed with a pencil for a while. He looked both embar-rassed and in some way compromised.

'It's something quite different, Box. I'll not beat about the bush.

It's about Bobby Fitz. Detective Inspector Fitzgerald of "J". You know all about his "light fantastic boys", don't you?'

'Yes, sir. They're sneak-thieves and petty informers, not above making a few shillings by breaking the law for Mr Fitz. What they're doing in sober fact is breaking and entering.'

'Exactly. Well, this Friday just gone, the 6 July, Bobby went out to Clapham to gather evidence against an up-and-coming receiver, Michael Stone. He took two of his light fantastic boys with him to break into Stone's house, and one of them fell through a sky-light and broke his leg. He began to squeal – and not just in pain!'

'What happened to Bobby Fitz?'

'Well, I'm telling you, aren't I? The upshot of all this was, that Bobby Fitz was caught red-handed at his illegal activities. We all knew what he was up to, and turned a blind eye because of the splendid results he'd got in the past. But once one of his boys grassed on him, Box, that was the end of him.'

'He's only two years off retirement,' said Box. 'I was talking to him only the other day. He's got an old mother to support—'

'And if he's dismissed – or worse – he'll lose not just his wages but his pension as well. I remember him well, Box. I worked with him twice when we were both uniformed inspectors, and you could sense his dedication to law and order. He was incorruptible. And now, this! He's utterly ruined, after thirty or more years' service to the Force.'

'Is there anything you think I can do to help? It's largely due to Bobby Fitz that Tower Bridge is still standing today.'

'You understand, Arnold, don't you, that I can't appear in the matter? My connections to the Royal Family preclude that. But I know that Bobby's superintendent at Bethnal Green Road, Mr Keating, wants to retire him early on health grounds – he has very bad lungs, you know. It'll be a difficult thing to do, and not strictly ethical, I suppose, but it'll save Bobby Fitz and his mother from penury. So I want you to visit Mr Keating at "J", and tell him how valuable poor Bobby's been to you over this Tower Bridge business. And then – do you know anyone at "W"?'

'I don't, sir.'

'Very well, I'll scribble a note to the superintendent at "W", asking him to grant you an interview. You'll understand that Bobby Fitz will be prosecuted – if it comes to that – from Clapham, where he and his precious light fantastic boys were taken up. Tell him the tale again, about Tower Bridge, and anything else you can think of that's relevant to poor Bobby's plight. If he can be persuaded to co-operate, we should be able to get Bobby Fitz retired, with his pension, on health grounds.'

Superintendent Radcliffe picked up one of the pile of printed wedding invitations, turned it over, and wrote: *Supt S. Lucas, Brixton Road Police Station.*

'There you are, Box,' he said. 'If all goes well, we'll have good news about Bobby before the week's out.'

At half past six that evening, Vanessa and Ellen examined the list of guests for the dinner that they would help to serve in half an hour's time. All twenty guests had arrived soon after six, and were being entertained to what Mr Quiller called 'pre-prandial drinks'. When time served, Vanessa would look up the word in a dictionary to find out what it meant.

Neither of them could even pronounce the names on the list that Quiller had pinned up on the staff notice board in the pantry. Monsieur and Madame Adamczyk. Monsieur and Madame Balonek. Monsieur and Madame Boruta. Monsieur and Madame Golombek. Monsieur and Madame Haremza. Doctor and Madame Jasionowski. Monsieur and Madame Malenkoff. Colonel and Madame Kropotkin. Doctor Franz Kessler. Herr Gerdler. Herr and Frau Eidenschenk.

Ellen giggled. 'Thank goodness we haven't got to announce them! Mr Quiller says they're mostly Poles, but that there are two Russian couples, and four Germans. Quite an affair!'

The solemn booming of a gong came to them from the entrance hall.

'That's the first gong,' said Ellen. 'Come on, it's time for us to take our places.'

In the dining-room the table had been extended to accommodate the twenty dinner guests. The long white damask cloth held a wealth of gleaming china and crystal, and four silver candelabra rose from islands of fresh flowers. Each setting or cover, as Quiller called it, was marked by a small china plaque, upon which was written the name of the guest who was to sit there. A nest of five wine glasses reposed beside each cover. To Vanessa it was an awesome sight. She noticed that young Ellen regarded it as nothing much out of the ordinary.

The two housemaids and Mary Partridge, the parlour-maid, took up their stations along the wall. Mr Quiller, in evening dress, and sporting white gloves, stood at the sideboard with Alexander, one of the liveried footmen. Despite her determination to remain calm, Vanessa found herself trembling. How much longer would she be able to sustain the fiction that she was a trained servant?

The gong rang out for a second time, and within the minute the guests, their host, and hostess, trooped into the room. They were all talking animatedly in English, and with a little discreet assistance from Quiller, they found their places. In a moment, a savoury would be served, and Quiller would pour out a small glass of chilled hock.

Vanessa allowed her eyes to rove across the seated guests. The baron and baroness seemed to have recovered their equanimity: each continued a conversation that had begun outside the room, the baron with Madame Boruta, an elderly lady who was rather deaf, and the baroness with an elegant and urbane gentleman, who, Vanessa thought, was probably Doctor Jasionowski.

At a sign from Quiller the savoury was served, the three maids being followed by Quiller and the footman, pouring the hock. The conversation at table continued unabated, a kind of low, rumbling murmur from people who had no inhibitions about talking in the presence of servants.

Snatches of their conversations came to Vanessa. There was talk of the latest Paris fashions, of Mr George Bernard Shaw's new play. Someone wanted to know what had happened to dear Helga, and whether young Josef had succeeded in securing a commission in the Imperial Guard. Nothing of world-shattering moment was being talked about.

They changed the plates, and served bowls of Brown Windsor soup without incident, even though Vanessa had convinced herself that serving soup would prove her downfall. Once again, Quiller and Alexander followed the maids with decanters, pouring the second wine. By this time, Vanessa had all but managed to remember the names written on the china plaques. The assembled guests were beginning to assume separate identities.

Sitting immediately in front of Vanessa where she stood motionless against the wall was one of the German guests, Doctor Franz Kessler. A tall, thin man, he dressed elegantly, and wore a small rosebud in the lapel of his evening coat. The light from the chandelier glanced off the rimless monocle that he wore in his right eye. His fierce moustache put Vanessa in mind of the pictures that she'd seen of Kaiser Bill.

Doctor Kessler had conducted a quiet, earnest conversation with his neighbour, Herr Gerdler, ever since they had entered the room. The two men seemed to be dwelling in a cocoon of their own making, paying little or no attention to the other guests.

'... I told him in Berlin what was likely to happen, but you know what Count von Donath's like.... True, His Excellency can be difficult.... The count has a brilliant mind, which one day soon will be able to realize its full potential....'

Time for the main course. Remember: roast lamb, cut at the sideboard and served directly to the table. Then, she and Ellen to bring round the gravy – you were allowed to talk at this stage, and ask, 'gravy, sir or madam?' Mary Partridge and Alexander would follow with the vegetables; then she and Ellen again, with the mint sauce. (You were allowed to talk for that, too). Quiller would come last, with the claret. Move forward now.

All was going well. The two Germans looked up briefly, and nodded impatiently when Vanessa offered the gravy. She served her side of the table, and returned to the sideboard. The mint sauce was the final ritual connected with the main course, and nothing, surely, could go wrong with that?

When Vanessa reached Doctor Kessler, she leaned forward at his shoulder, ready to offer him the sauce. It was at that very moment that Kessler uttered the words: 'He was snooping around at your shop that day. He was in on the attempt to arrest Grunwalski. He's dangerous, I tell you. His name's Box. Inspector Arnold Box.'

Vanessa's start of surprise jolted her tray, sending a spray of mint sauce down the lapel of Doctor Kessler's suit. The man bellowed with rage, his face white and contorted as he sprang up from his chair.

'You stupid little fool! Look what you have done! Clumsy, clodhopping girl!'

The other guests stopped speaking. Baroness Augustyniak permitted herself a smirk of satisfaction. Vanessa tried to sponge down the frantic German's coat with her napkin, but he seized it from her and flung it to the floor. All eyes were on her, and nobody spoke.

'No real harm done, I think, Doctor?' The powerful, genial voice of Baron Augustyniak came from the end of the long table, bringing with it a sudden calm. 'Quiller,' he continued, 'you'd better get that girl out of the room. Ladies and gentlemen, let us all do justice to this excellent Welsh lamb.'

Within moments 'Susan Moore' had been forgotten, and the conversations were resumed. Doctor Kessler still looked indignant, and treated Vanessa to a vicious glance, but he held his peace. Vanessa felt the tears stinging her eyes. How rotten it all was! Although she was not really a servant, she felt second-rate and inadequate. She saw little Ellen looking at her with a mixture of mute sympathy and bewilderment.

Mr Quiller escorted Vanessa to the door, speaking in low tones. 'Alexander, you take over Moore's duties. Moore, you'd better make yourself scarce for the rest of the evening.'

'Yes, Mr Quiller.'

The butler quietly opened the door, and Vanessa slipped through into the hallway.

'I'm disappointed in you, my girl,' he whispered, and then shut her out of the room.

9

The Arrest of Gertie Miller

VANESSA STOOD FOR a moment in the deserted hallway of White Eagle Lodge, and attempted to master her rising inclination to scream with impotent rage. How dare that arrogant foreigner call her stupid! She was not afraid of his ill-bred rages. Why, he looked like a comic parody of the Kaiser! And how dare Baron Augustyniak, her master, dismiss her from the room as though she were someone beneath his notice!

It took her some time to master her rage, but when she did, it was succeeded by a sudden and alarming flood of tears. She was not the crying kind; these tears were for her humiliation in front of her young friend Ellen, and her sense of failure in having let down Mr Quiller. She had only been in the house four days, but she was already beginning to think of herself as a bona fide member of the household.

She heard someone push open the green baize door from the kitchen, and hastily hid herself in the recess beneath the staircase. Albert, the second footman, appeared, pushing a trolley laden with glasses and decanters. Rage and tears forgotten, Vanessa joined him. She realized that he was setting out the refreshments for the baron's private meeting in the study after dinner.

'Do you want any help, Albert?' she asked.

'Why aren't you in the dining-room?' Albert, a stout and stolid young man, was looking straight ahead, intent on manoeuvring his rattling burden across the tiled floor and into the carpeted corridor.

'I spilt mint sauce on one of those Germans,' Vanessa replied, 'and the master had me thrown out! So I've nothing to do.'

'Thrown out, hey?' Albert smiled, and glanced at Vanessa. 'Come on, then, Susan,' he said. 'You can help me set this lot out, and then wait for me to come back with the coffee. You've been crying, haven't you? Don't take any notice of that kind of thing. It's all forgotten by the next morning, and you learn from the experience.'

A temporary buffet had been set up against one wall of the baron's study, and it was here that they set out two crystal decanters, six brandy glasses, and several boxes of cigars. Vanessa opened the door for Albert, and he pushed the trolley out into the corridor. When he was out of sight, she quickly surveyed her surroundings.

The study was the last room along the corridor, which ended in a glazed door giving on to the garden at the side of the house. Directly opposite the study door was the entrance to a chilly, unlit room, evidently used for flower arrangements. Like the garden door, it was glazed with small square panes of frosted glass.

She returned to the study, and moved swiftly across the room to the door of the little chamber beside the fireplace. It was still open, and a swift inspection showed her that, even when closed, it was possible to see parts of the study by squinting through a small aperture made in the wall to carry a gas pipe through to the overhead mantle. It was hardly a perfect hiding place, but it would serve its turn: if she could see, then she could also hear. She felt afraid, but behind the fear lurked a kind of pleasurable excitement. She was about to hear whatever secrets Baron Augustyniak shared with his select group of associates.

When Albert returned with the silver coffee jugs, he placed them on a warming tray, igniting the wicks of two small spirit lamps arranged beneath it. She helped him to set out the coffee cups, the cream jugs, and the bowls of demerara sugar. When he moved towards the door, she said, 'I'll just plump up the cushions in these chairs, and join you later in the kitchen.'

'All right, Susan,' said Albert, and left the room, pushing the trolley in front of him. Vanessa listened as it rumbled away towards the hall. It was time to conceal herself, and wait for the baron and his friends to arrive from the dining-room.

After what seemed like an hour, Vanessa heard the door open, and the murmur of voices as the baron and his friends came in from the corridor. She could see the door from her vantage point behind the gas pipe outlet. The baron entered first, holding the door open for his guests. He was followed immediately by Doctor Kessler and his friend Herr Gerdler, faded, stooping, with a mean, thin-lipped mouth. They were still talking earnestly together, as they had done at the table.

The two Polish gentlemen, Monsieur Balonek and Monsieur Haremza, came in separately from the passage. Herr Eidenschenk came last, looking grave and thoughtful. Baron Augustyniak closed the door.

Vanessa could see part of the baron's desk, and the two armchairs placed near it, but the rest of the room was hidden from her view. For some minutes, everyone passed out of sight, and she could hear the tinkle of cups and glasses, followed soon afterwards by the reek of cigar smoke. Presently the baron appeared, clutching a glass of brandy. He sat down at his desk, and motioned with his free hand to the two armchairs. In a moment, Doctor Kessler and Herr Gerdler came into view, and sat down. The others, presumably, had settled themselves elsewhere in the room.

'Gentlemen,' said the baron without preamble, 'As some of us are Poles, and others Germans, I suggest that we speak English at this meeting. This will not be a long meeting, as we do not want the others to think that it's anything other than a chance for a few old friends to indulge their nostalgia in intimate reminiscences. So let us begin. The fateful day, the 21 July, is not far away.

Everything is ready for the momentous event of that day, which we have called The Aquila Project. I am what the English call an "anchor man", ostensibly the man of power, but in fact at the service of more powerful forces. Herr Gerdler, would you like to remind us of what you see as the salient details of our mission?'

'I will do so,' Gerdler replied. 'This very morning, the 9 July, the action group set out for Poland, taking Grunwalski with them. He is fully primed, and has the necessary weapons at his command – weapons that I have been able to supply.'

'Has he been amenable to our aims since we freed him from his prison?'

'Entirely so, Baron. Indeed, the man seems dedicated to the task ahead. I gather there are family reasons why he should be so loyal. We feel that Grunwalski is something more than a mere mercenary.'

Vanessa saw Doctor Kessler attempt to hide an amused smile behind his hand.

'So,' Gerdler continued, 'they have left England, and will be moving across France. You understand that the French route is the right one for them at such a time. Accommodation has been arranged at every stage of the journey, including its ultimate destination.' Gerdler glanced briefly at Doctor Kessler, who once again smiled at some secret amusement, but said nothing.

'You mean Polanska Gory?' asked the baron.

'Precisely. As for what happens to Grunwalski after the mission has proved successful – well, you will want to hear from Herr Eidenschenk about that.'

Vanessa could not see Eidenschenk, but she could hear him clearly enough, though his English was heavily accented.

'As you know, gentlemen,' he said, 'although I am by nationality German, my family has its roots in Poland, and I am fluent in Polish and Russian. I am also one of the original members of The Thirty. I have already put in place a little coterie of friends, all of German-Polish lineage, who will assume the role of uniformed police, and, after the great event has taken place, will take Grunwalski into protective custody immediately. They will transport him swiftly out of the Polish lands and back to France. He will be conveyed to Spain through a route that most of you will know about, and lie low there in Madrid until it is prudent for him to return to England, where he prefers to be based.'

'What will he be paid? And who will pay it?' asked a voice from somewhere in the room. It may have been Monsieur Haremza.

'He will be paid ten thousand pounds. The money will come from the gold reserves of a nation which must remain unidentified. I know you will all see the necessity for that.'

There was a general murmur of agreement, and then the baron spoke again.

'Herr Doctor Kessler,' he said, 'I should like to say on behalf of us all how honoured we are to have you with us tonight, and to congratulate you on your appointment as Second Secretary at Prussia House. Will you please give us your views on the security aspects of The Aquila Project?'

Doctor Kessler cleared his throat. He was looking straight ahead, and rather disconcertingly seemed to be staring straight into Vanessa's eyes.

'Thank you, Baron,' said Kessler, 'for your kind words. Concerning security, I will mention two points only. First, I think that someone should be detailed to keep a constant eye on a man called Detective Inspector Arnold Box, of Scotland Yard. He was concerned with the arrest of Grunwalski on Tower Bridge. He was seen questioning Peter Rosanski before his convenient demise, and I actually met him myself when he came to question Herr Gerdler here at his shop in Covent Garden. He's appearing too often in our affairs for comfort. He needs watching.'

'That can easily be arranged, Doctor Kessler,' said Augustyniak. 'I will see to it myself. And what is your second point?'

'I want you to be assured, gentlemen, that all our sympathizers here in England, people who have smoothed our way during the last year, are being kept from having second thoughts by the knowledge that I hold compromising papers on every one of them. One or two of these people are very highly placed, and fully capable of bribing or cajoling servants and other lesser fry to betray their trust. To make absolutely sure that these papers are out of the reach of such people, I have placed them all in the safe in my study at Prussia House, a safe to which I alone hold the key. Diplomatic immunity, gentlemen, is a sure guarantee against what the English call light-fingered gentry!'

'Excellent, Doctor Kessler,' said the baron. 'But you mention one or two high-placed Englishmen who are helping to fund The Aquila Project. I'm intrigued! Would it be in order to say who they are?'

'Well, Baron, under normal circumstances I'd say nothing, but yes, I'll tell you their names. One of them, you'll be surprised to hear, is—'

Vanessa, numb and cramped with standing so long, suddenly slipped. She put out a hand to steady herself, and sent a number of silver trophies crashing to the floor. She saw the baron spring up from his chair with a cry of rage, and in a moment he had flung open the door. He seized Vanessa by the arm, and dragged her trembling into the room.

'Thief!' he cried. 'I thought so.... You are no trained servant, Susan Moore! You came here for my silver, you little thief!'

Still holding her by the arm, he all but dragged her across the room to the fireplace, and pulled the bell. His audience stood aghast, some shocked, some embarrassed. Doctor Kessler had sprung to his feet, his face once more white with rage, but some instinct concerning his place as a guest in the baron's house kept him silent.

Almost immediately the door opened, and Joseph Doyle, the surly coachman, came into the room. His cold eyes glanced briefly at Vanessa before fixing themselves on his master.

'What's amiss, Baron?' he asked in his usual surly tones. 'I heard a commotion in here as I came in just now from the mews.'

'Doyle,' said Baron Augustyniak, 'this young woman is a thief. She had concealed herself in my trophy-cupboard with the intention of stealing my silver when my friends and I had left the study. Lock her up in the flower-room, and run for the police.'

'A thief, hey?' said Doyle. 'Well, I'm not surprised, sir. Some of us suspected her already of being up to no good. She's no trained servant, that's for sure. Come on, you,' he said roughly, seizing Vanessa by the arm. He pushed her in front of him over the threshold into the corridor. Alexander, the head footman, had come hurrying from the kitchen to answer the bell. Doyle waved him away, and led Vanessa into the cold flower-room across the corridor.

'You'll stay here, see?' he growled. 'I'm going to fetch the constable, and I'm going to lock you in here till I get back. A thief, hey? Is it just you, or have you got a damned accomplice waiting on the outside?'

Doyle did not wait for an answer, but hurried away, locking Vanessa in the room by turning the key on the other side of the door. Vanessa rubbed her arm. First the baron, then this rough coachman – why did men always seize women by the arm? Still, it could have been worse. It might have been her throat.

Despite the hot summer weather, it was chilly in the flower-room. Some light filtered in through the frosted glass panes in the door, and she could see shelves full of glass and metal flower vases, and near them a depressing brownstone sink. She had felt afraid when the baron had dragged her from her hiding place, but that fear was rapidly being replaced by the exhilaration of success. She knew that what she had overheard would be of the utmost value to Colonel Kershaw – if, that is, he didn't dismiss her on the spot for taking an unauthorized initiative. Perhaps—

She heard the key turn in the lock, and in a moment Doctor Kessler had erupted into the room. His face was dark with anger, and his waxed moustache bristled with what seemed to be its own belligerence.

Vanessa backed away from him in fright. He looked half-crazed, and she wondered whether he was about to foam at the mouth. She could smell the mint sauce that still clung to his jacket, and in the midst of her fear came a sudden inclination to laugh.

'If you lay a hand on me, Doctor Kessler,' she said, 'I'll scream the place down.'

'You little fool!' Kessler's voice came low and menacing. 'You may have deceived Augustyniak and the others, but not me. You're no thief. You're too clumsy and gauche for that particular trade. No, you are one of Napier's spies, insinuated into the baron's household to spy on him—'

'I don't know what you mean! Spy on him for what? What's he supposed to have done?'

She saw Kessler hesitate as he realized that he had spoken indiscreetly and, at the same moment they both heard the door from the garden pushed open. A young police constable walked into the flower-room, accompanied by Joseph Doyle. The study door opened, and the baron and his guests came out into the corridor.

'Ah! Constable!' cried Baron Augustyniak. 'You've arrived here commendably quickly. I want you to take this girl in charge. I accuse her of being a thief.'

The constable glanced at Vanessa, looked carefully at her face, and then took a notebook and pencil from his pocket.

'What's your name?' he asked, and when she told him that it was Susan Moore, he wrote it down slowly and laboriously. Then he turned to face the baron.

'Sir,' he said, 'there's a Scotland Yard officer working at a case close by, and I've asked him to come here to help. I can't arrest this young woman without some evidence, and this officer from the Yard will be a great help.'

'Very well,' said the baron. 'Is it in order for my guests to leave, now? It's almost half past ten.'

'That will be quite in order, sir,' said the constable, 'provided that you will be available for questioning. It's really a matter of routine, nothing more than that. If your coachman will keep an eye on the girl, I'll fetch the Scotland Yard officer straight away.'

A moment later, the baron had ushered his guests along the corridor, and the constable had disappeared through the garden door. Vanessa and Joseph Doyle stood in a kind of embarrassed silence for a while, and then the coachman spoke.

'You'd better admit to being a thief, Miss Drake,' he said, 'so that by arresting you the police will be able to spirit you away from this lion's den—'

'You know who I am?' cried Vanessa. 'But how—'

Joseph Doyle chuckled to himself. 'Well, of course I know who you are! Just do as I say, and play up to this Scotland Yarder when he comes. The colonel wouldn't like anything nasty to happen to you. That's why I came here in the first place.'

'What happened to the original coachman? Mr Quiller said he's gone off in a huff.'

'He went off, miss, because someone paid him to do so. You know who I mean.'

'But how could you get away with pretending to be a coachman?'

'I *am* a coachman,' Doyle replied, 'and I'm minded to stay here for a while. It's a nice billet. But look! That constable's returned with his Scotland Yard friend. I'll make myself scarce. Remember what I told you: admit to being a thief. That'll get you out of here.'

As he was speaking, the garden door had opened to admit the constable, followed immediately by the Scotland Yard officer. Vanessa almost cried out in surprise. It was her fiancé, Jack Knollys. Joseph Doyle smiled to himself, and slipped out the room. At the same time, Baron Augustyniak came up from the entrance hall, where he had been bidding his guests farewell.

Jack Knollys turned to look at Vanessa, and his face broke into a smile of triumph.

'Well, well,' he said, 'if it isn't Gertie Miller! A little bird told me that you might be up to your tricks in St John's Wood. The game's up, Gert. Have you got Johnny the Stoat with you?'

'I'm saying nothing, Mr Knollys,' said Vanessa sulkily. Knollys turned away from her impatiently, and addressed Baron Augustyniak, who had not taken his eyes off Vanessa. His face held an expression which was an uncomfortable mixture of mockery and relief. It was impossible, thought Vanessa, to know what that enigmatic man really thought of his erring housemaid.

'Sir,' said Knollys in low tones, 'this young woman is well known to us, and in the normal course of things she'll be held overnight, and brought up before the magistrate in the morning. But you, or a member of your household, will need to lay a complaint against her, and will be called as a witness, as she was seized by you on suspicion, and not caught *in flagrante delicto*.'

A little shadow of anxiety crossed the baron's brow, which Knollys took as a cue to make a suggestion.

'Now, I appreciate, sir,' he said, 'that this is a Diplomatic household, and if you wish, I can prosecute this case myself, and make a brief statement to the press. I shall have to identify the house, but nobody will need to be called as a witness. I will leave you to decide what course of action to take.'

'I should be glad to hand the whole squalid affair over to you, Sergeant,' said the baron. 'The Russian Ambassador would, I know, take it as a great favour if I was allowed not to appear personally in the business.'

'The Russian Ambassador, sir? I understood that you were a Polish gentleman?'

'It's the same thing,' replied the baron, shortly. 'See to the matter, will you, Sergeant?' He suddenly turned on his heel and hurried away.

Knollys turned to the constable, who was standing guard over Vanessa.

'Constable,' he said, I want you to look around the grounds, just in case her accomplice, Johnny the Stoat, is with her. Come on, Gertie, I'm going to search your room, just in case you've helped yourself to anything else of the baron's, and then you pack your things. It's a night in the cells for you, my girl, and up before the beak in the morning.'

Vanessa led her captor to a door in the hall that took them up the servants' staircase to the third floor. She opened the door of her room, and hurried in, closely followed by Knollys. She was immediately all but smothered in one of Jack Knollys' powerful embraces.

'He knew you'd overstep the mark,' he said, when he had released her. 'That's why he made sure that I was here most nights. He'll give you what for, when he sees you next.'

'Jack,' Vanessa whispered, 'he'll forgive me immediately when he hears what I have to tell him. This Baron—'

'Don't say anything now, Cornflower,' said Jack. 'You never know who's listening. Just pack up all your things, and I'll get you out of here. I've got a cab waiting at the end of the road.'

It had been a great adventure, Vanessa mused, as she began to pack. Her only regret would be not seeing her young friend Ellen again, and leaving behind her the belief that she was a common thief and criminal. Somehow, the idea of Mr Quiller thinking that to be the truth filled her with an almost painful regret.

10

Conclave at Lipton's Hotel

VANESSA SAT BACK on the stuffed horsehair seat of the cab, and sighed with relief. It was quite dark, and the elegant streets of St John's Wood were radiant with gaslight. Mixed with the smell of stale tobacco and damp, she could just discern the perfume of night-scented stock. The cab driver had not waited for instructions, but had driven swiftly out of Cavendish Gardens and into the dark expanse of Regent's Park. Despite her excitement, Vanessa found that her eyelids were too heavy to keep open, and she slept.

She awoke with a start to find that they had crossed Marylebone Road, and were making their way along Harley Street. She glanced at Jack Knollys, who was separated from her by her bulky carpet bag. He looked stern and preoccupied.

'Where are we going, Jack?' she asked. Her fiancé seemed to wake up from a kind of trance.

'What? Oh, it's you, Cornflower. Is this your little carpet bag? What do you want to know?'

'I want to know where we're going. We'll be in Mayfair, soon, at this rate.'

'We're going to Lipton's Hotel, in George Street, just off Hanover Square. As soon as Baron Augustyniak sent for the police – and that was providential, if you like! – I alerted the colonel to the situation, and he said that he would see you straight away.

Lipton's Hotel is one of his bases, apparently. A bit like Bagot's, only on a more modest scale.'

'I don't want him to see me dressed like this,' said Vanessa. 'In this housemaid's dress, and old black coat. He's always seen me smart and well turned out.'

'He doesn't care what you're wearing, Cornflower. Neither do I, for that matter. You look all right to me. You always have, and you always will. Here we are now, turning in to Hanover Square.'

It was rather gloomy in the entrance hall to Lipton's Hotel, as the gaslights had been turned down to a glimmer. A young man seated in a kind of mahogany and glass cabinet near the door glanced up at them as they came in from George Street.

'He's upstairs,' said the young man. 'Number 6, on the first floor.'

At Jack's insistence, Vanessa preceded him up the staircase, which was thickly carpeted. She had never been in Lipton's Hotel before. From what she could see of it, it was very comfortable, and of a high standard. They found Number 6, and Knollys knocked quietly on the door. A voice bade them come in, and Vanessa and Jack entered the room.

Colonel Kershaw rose from a chair near the fireplace of what was evidently a sitting-room. Vanessa noticed that coffee and sandwiches had been set out on a small table, and suddenly felt hungry. Sitting opposite the colonel was Arnold Box, and standing at one of the windows overlooking George Street was a man in his late thirties, his face adorned with a clipped moustache, and with lines of good humour at the corners of his deep-set blue eyes.

'Missy!' cried Colonel Kershaw, 'so you've been successfully abducted from the clutches of the foe! I expect you've a lot of things to tell me, but first you'd better fortify yourself from the food and drink laid ready on that table. And you, Mr Knollys. Of course, you both know Inspector Box. This other gentleman is Major Blythe, from the Home Office. Major Blythe and I occasionally work together. So sit down, both of you, and sustain the inner man – and woman. Then we will talk.'

Vanessa did as she was bid, and poured out two steaming cups of coffee for Jack Knollys and herself. The sandwiches, a selection of ham, chicken and cucumber, were very fresh, and they both did full justice to them. Meanwhile, Kershaw, Box and Major Blythe talked in low tones among themselves. It was only when the colonel had seen that Vanessa and Jack had both finished their refreshments that he spoke to them.

'And now, Miss Drake,' he said, 'the time's come for you to tell me all that happened to you since you set foot in White Eagle Lodge on Friday, the 6th. Take your time, and try to recall everything concerning Baron Augustyniak, his wife, and his guests. I will not interrupt your story unless it's absolutely necessary.'

Vanessa told her audience all about the master and mistress of White Eagle Lodge. She gave a complete set of verbal portraits of all the servants, what they said and what they did. She dwelt in great detail on the fateful dinner party, describing and naming the guests, and repeating word for word what Doctor Kessler had said about Arnold Box. She saw Box pull a wry face, and when she described how she had spilt the mint sauce, she saw a fleeting smile cross Colonel Kershaw's face.

He leaned forward in his chair when she began her account of the scene in the study, which had culminated in her exposure. She concluded her tale by asserting that although Baron Augustyniak had treated her roughly when he had found her in the silver-cupboard, she still thought that he was normally a considerate gentleman, with a kindly regard for his servants. He seemed to be both patient and resigned in the matter of his wife's jealousy.

When Vanessa had finished her tale, Colonel Kershaw sat in absorbed silence for what seemed like minutes. For a brief moment she wondered whether he was going to dismiss her from his service for exceeding her brief. It would not have been the first occasion that he had almost decided to do so. The thought troubled her more than she had realized. Did he know that her loyalty to him was total and unconditional?

She saw Jack Knollys looking at her with quiet amusement, and realized that he had read her thoughts. She loved Jack Knollys, and hoped that one day soon he would name the day. As for Colonel Kershaw – well, she had special feelings for him, too, and had long ago sensed that he regarded her as a kind of surrogate daughter....

Colonel Kershaw pulled himself up straight in his chair beside the fireplace.

'Well, Miss Drake,' he said, in his quiet voice, 'I think you have excelled yourself on this particular mission. The information that you have brought me is quite invaluable, and I cannot see any other way in which I could have obtained it. Well done, missy!'

Vanessa felt herself blushing with pleasure. He was going to keep her, and something told her that there would never again be talk of a parting of the ways. She muttered a quiet 'Thank you, sir'.

'You have witnessed this evening,' Kershaw continued, 'a gathering of some of the most dangerous men who have ever assembled in an English house to plot treason and anarchy, and rather than exclude you from this conference, I will ask you to remain for a little while and listen to what I have to say.

'First, I knew nothing of evil report about Baron Augustyniak, but now I see him as what he himself called the "anchor man" of this organization, The Thirty. Incidentally, Miss Drake, what a very good memory you have! All those foreign names, and whole sentences of dialogue. That's an invaluable asset, which could be of special use in the future.

'Second, let me talk about Doctor Franz Kessler. I know a great deal about him. Mr Box here has met him, and so has Sir Charles Napier. Kessler has recently been appointed Second Secretary at Prussia House. This man, a Doctor of Law from Heidelberg University, is an expert swordsman and a crack shot with a rifle. He is a man with blood on his hands, and a ruthless determination to see any project with which he's associated carried through to success.'

Vanessa listened, fascinated. It was not often that she was allowed to share in this kind of consultation. It was as though the colonel felt that she was now ready for greater trust and responsibility than he had seen fit to bestow upon her in the past.

'There are some people,' Kershaw continued, 'myself included, who wonder why such a man has been given a post carrying diplomatic immunity. Sir Charles Napier believes that Kessler has powerful friends in the higher German Establishment. Whatever the truth of the matter, Kessler is now a diplomat, and therefore not subject to the stringencies of our British law. As you yourself have witnessed, Miss Drake, Kessler has a violent temper – hardly a diplomatic trait.'

'And he's a crack shot with a rifle, sir?' said Box. 'That's very interesting.'

'It is, Box. He is also a killer. I know for a fact that he had committed two violent murders for political purposes, as the agent of a third party. I know who that third party is. So does Napier. I am convinced now that Kessler was sent here to London purely to fulfil some nefarious purpose of this nest of assassins and dreamers calling themselves The Thirty. It seems that he's the blackmailer-in-chief of this precious gang, and that he has a hold over a number of English collaborators....'

Colonel Kershaw stopped speaking, and turned to look at Major Blythe, who, so far, had sat silently, listening intently to what he was saying.

'Blythe,' said the Colonel, 'in connection with that other matter – the police business that we talked about – do you think there's anything doing in that direction? About Kessler and his diplomatic safe, you know?'

'I'd say yes, Colonel; very decidedly. After all, there'd be nothing to lose for all parties on our side. What do you think, Mr Box?'

'About – oh, yes, I see. Well, I've no objection, gentlemen, as long as you don't tell me anything about it. Or Sergeant Knollys.'

'There you are, Colonel,' said Major Blythe. 'Everybody's in agreement on that matter. Do you want me to put it in train when I see him?'

'Please. If you will. I'm infinitely obliged to you, Blythe.'

I wonder what they're talking about? thought Vanessa. Whatever it is, Jack and I are not to be privy to it. Well, that was how people worked in Colonel Kershaw's organization. You were told only what you needed to know, and there was no point in going into tantrums about it.

'Now,' said Kershaw, turning towards Vanessa once again, 'let me just conclude what I have to say about the other folk at Baron Augustyniak's dinner party. The man called Gerdler is probably the quartermaster of The Aquila Project. I know about him, too. He is a brilliant organizer, and an arranger of comings and goings, with a whole coterie of people employed by him for various nefarious purposes. He keeps just within the law of whatever country he's operating in, but is nonetheless a man of deep criminal tendencies. He's also an expert in firearms, and keeps a gunsmith's shop near Covent Garden. His political views are those of his friend and fellow conspirator, Kessler.

'As for Eidenschenk, well, he sounds like another Gerdler, an organizer, with men of his own, but I'd say that he's much more of a Polish patriot than the other Poles who were present at that dinner. He is also a liar. There is no "unidentified nation" paying Grunwalski ten thousand pounds. That money is probably coming from a cartel of European business interests, notably the armaments manufacturers of Bohemia and the Ruhr. If The Aquila Project succeeds, there will be plenty of work to keep the armaments factories busy. There are other conclusions that I can draw from Miss Drake's intelligence report, but I need to keep them to myself for the moment.'

Kershaw stood up, and looked gravely at Vanessa.

'Miss Drake,' he said, 'I don't want to alarm you, but I'm concerned that Doctor Franz Kessler might want to finish his business with you. Although you were at White Eagle Lodge under an incognito, men like that have ways of finding things out. I want you to stay here, in Lipton's Hotel for tonight. It's nearly twelve, and I'm sure you'd appreciate a good night's rest. Sergeant Knollys, would you care to remain here also, in order to keep watch over Miss Drake during the dark hours? Tomorrow, missy, we'll arrange for you to be taken to a place of safety. It's only for a little while, because, unless I'm very much mistaken, Doctor Kessler will have quit these shores before many days have elapsed.'

Kershaw pulled the bell, and almost immediately a housekeeper knocked and entered the room. She was accompanied by the young man from the reception booth on the ground floor.

'Miss Drake is ready to retire, Mrs Wade,' he said. 'Please show her to her room. Mr Davies, would you show Sergeant Knollys where he can camp for the night?'

He took Vanessa gravely by the hand, and bowed briefly over it.

'Good night, missy,' he said, 'we shall meet again before the month is out. And once again, well done!'

'I didn't expect her to remain undetected for more than a few days,' said Kershaw when Vanessa and Jack Knollys had left the room. 'It's particularly difficult to sustain the fiction that you are a trained servant when, in fact, you're something quite different. She's a valiant girl.... Franz Kessler is a ruthless foe, and there are some people who think he's slightly mad. It's odd, you know, to find someone as German as Kessler – or Gerdler, for that matter – being so deeply involved in one of these Polish conspiracies. Still, we must face the fact that he is so involved, and act accordingly.

'Box,' Kershaw continued, 'can you arrange a place of safety for Miss Drake? I don't want to draw her into one of my secret places: that would be to continue the alarm and anxiety of her situation. It would have to be somewhere where she could stay while you and I are – er – otherwise engaged.'

'I know just the place, sir,' said Box. 'I shall take her there first thing in the morning.'

'Excellent. Now, I don't want to detain Major Blythe much longer, as it's getting very late. So can we just complete this piece of police business that we were discussing before Miss Drake arrived? Are you sure, Mr Box, that you can arrange the enquiry to take place where Major Blythe's presence would seem quite natural?'

'I see no problem at all, sir. The enquiry can be held in Albany Street Police Station, which is near Regent's Park, and the head-quarters of "S" Division. Superintendent Harris already knows about it, and has agreed to let Superintendent Keating chair the committee on his patch, as we say. He also knows that Major Blythe is something more than just a member of the Hampstead Watch Committee.'

'Well done, Box. It's essential that the matter is cleared up immediately, so that any steps that have to be taken can be made by Major Blythe, who has full powers in the matter. You and I can go about our particular business secure in the knowledge that all should be well at Albany Street Police Station.'

'And when all the police business is over, Colonel,' said Major Blythe, 'I'll be able to give my attention to that business of Herr Kessler's private safe in Prussia House.'

Major Blythe bade Kershaw and Box goodnight, and quietly left the room. Box saw how he drew himself briefly to attention on the threshold. Whatever else he was, Major Blythe was evidently still a serving officer.

'Now, Box,' said Kershaw, 'Grunwalski and his associates left England on Monday, which was the ninth. You and I must set out for Poland on Thursday, the twelfth – just ten days before Project

Aquila reaches its climax at Polanska Gory. We will travel by railway up to Scotland, and make our way to Sir Hamish Bull's house, Craigarvon Tower—'

'Ah! I see, sir!'

'I thought you would, Box. It's a short walk from there to the Northern Fleet headquarters at Dunnock Sound, where we will step aboard the light cruiser *Albion*, which is due to make a courtesy visit to the German Baltic Flotilla at Danzig. The *Albion* will raise anchor and steam out of Dunnock Sound at eight o'clock on Thursday evening. It's a long haul – seventy-two hours – but it's the safest way for us to get into Poland undetected. We should drop anchor in Danzig harbour on Sunday evening, the fifteenth of July.'

'Will there just be the two of us, sir?' asked Box. It was a deliberately naïve question, and Kershaw smiled in recognition of the fact.

'No, Mr Box, there will be others. I'm taking a sergeant-armourer with me, a man called Morrison, and another man, Kolinsky, who is a Polish-speaking military interpreter. The four of us will travel together on HMS *Albion*. I have a few other people already on the alert in both Germany and the Polish lands of the Russian Empire – people who will be shadowing us, and who will come to our aid immediately if the need arises. I have passable papers for the four of us, though I'm hoping that we won't need to make use of them. So prepare yourself, Mr Box! On Thursday, we go a-hunting, and our quarry is a gang of madmen who aim to take the life of an emperor, and throw the peace of Europe to the dogs of war.'

Extract from *The Daily Chronicle*, Tuesday, 10 July 1894.

St John's Wood. Yesterday evening, the ninth inst., an attempted robbery took place at the residence of Baron and Baroness Augustyniak in Cavendish Gardens. It would seem that a female thief, alleged to be one Gertrude Miller, had gained fraudulent access to the house, White Eagle Lodge, by giving herself out to be a trained housemaid. Miller purported to have been on the books of Thompson's Domestic Agency, in the name of Susan Moore, but the proprietor of that establishment denies all knowledge of any such person.

Miller was apprehended by Baron Augustyniak himself, as he was entertaining a few friends to drinks in his study. We would commend this gentleman's prompt and decisive action, and the subsequent actions of PC Williams and Detective Sergeant Knollys in securing the woman, and conveying her to the Bridewell. Miller will appear before one or other of the stipendiary magistrates this morning.

Superintendent Keating of 'J' Division looked gravely at the man sitting before him on an upright chair. He had known him for over thirty years, but now, if the matter was not handled carefully and subtly, he would lose not only his pension, but almost certainly his liberty. Keating glanced at the four assessors whom he had chosen to help him judge the case. They sat with him in the upstairs office at Albany Street Police Station, two on either side of him, facing the man in the upright chair. Keating rather self-consciously cleared his throat.

'Detective Inspector Robert Fitzgerald,' he said, 'after a long and distinguished career in the Metropolitan Police, you were detected in the instigation and committal of an illegal act, namely, breaking and entering. The officer who arrested you, Police Constable Thomas Philips of "W" Division, Brixton Road, reported the matter to me, and at my instigation delivered you into my custody.'

Bobby Fitz thought to himself: if I go to gaol, Mother will be sent to the workhouse. If I'm spared gaol, but dismissed in disgrace, I will lose my pension, and I'll be barred from working as a private detective. But whatever happens, I'll find something to do.

'I've summoned you here today, Fitzgerald, to tell you the decision of this panel concerning your future. On my left, are Chief Superintendent Slessor, and Detective Chief Inspector Langham. On my right is Major Ronald Blythe, of the Hampstead Watch Committee, and Mr Creighton Carr, a stipendiary magistrate. You know none of these gentleman either personally or professionally, which is why I invited them to consider your case, and to advise me as to an appropriate course of action. They have done so, and have communicated their recommendation to me this morning, Thursday, 12 July, 1894. They have seen all the papers in the case, and also written pleas in mitigation from Superintendent Radcliffe of the Home Office, Superintendent Lucas of "W" Division, and Detective Inspector Box, of Scotland Yard, currently based at King James's Rents, Whitehall Place. Those pleas in mitigation have also been taken into account.'

Superintendent Keating paused, and began to speak in low tones to the men on his right and left. Bobby Fitz could hear nothing of what they were saying, and the faces of the five men remained inscrutable. Thirty years of dedicated policing, and it had all come to this!

'Detective Inspector Fitzgerald,' the superintendent continued, 'it is clear that you cannot remain as a member of the Metropolitan Police, and that you will be barred from joining any other police force in England, Scotland, and the Principality of Wales. However, in consideration of your many years of dedicated service, we have decided not to institute a prosecution against you, but instead, to demand your immediate resignation, on the grounds of ill health. It is understood that you have an aged mother to support, and that the loss of your police pension would have a grave effect upon your wellbeing. That is our decision. You must come up here at once, and sign the letter of resignation that I have written on your behalf.'

Bobby Fitz rose from his chair. He walked stiffly, as though in a trance, and stood before his superintendent's table. He glanced briefly at the letter, which said that, on the advice of Doctor E.A. Thompson, police surgeon, he offered his resignation, owing to chronic congestion of the lungs. His hand trembled with relief as he signed the letter.

The committee rose noisily from their chairs, pointedly avoiding eye contact with the man whom they had judged unfit for public service. All but Superintendent Keating quickly left the room.

'Sir, how can I thank you enough—'

'You damned fool, Bobby,' Keating interrupted. 'You went too far, didn't you? You thought you were impregnable. Well, nobody is. I'll miss you back in "J" – you're a good man gone to seed. We've all taken risks here today to find a way out for you. Did you know that Inspector Box has volunteered to deal with the press if any inconvenient questions are asked? Well, it's true. Now, what are you going to do?'

'I'll see if one of the detective agencies will take me on. It's something that I could do to earn enough to keep Mother and me.'

Superintendent Keating gathered up the papers from the table where he had sat.

'Listen, Bobby,' he said. 'When I go out of this room, you'll find that Major Ronald Blythe will come in to see you. He wants to talk to you, and I'd advise you to gather your wits together and listen to him very carefully. That's all. When all this has blown over, we'll hope to see you from time to time in Bethnal Green Road.'

Keating shook hands briefly with his former inspector, turned abruptly to the door, and went out into the corridor.

Before Bobby Fitz had had time to recover from the enervating interview that had effectively handed him back his life, Major Ronald Blythe came into the room, closing the door behind him. Until that moment, he had been nothing more to Bobby Fitzgerald than the vague shape of a man sitting in judgement upon him behind the table. Now he saw him as he was, a man in his late thirties, fresh-faced and with a military moustache, and shrewd but good-humoured eyes. He was informally dressed in a light tweed hacking jacket and dark trousers.

Blythe drew two chairs out from a row arranged along one of the walls of the room, and motioned to Bobby Fitz to sit down beside him. There was to be no hint of the tribunal about this meeting.

'Mr Fitzgerald,' said Blythe, 'I have read about your exploits, and your use of a group of criminal experts, called by you the "light fantastic boys". I've also heard that you are a very loyal and patriotic man, devoted to Queen and country. Now, I can here and now enlist you into another branch of the public service which owes direct and personal allegiance to Her Majesty, an organization in which a man of your particular abilities would be a valued asset.'

'My particular abilities, sir?'

'Yes. The kind of talent for detection that revealed the existence of the assassin Grunwalski to the security services, and thus averted what could have been an embarrassing incident on Tower Bridge. Not only you, but your boys would have a role to play. Are you interested in my proposition? I would have immediate work for you, if you accept my offer of membership.' He added, in a more confiding tone, 'The position is salaried, and totally secure. In all that you do, you have the Queen and the State behind you.'

'I should very much like to join your organization, sir. You'll find that I'll not let you down.'

'Very well. You'll understand that I am only the agent of another. In a few weeks' time, I'll take you to meet the head of our organization. Now, listen very carefully while I tell you about the little enterprise in which you will play the major part. Write nothing down, but try to commit everything I tell you to memory. There is a German diplomat who came very recently to England, a man called Franz Kessler....'

The former Detective Inspector Fitzgerald leaned forward in his chair, and gave his full attention to the man who had just given him back his future.

11

From Berlin to Danzig

IN HIS OFFICE in the house of the Prussian Landtag in the
Albrechtstrasse, Count von Donath sat at his desk and stared
into vacancy, envisioning his own desired version of the future. In
his mind's eye he saw the great and gracious city of Berlin spread
out as in a map, its palaces, its churches, its museums, and its
thronging thoroughfares. It was here, in the capital of the Second
Reich, that a new world was being fashioned.

Beyond and around the great city stretched the mighty land of
the German Nation, straining at its borders with France and the
vast territory of the Austrian Empire. Germany was hemmed in,
choking, constrained like a great stallion longing to gallop in open
terrain, but champing at the bit, and held in check by a bridle
fashioned from the fossilized conventions of diplomacy.

But in the coming month of July, 1894, and upon the 21st day
of the month, an event would occur that would cause the greatest
convulsion seen in Europe since the demise of Napoleon....

'Excellency, you are due at the Prussian Chamber of Deputies in
half an hour.'

One of his secretaries had entered the room without his being
aware of it. Von Donath pulled himself back into the present long
enough to thank the man curtly, and dismiss him. He glanced out
of the high window at the buildings of the Prussian Chamber
across the street. It would take him only minutes to get there.

Above the fireplace hung two portraits, the likenesses of a father and his son. Frederick I, Emperor of Germany, had been a humane and kindly man, modest in peacetime and a lion in war. To many he was known by his second title, Frederick III, King of Prussia, and that was how he, von Donath, thought of him. Frederick had fought in person at Sadowa, Wörth, and Sedan, and he had taken part in the Siege of Paris. He had come to the imperial throne in March, 1888, and was dead of throat cancer by June: King and Emperor for ninety-nine days.

There was a finely carved ivory chess set on von Donath's desk. He picked up the black king, examined it thoughtfully, and then placed it carefully back on its square. As in human life, each chess piece had its rank and its ordered place in the scheme of things.

Next to the portrait of Emperor Frederick was that of the current occupant of the throne, William II. It was he who had dismissed Bismarck, giving the signal to men like von Donath that the old order of things was about to change. Young, and headstrong, he was both loved and revered by the German people and nation.

All was going well. The Thirty were little more than a rumour to most people. Some members of the Imperial Chancellery regarded it as a fictional bogey, thought up by foreign rivals to create instability in the Reich. Well, let them go on thinking so, until the 21st.

He had introduced the 2 zloty coins as a kind of identity token at Augustyniak's instigation. That kind of romantic nonsense appealed to his Polish nature. Well, it was harmless enough. Augustyniak had proved to be a first-rate organizer, although he could have no idea that he was being used for a secret nefarious purpose. When the map of Europe was reshaped, he would receive his just reward.

Yes, Augustyniak had done well, and so had devoted, deadly Franz Kessler. He had received Kessler's long telegram from London only the day before. Kessler had minor worries, but then, he was a worrier by nature. He feared that Sir Charles Napier had seen through Augustyniak, and had insinuated a Foreign Office agent into the Baron's household in the guise of a servant – a housemaid, so Kessler said, and a clumsy one at that. This was highly unlikely: Napier employed couriers to do his bidding. Sending out young girls dressed up as housemaids was hardly his *modus operandi*.

Von Donath rose from his desk, and gathered up the notes for his coming speech to the Deputies of the Prussian Chamber. It was on the concept of legal appeals in the Code Napoleon. He suddenly stopped, as an unpleasant, but exciting, memory came to the fore in his crowded mind. That day in Berlin, that wet day last May, had been the moment when the whole project became possible, with the elimination of the treacherous double agent, Paul Claus.

Franz Kessler himself had volunteered to be the assassin. It was he who had arranged for Claus to be surrounded by a crowd of accomplices – he remembered how they had sheltered all the time beneath their wet umbrellas – and had then stabbed him to the heart. By prior arrangement, Kessler had slipped the still reeking knife into von Donath's pocket. The police would never have even considered questioning, let alone searching, a man of von Donath's eminence. He had dropped the knife into the Spree, as he crossed the Kaiser Wilhelm Bridge.

Surely it had been an act of fate that Claus's Polish coin had dropped from his pocket into the street, where he, von Donath, had retrieved it? Yes, it had been a signal from the gods to proceed as planned with Project Aquila – the elimination of an emperor, and the dawn of a new era in Europe. All was in readiness. The positions at the bridge had been carefully worked out, and the chosen assassin had been fully primed. Nothing could go wrong. And after that fateful hour, they would fill the prisons with their political foes.

Von Donath picked up the white king, and subjected it to

careful scrutiny. Then he placed it back precisely upon its square. A clock in the room chimed the quarter before eleven. With a sudden movement of his hand, von Donath swept the chess pieces off the board, and watched as the little ivory kings rolled helplessly across his desk.

It was time for people to leave their preordained ranks and make a bold bid to secure the future. That would happen on the 21st.

Von Donath left the room, descended the stairs, and strolled across the Albrechtstrasse to the Prussian Chamber of Deputies.

Colonel Kershaw and Inspector Box stood together on the foredeck of HMS *Albion*, watching the armoured prow of the cruiser cutting its path through the choppy waters of the North Sea. Above them, screaming gulls wheeled about in a sky filled with sullen clouds. A following wind blew down swaths of acrid black smoke from the vessel's two tall, raked stacks across the decks. It was the early morning of Friday, 13 July.

'An unlucky day? Perhaps so, Mr Box,' Kershaw was saying, 'but not for us, surely? It's The Thirty who will remember this as an inauspicious day – the day when you and I, and our companions, set out to frustrate their knavish tricks.'

Colonel Kershaw was wearing his favourite long black overcoat with the astrakhan collar, but instead of his usual silk hat, he had donned a flapped cap, which buttoned beneath his chin. Box himself had chosen to appear in his usual day clothes, with his fashionable overcoat and curly-brimmed bowler. After all, Danzig was a big city, full of civilized folk going about their daily business – or was it?

'Sir,' asked Box, 'what kind of a place is Danzig? Would you say that it's similar to London?'

'Well, Box, it's a great port, and a vital gateway for German trade into the Baltic. It's also the capital of Western Prussia. So, yes, it has some points of similarity with London, though, of course, it's only a fraction of its size. Its population is about two hundred thousand. It's been part of Prussia since 1814, so you can see why these wild notions of an independent Poland – which would have to include Danzig, or Gdansk, as the Poles call it – are dangerously destabilizing. It's a city where many Germans think they are Poles, and some Poles think they are Germans. A rather sturdy minority of both nationalities think they're Russian.... But you may be sure of this: any hint of Danzig ceasing to be German would set the whole of Germany in arms.'

'What will happen when we arrive there?'

'The *Albion* will tie up at one of the wharfs of the German Northern Flotilla in the Naval Dockyard facing on to the Gulf of Danzig. It's a goodwill visit, so there will be an official reception for the ship at the dockside, but that won't take place until Monday morning. Meanwhile, we will be met by someone who will convey us from the *Albion* to a house in a little street near the artillery barracks in the Wall Gasse, where we will spend the night.'

'This house, sir—'

'It belongs to a man called Roger Besnasse, a Lithuanian oil and tar merchant. It's by way of being an intelligence exchange for people engaged on discreet missions. The German authorities know it's there, but see the wisdom of letting it operate. Prussian State Intelligence uses it quite frequently. It's a useful staging-post for ventures like ours.

'Early the next morning we shall travel by railway to Posen, and from there by a single-track branch line to a place called Limburg, which is little more than a fortified railway station a quarter of a mile from the Russian border. We cross into Russian Poland from there.'

Arnold Box digested this information, but made no reply. He looked ahead of him at the restless waves of the North Sea. They would be sailing past Holland by now, he mused, and in another hour, perhaps, they would be skirting German Heligoland.

Next year, if all went well, the great Kiel Canal, linking the North Sea to the Baltic, would be open. Until then, access by ship to Danzig entailed a wearisome journey around Denmark's Jutland Peninsula via the Skagerrak. Evidently, Colonel Kershaw thought that this long, slow haul by sea was necessary.

'What exactly do you propose to do, sir, when we arrive at Polanska Gory? As we are entering Russia illegally—'

'Listen, Box,' said Kershaw, his face flushing with an uncharacteristic anger, 'Grunwalski was one of my agents, selected and groomed by me to infiltrate himself into this rotten gang, and help me to destroy it. I chose him, and then I lost him! I want that gang destroyed, and I want Grunwalski back. All this affair is *my* fault.'

Colonel Kershaw frowned, and bit his lip. Box remained silent, waiting for him to speak. He had never before heard the colonel be so bitterly self-critical.

'Yes,' Kershaw continued, 'I want Grunwalski back safely in England, but I don't want any of the listeners for foreign intelligence services to know that I'm in pursuit of him. I must not appear in the affair. And that's why we're travelling incognito through Germany, and then into the Russian Empire, without the knowledge of the external authorities. I can't call on the conventional forces of law and order to assist me. But I have my ways, Box, and what I can't plan beforehand, I'll contrive on the spur of the moment. Do you understand?'

'Yes, sir, I do. And it's not entirely your fault, you know. The Metropolitan Police had arrested Grunwalski, and were actually holding him in custody. We let him be sprung by Augustyniak and his conspirators, because we'd failed to realize the full seriousness of the situation. So let's share the responsibility, sir, and get on with ensuring the solution.'

Colonel Kershaw chuckled, and clapped Box on the back. The inspector's words seemed to have restored his good humour. He talked more optimistically of the coming adventure, and some minutes later the two men parted company. The *Albion* continued to cruise steadily at fifteen knots on a voyage that would take them out of the North Sea, and into the Strait of Jutland.

In a room on the top floor of one of the buildings constituting the Berlin barracks of the 32nd Imperial Field Regiment, Count von und zu Thalberg, Head of Prussian Military Intelligence, was reading a report from one of his discreet agents resident in England. It was a matter of wry amusement to Thalberg that such a passionate Anglophile as himself should be receiving intelligence reports of this nature from the heart of the British Empire. But it was a dangerous time, this last decade of the nineteenth century, and of all the enemies of stability in Europe, complacency was probably the most deadly. There were hotheads everywhere.

Count von und zu Thalberg was a distinguished man in his late forties, smartly dressed, but with the easy elegance of the old Prussian aristocracy about him. At one time a field commander, he had been for many years one of the principal officers of the German Military Intelligence. Three years earlier, he had become its head.

'Augustyniak's Polish Institute in London,' he said aloud, 'is already well established as a front for the conspirators in their crazed attempt to establish an independent Poland. Augustyniak is a bit of a romantic dreamer, as we know, but none the less effective for that. On the 9 July, the baron hosted a dinner party at his house in London, at which some core members of The Thirty were present. Franz Kessler was there. So were Balonek and Haremza, the poisonous Gerdler, and that fanatic, Eidenschenk.'

Thalberg had addressed his remarks to a stocky little man dressed in a rusty old black frock coat, who sat upright at a small wooden table on the far side of the high-ceilinged room. He had a wide, wooden countenance, adorned with an old-fashioned German moustache. He looked like a weather-beaten old farmer. The man paused in his examination of a number of maps which he had spread out on the table.

'And what did they do, Excellency?' he asked.

'Each man gave an account of himself, and then they all talked treason until some domestic incident interrupted them – something about a thieving servant. The most important piece of information gleaned from their meeting, was that Grunwalski and his keepers left London for Poland on the very same day, 9 July. It seems that Grunwalski may have thrown in his lot with The Thirty – I say "seems", because, of course, men like Grunwalski are trained to dissemble. Another very interesting point is that Doctor Kessler is convinced that our old friend Detective Inspector Box is on their track. You remember him, do you not, *Oberfeldwebel*?'

The sergeant-major permitted himself a little throaty chuckle.

'Herr Box! Yes, Excellency, he and I became good friends. I first met him, I recall, when you and I were staying at Minster Priory, in the English county of Wiltshire, where you conferred with the *Herr Oberst* Kershaw. That was the beginning of the business that had its dramatic finale at the Rundstedt Channel.* Do you intend to inform Colonel Kershaw of your interest in this Polish business?'

'I would like to, Sergeant-Major Schmidt,' Thalberg replied, 'but I don't think I will. Colonel Kershaw's a wily bird, as you know, and it may be that he has plans of his own. He'll certainly know about Augustyniak and his circle. And there's something else.'

Count von und zu Thalberg picked up another slip of paper from his desk, and read it through quickly. Schmidt saw that it was a pale blue telegraph form of the type used by Military Intelligence's private wires. It would not do for people like them to use the Prussian State Telegraph system.

'My informant tells me here, *Oberfeldwebel*, that Colonel Kershaw left London by train on 11 July, bound for Scotland, where he is to stay for a while as a guest of his friend Sir Hamish Bull at Craigarvon Tower. Does that ring any bells for you, Schmidt?'

* *Web of Discord.*

The old warrant officer chuckled to himself, and watched as his master smiled.

'Why, yes, Excellency. It's but a little walk from Craigarvon Tower to Dunnock Sound, where part of the great British Fleet lies at anchor. The good colonel could easily step on board a Royal Naval cruiser, and make his way up through the German Ocean to Danzig. And from there – well, who knows?'

'Precisely. So let us leave Colonel Kershaw alone for a moment, and consider our own movements. You and I, Schmidt, will go to Polanska Gory ourselves, as arranged, and see what we can do to rein in this madman, Grunwalski. We've already got a few men posted in the district, keeping a benevolent eye on the situation, and I have been given a detachment of the 4th Brandenburg Lancers, who have been billeted in the cavalry barracks at Posen. They could be of great value to us if this affair suddenly explodes into the Reich. It's going to be a tricky business, but we must succeed. No crazed fanatics must be allowed to assassinate Tsar Alexander III, and plunge Europe into the dark night of war.'

Sergeant-Major Schmidt frowned, and shook his head.

'It's a strange, obscure affair, Excellency. The Tsar is clearly in very poor health – all Europe knows that – and there are some who say that he cannot last the year. He's a curious target for the assassin, in my estimation. Why not wait for the Crown Heir to succeed him? Grand Duke Nicholas? He would be a much bigger prize. A young man, poised to rule, suddenly blown to oblivion.'

'You're right, Schmidt. I've had the same thought myself. But the reality is different, as you see, and it is with reality that we must deal. What have you to tell me from your examination of those maps? You've been poring over them for the last hour without speaking a single word.'

Sergeant-Major Schmidt put on a pair of little gold-rimmed spectacles, and picked up one of his maps.

'Polanska Gory lies in a hollow at the centre of a range of shallow hills in the westernmost part of the north Polish plain.

Latitude, so-and-so, longitude, that. It is five German miles from Lublin. It was built in the eighteenth century, and for a little while, in 1865, was within the German pale, and known as Bad Polenburg—'

'You can spare me the history, *Oberfeldwebel*. Just give me the facts.'

'Yes, sir. If we were to journey by railway from Danzig to Breslau, we could then go by road across an area of flat country-side to the north of Lublin, largely occupied by farmland and small villages. Polanska Gory is surrounded by birch woods, planted along the flanks of the low hills surrounding it.'

Schmidt picked up a magnifying glass, and bent down low over the map.

'But here, half a mile away from the spa, and on the skirts of one of those woods, there is what looks like a fortified church or monastery, with a straggling village in front of it. Our road would lie that way, and it occurs to me, Excellency, that our opponents could occupy such a place, and hold it easily against us—'

'I've heard of that place, Sergeant-Major,' said Thalberg. 'St Mary of the Icon, it's called, part church and part fort. It belongs to the old Polish-German family of Hardenberg. They're impov-erished now, little more than peasant farmers. But they're revered in that part of Poland because of their role in the Battle of Tannenberg in 1410.'

Thalberg saw his sergeant-major looking at him critically, and smiled.

'Yes, I know what you're thinking – why all this history? Why doesn't he confine himself to facts? Well, one of my kinswomen married into the Hardenberg family a few generations ago. But I am interrupting you. I agree that St Mary of the Icon is a dangerous place. What do you suggest?'

'I suggest, Excellency, that we travel by train from Danzig to the Russian town of Brest-Litovsk. From there, it will be an easy journey to Lublin, and from there, we will be able to strike north through the pine woods and down into Polanska Gory. This large-scale map of the area shows a wide road, evidently used by carriage-folk on their way to take the waters at the spa.'

'Excellent! We have a few days to finalize our arrangements, and then you and I will set out for Danzig. We will travel as ourselves – there's no reason for covert action at this stage – and take the railway via Stettin.'

'How will this Grunwalski be silenced?'

'He and his friends must walk into a trap of our devising, and so be rendered harmless immediately. We can call in our people dispersed throughout the area if we have to. But you know, *Oberfeldwebel*, I'm quite certain in my own mind that the Russian authorities will be able to deal with the matter themselves. Still, our presence in Polanska Gory will show the Russians that Germany will not countenance any potential threat against the life of the Tsar. When faced by anarchist assassins, Russia and Germany are on the same side.'

HMS *Albion* steamed into the dockyard of the Imperial Northern Flotilla some minutes after eight o'clock on the evening of Sunday, 15 July. During her long journey through the Strait of Jutland, she had hoisted lines of festive flags as a tribute to the people of Southern Denmark, and many of the commercial vessels in the Strait had sounded their whistles in reply. The *Albion* was still in festive array when she anchored at the naval dock.

The ancient mercantile city of Danzig glowed under a spectacular sunset, which tipped the many tall spires and steeples with glowing red. The wharfs and wide quays were lined with tall, many-windowed houses and business premises, rising four storeys to fancifully carved gables backed by steep, red-tiled roofs. The old town was an impressive sight as viewed from the decks of the *Albion*, because from there they could see how many of the wide and winding inlets from the sea had been tamed into canals to serve the busy wharfs. As well as medieval towers and spires, the visitors could see the tall chimneys of factories, and the crowding masts of commercial shipping anchored off the shore.

The magnificent sunset glowed for another half-hour, and then the dark clouds of night came in from the east. A small party of German officers had appeared on the quay, and the *Albion*'s captain had come down the gang plank to welcome them aboard. A smaller plank had been pushed out near the exit from the ship's galleys, and it was down this second plank that Kershaw, Box, and their two companions walked as darkness fell across the quays.

A respectable man in overcoat and bowler hat appeared from behind some bales of jute and approached them. He raised his hat politely, and addressed himself to Colonel Kershaw, speaking in German.

'Come, gentlemen,' said the colonel, 'this man will be our guide to the house of the Lithuanian Besnasse. It would seem that our somewhat irregular entry into Germany has been successful.'

They followed their guide off the quay, and through a wicket gate that took them on to a long, narrow pathway bordering one of the many canals of the dock area. To their left rose the frontages of picturesque ancient houses, evidently both homes and places of business to the many merchants who dealt in timber, corn and sugar. From time to time the row of houses was interrupted by massive buildings of stone, brick and wood, which frowned darkly over the waterway to their right, and looking as though they would collapse at any moment. These buildings housed the great hoists used for lifting cargo from the many barges tethered at the canal-side. By now, the sunset had faded, and it was getting dark.

Box stole a glance at his companions. Colonel Kershaw, who was carrying a stout carpet bag, looked straight ahead, and walked rapidly, as though anxious for them to reach their safe house. Behind him on the narrow pavement his sergeant-armourer, Morrison, a cheerful but taciturn man, was burdened with a long canvas case slung over his shoulder. Box wondered what the case contained. The fourth member of the party, Kolinsky, had a knapsack slung across his back. A quiet, modest man with little conversation, he was the only one of the party who looked around him with an obvious interest in his surroundings. Kershaw had told Box that Kolinsky spoke fluent German, Russian and Polish.

The guide suddenly turned left, and they found themselves on yet another waterside pathway, above which rose a line of eight-storeyed warehouses, decorated in black and white bands of painted wood, like old Tudor buildings. At the end of this path a narrow alley took them abruptly from the world of waterways and into one of the streets of the old town. Here they stopped at a tall wooden house, and the guide knocked at the door. Soon, thought Box, they would be safe from prying eyes.

Towards ten o'clock, Arnold Box sought out Morrison, the sergeant-armourer. He found him in a little attic room of the lodging house. He was sitting on a stool, and across his knees lay a rifle, which he was cleaning by the flickering light of a candle. Beside him on the window sill stood a can of oil and a number of well-used rags.

'How are you, Mr Morrison?' asked Box. 'These little bedrooms are a change from the Royal Navy's hammocks!'

'They are, Mr Box, and very welcome, after three days and nights at sea. Kolinsky tells me that this is a licensed lodging house, but we're the only lodgers, or so it seems to me. But then, the colonel knows some very peculiar places.'

Morrison took up one of the rags, and turned his attention to the rifle. Box saw that the long canvas case that Morrison had carried slung over his shoulder lay on the floor beside the stool. Why was this man carrying a rifle? Was he contemplating some kind of fight? He saw that the sergeant-armourer had read the query in Box's eyes.

'You're wondering about this weapon, aren't you, Mr Box?

This is Colonel Kershaw's favourite rifle, one of the 1892 models of the Lee-Metford Magazine Rifle Mark 1. Beautiful, isn't it? This one always polishes up to look like purple mahogany! Just over four feet long, as you can see, with its own magazine of .303 calibre bullets, and a specially designed hair trigger. That little brass tube mounted above the stock is a telescopic sight, with cross-wires between the lenses.'

'And this rifle was made especially for Colonel Kershaw?'

'Well, it's standard British Army issue, but the trigger, and the special sight, were made to the colonel's own specifications.'

'Why should Colonel Kershaw want to bring a rifle with him?' asked Box. He had already postulated a rather unpleasant answer to his own question, and wondered what Morrison would suggest.

'Well, Mr Box,' Morrison replied, looking steadily at the inspector with a quizzical smile, 'the Lee-Metford is a fine hunting weapon, so maybe the colonel hopes to get a bit of hunting in before he returns to England. I believe that you can bag wild boar in these parts.'

Yes, thought Box, I expect you can; but Colonel Kershaw's idea of what constituted a wild boar was almost certainly different from the usual definition. It would be wise to ask no more questions.

They rose just after dawn the next morning, and breakfasted on hot coffee and soft bread rolls and butter in the kitchen of the lodging-house. Box thought of his snug sitting-room in Mrs Peach's house in Cardinal Court, off Fleet Street, where he would have been served bacon and egg, or a nice kipper, washed down with two cups of tea – proper London tea, that you could stand your spoon up in.

They left the house just after seven o'clock, and followed their guide through a number of thronging streets until they came to a busy railway station. Box saw the man hand a number of tickets to Kershaw, bow his head in the Prussian fashion, and disappear rapidly into the crowds. Within minutes the colonel had found the correct platform, and they had climbed up into the 8.15 stopping-train to Posen. Their adventure had begun.

12

Encounter at St Mary of the Icon

T HE CARRIAGE OF the 8.15 train to Posen was arranged as a single long compartment, with wooden seats on either side of a wide gangway. Box and Kershaw sat together, facing their two companions. Their luggage rested on the floor beside them, as there seemed to be no luggage racks. Colonel Kershaw held their tickets, and it had been agreed that he and Kolinsky would do any necessary talking.

With a sudden jolt, the train started, and began to move slowly out of the station.

The carriage was half full and, glancing round him, Box saw that most of their fellow-passengers looked like businessmen or merchants, though there were a number of country folk as well, men and women dressed in what was evidently national costume. A group of soldiers, in the field-grey uniform of the German Army, sat by themselves at the back of the carriage, talking quietly to each other.

They journeyed through a flat, uninteresting landscape, where arable farmland and small factory estates existed uneasily together. The route seemed to be sparsely wooded, and the trees stunted and twisted. A phrase came into Box's mind as he looked at the scene from the carriage window: *ruined woodlands*. He'd seen that expression once, in a poem. *The flying gold of the ruined woodlands*. Maybe it was by Tennyson.

The train stopped at a small station, the soldiers alighted, and a ticket inspector in a very smart uniform climbed up into the carriage. There was a little stir as everybody produced their tickets, and the inspector passed along the gangway, punching a hole in each ticket as it was presented to him. Colonel Kershaw handed their four tickets to the smart man, who punched them, and gave them back. Kershaw made some comment in German, and the man replied, clicking his heels and bowing stiffly before passing further along the gangway.

'What did you say, sir?' whispered Box.

'I said it was warm for the time of the year, and he agreed that it was.'

As the four men were virtually cocooned in their island of facing seats, they began to speak to each other in English. None of the other passengers seemed to notice.

'This place that we're going to, sir,' said Box, 'Posen. What kind of a place is it? These foreign towns all sound so sinister, don't they?'

Colonel Kershaw smiled.

'Well, Mr Box,' he said, 'it's all a matter of familiarity, I suppose. Posen sounds quite harmless to me. Why not ask Mr Kolinsky? He'll know more about Posen than I do.'

The interpreter leaned forward in his seat. His eyes glowed with a light of interest.

'Posen, Mr Box,' he said, 'is one of the finest provincial capitals in Germany, with a famous town hall, and many thriving industries. There is talk of a magnificent Royal residence to be built there for the enjoyment of the Kaiser and his Empress. Posen is where my own ancestors are buried, in the Cemetery of St Martin.'

'So it was Polish at one time?' asked Box. 'I gather from your name, Mr Kolinsky, that you are yourself of Polish origin.'

'Posen, or Poznan, as we Poles call it, was the seat of the early Polish rulers, but it has changed hands many times over the centuries. The Swedes captured it in 1703, the French came in 1803, and it was ceded to Prussia in 1815. The whole of this area, Mr Box, is a melting-pot, waiting to boil over. Posen is a city populated by Poles who are forbidden by edict to speak their own language. German is fast becoming compulsory as the only language in the province. The Germans are storing up a nightmare of revolution for themselves in Posen—'

'That's enough, Kolinsky,' said Kershaw. 'It's quite possible that there are some English-speakers in this carriage. If people start to notice us, it could prove very inconvenient. Remember, we are travelling on false papers.'

The interpreter blushed, and lowered his eyes. He's allowed his feelings to get the better of him, thought Box. And I don't blame him, either. Thank goodness England had always been English, and was likely to remain so!

It was hot in the train, and the stunted landscape seen from the windows seemed to be lying exhausted in the summer heat. Box dozed off for a while, lulled asleep by the regular rhythm of the wheels. He could hear the quiet murmur of conversation, and was dimly aware of the aroma of drifting tobacco smoke.

He was jerked awake as the train halted at another little station, which proclaimed itself to be Niederstadt. The ticket collector alighted – and Major Ronald Blythe stepped up into the carriage. Surely he was still dreaming? No, it was Major Blythe in the flesh, making a show of greeting the colonel as though he were a long-lost friend.

'My dear man!' cried Major Blythe, holding out a friendly hand to Kershaw. 'Fancy seeing you here! Push up, won't you, and let me sit down for a minute. I'm getting off at the next station.'

Colonel Kershaw seemed to accept Blythe's presence on a train hundreds of miles away from England as perfectly natural.

'Why, Mr Robinson,' he said, shaking hands with Blythe, 'I didn't know the firm had sent you out this far on business. Or did you come to find me specifically?'

'Well, I've been promoted as chief salesman for Northern Germany, you see, after old Bobby Fitzgerald retired. By the way, he gave me some papers for you – said you'd want them. Diagrams of the new tractors, and things of that nature, which he'd found lying around in a safe.'

Major Blythe took a bulky brown envelope from his pocket and handed it to Kershaw. Hearty and cheerful, rather loudly dressed in a light check suit, he looked decidedly more like a salesman than a serving officer in the British Army.

'And you're branching out into sanitary ware, I believe?' asked Blythe. 'You're very wise. It's going to be a thriving market. Well, here's my stop. Marvellous to have seen you again. Are these your friends? How do you do? Sorry I can't stay. Good morning!'

Major Blythe swung down from the train on to the platform, and stood for a while waving as they began the last section of the journey to Posen. Colonel Kershaw thought: Good for him! He must have travelled like lightning across Europe by fast train to intercept me here. Sanitary ware, indeed! Cheeky man.... And that insubordinate police inspector, Bobby Fitz.... He must have undertaken his dangerous commission immediately, and with complete success. Mr Fitzgerald was going to be an invaluable asset. He would have to be cultivated, and suitably rewarded. In a dangerous world, there would always be a need for such reckless and resourceful men.

The train drew into the main railway station of Posen towards noon, and the four men gratefully climbed down on to the track. It had been a long, tedious journey. The concourse was crowded with travellers too busy to notice four foreigners pushing their way towards one of the remoter platforms, so they arrived at the Limburg departure gate without incident. A small engine, coupled to a single coach, stood on the track with steam up.

Colonel Kershaw handed a fresh batch of tickets to the

uniformed man at the gate, who examined each one carefully before punching them all with four vicious jabs.

'Change at Sheinberg for the Ten Farms,' said the man, handing back the tickets. Box found the fact that he spoke in English rather unnerving.

'We intend to go straight through to Limburg,' Kershaw replied.

'Then you'll have to show me your military pass,' said the man, stolidly. 'You can't go through to Limburg without a pass. If you're not going to the Ten Farms, you'll have to get off the train at Sheinberg, and walk the two miles into Limburg village.'

The man seemed to lose interest in the matter, and retreated into his glazed booth beside the gate. Taking their cue from Kershaw, the other three followed him along the track and climbed up into the single carriage. There were no other passengers. The carriage smelt of stale tobacco smoke, and the windows were dirty. But the seats were upholstered in faded blue cloth, and the four men sank gratefully into the cushions. In a few moments a whistle sounded, and a man in railway uniform held aloft a white disc fixed to the end of a rod. The engine juddered into life, and they were soon moving out of the Posen station.

'Sheinberg was an unforeseen hitch in the proceedings, gentlemen,' said Kershaw. 'However, it's not really surprising. I'm told that there are only a few houses at Limburg, where the main building is the fortified railway station. It's probably alive with German soldiers. We'll just have to trek the couple of miles from Sheinberg to meet our contact on the outskirts of Limburg village. Limburg's only a quarter of a mile from the Russian border, and it's from Limburg that we shall cross discreetly into Poland.'

'Why did the ticket collector speak to you in English?' asked Box.

'I suppose it's because we *look* English,' the colonel replied. 'At least, you and I do, and Morrison there. I can't speak for Kolinsky.'

'Well, sir,' said Kolinsky, smiling, 'I grant I'm of Polish extraction, but I was born in the Isle of Dogs. So I reckon I'm as English as anyone else!'

'That ticket inspector,' Box persisted, 'do you think he knew who we were?'

'Well, anything's possible, Mr Box,' Kershaw replied, 'but I think it highly unlikely. We just looked English, that's all. Don't look for difficulties where none exist.'

The four men fell silent, each occupied once more with his own thoughts. Arnold Box was beginning to experience an unsettling disquiet. Colonel Kershaw was too dismissive. Why were things going so smoothly? No one had asked them for their papers, no one had subjected them to any questions. It was true that they were not travelling in an enemy country, but they were foreigners to a man, and foreigners attempting to journey into what was very obviously a restricted area. But no one had stopped them....

Kershaw thought to himself: What is Mr Box thinking about? He looked worried. I'm glad I brought him with me on this journey. While I try to hold the whole picture of Europe in my mind, predicting its crises and their possible solutions, Box is beavering away at the minutiae of the present moment. Box's mind supplements my own. He thinks quite differently from me, and that's his great value. Yes, he looks worried. I'll have to reassure him, when we get a private moment together, that everything's going as I expected.

Morrison, the sergeant-armourer, was preoccupied with his own professional thoughts. Why had the colonel insisted on bringing the Lee-Metford with him? He'd joked about hunting to the policeman, Inspector Box, but he'd not specified what kind of hunting the colonel liked. They were going secretly into Russia to frustrate an attempt on the life of the Tsar. Apparently, it was to be carried out either with a bomb or a fusillade. Morrison had an uneasy feeling that Colonel Kershaw had come equipped to prevent the assassination by the desperate expedient of shooting the assassin.

The interpreter Kolinsky gazed out of the window at the Prussian countryside. The terrain this far east was flat and uninteresting, and although the soil was fertile, there was a listless air about the farms stretching on either side of the track. It was as though the malaise of the impoverished Polish peasantry had crept out beyond the Russian-Polish border to infect the German farmers. It was only an illusion, of course; the German landowners valued their lands, and what they could produce, and their tenant farmers were free citizens of the Reich. Serfdom had been abolished in Prussia in 1807.

The Polish aristocracy, though, were preoccupied with dreams of independence, and the plight of their peasants was very much a minor consideration. The Russian peasantry had been reduced to a position of serfdom in the seventeenth century, and their condition had been imposed by statute in 1648. When eastern Poland had fallen under the Russian yoke, the Polish peasantry joined the ranks of the serfs. Tsar Alexander II had liberated the serfs – all twenty-three million of them – and serfdom had disappeared in the Russian Empire by 1863.

In the Polish lands beyond the Russian borders, though, serfdom remained a habit of mind, common to both *magnat* and peasant. It was said that after emancipation, the Russian peasant was allowed to stand up on his own two feet, while the Polish peasant remained on all fours.

Would Poland ever be free? If it were, then it would have to look westward towards Germany, and forge strong alliances with the German Empire. Such a move would at least allow for the new Poland to progress as a modern state. It was with Germany, not Russia, that the Polish future lay.

Meanwhile, thought Kolinsky, he had the incredible good fortune to be British, and a Londoner into the bargain. He sat back in his seat, and thought of the Isle of Dogs.

The train arrived at Sheinberg just after two o'clock in the afternoon. The station was a single wooden building rising above the track. The village consisted of a few red-roofed cottages near the station, and a small wooden church with a tall spire. All around it lay deserted fields of wheat and barley. The four men alighted. A group of soldiers came out of the station building, and boarded the train. They were all carrying rifles, and were evidently on their way to the fortified railway station at Limburg.

A dusty winding road led out of the village, and after Kolinsky had ascertained from the station master that it was the road to Limburg, they set out for the two-mile walk in the heat of the summer afternoon. Colonel Kershaw fell into step beside Arnold Box, while their two companions trudged on doggedly ahead. It was very quiet: there seemed to be neither man nor beast for miles around.

'What's the matter, Mr Box?' asked Kershaw. 'You're not your usual chirpy self.'

'I don't like the feel of things, sir,' Box replied. 'Everything's too easy, if you get my meaning. Nobody's asked for our documents. Nobody seems curious about four foreigners travelling towards a restricted area. It's as though somebody's given the word to leave us alone, until—'

'Until what, Box? What are you expecting to happen?'

'Let me tell you a little story, sir. A couple of years ago, we got word at the Yard that a celebrated smasher – by which we mean a high-class forger of coins – had gone to ground somewhere in Bermondsey. We made our usual enquiries, and alerted a few choice informers that there was money to be made. Within the day, we were given six definite leads, each one following from the one before, like a chain of events. Those leads told us that our quarry was holed up in a house in Black Swan Yard, near Crucifix Lane. Towards dawn, three of us went to this house, forced the door, and rushed in with the darbies at the ready.'

'And what happened?'

'We were rushed by a gang of ten real bruisers who were lying in wait for us. We were battered soft, the three of us, and the smasher got clean away. And that's how it feels like to me, sir. I wonder if we're being helped on our way into a trap.'

Colonel Kershaw glanced at Box, and for a moment made no reply. He's wondering whether to tell me something, Box thought, something unpleasant, I'll be bound! Yes, he's going to tell me.

'Listen, Box,' said Kershaw in a low voice, 'I've no doubt whatever that we have been secretly observed ever since we docked at Danzig, observed, that is, by our enemies, and perhaps by our friends. When we were at Danzig station, I saw an agent of Count von und zu Thalberg boarding a train. It's just possible that he had been sent to keep an eye on *us*.'

'Count von und zu Thalberg's a trusted friend, sir. No harm can come from being trailed by one of his people.'

'True; but like you, I'm certain that our enemies will have seen us, too. Well, I planned this trip in such a way as to make surveillance by the enemy virtually inevitable. We are not dealing here with amateurs. The simplest way of coming face to face with poor Grunwalski and his captors – for that's what they are – is to allow them to lead us to where he is. Let The Thirty do part of our work for us. It may be a counsel of desperation, or it may be a sound move on my part. Are you with me, or do you think I've made a wrong move?'

'I'm with you, sir,' Box replied. 'I don't mind telling you that I'm relieved to hear what you've just told me. For a while, I thought—'

'You thought I'd lost my touch?' Kershaw laughed. 'Well, the fact that you thought so proves that I haven't! Come, Mr Box, let us give all our attention now to the task at hand.'

The four men trudged along the dusty path of beaten earth, which wound between overgrown hedges on its way to Limburg. Eventually they rounded a curve and came quite suddenly into a small village, larger than Sheinberg, and boasting a stone church and a high-fronted timber inn. Across a large field of root crops they could see some railway buildings surrounded by a wooden stockade.

'That's the fortified railway station we've heard so much about,' said Kershaw to Box. 'From there, a single-track line crosses the border into Russia half a mile from here. It stops at a customs control post, and then makes its way to the Russian town of Brest-Litovsk. But that's not the route for us. Ah! I rather think that our contact is already waiting for us.'

He motioned to a stocky man in the dress of a gamekeeper, who was standing near what seemed to be a market cross. He was smoking a curly pipe, and glanced from time to time at the church clock. As the four men emerged from the lane into the village street, the man joined them, and walked silently beside them, puffing away at his pipe, and looking fixedly ahead of him.

As soon as they had left the village, and entered a straggling beech wood, he spoke to them in halting English.

'Good day, *Herr Oberst*. Within another hour, you will have reached the spot where I can spirit you away from Germany and into the Polish territories of Russia. That is my task, you understand? It is for you to find a way to return when your business is done. Come.'

It soon became clear to Box that the beech wood was never tended by a forester. The few paths were overgrown, and from time to time their way was blocked by a fallen tree. The atmosphere was dry and fetid. They were plunging into one of those desolate areas where the line of demarcation between two nations led to the creation of an untenanted wilderness.

The guide all but ignored them. He had extinguished his pipe, and had taken to humming a rather mirthless tune to himself as he led them steadily to their destination. Box, by now tired himself, could sense the weariness of his companions. The two-mile walk from Sheinberg had been unlooked-for, and this further weary traipse through a wood added to the tedium of a journey that had begun early that day in far-off Danzig.

Presently, they emerged into a clearing in the wood, a lonely, deserted place, containing a ruined hut, and the overgrown remains of a collapsed cottage. The ground was wild with sinuous creeper and rotting logs. The guide stooped low, and disappeared into the undergrowth. In a moment they heard him whispering to them to follow. They did so, pushing aside the clinging tendrils and massive dock plants, and found themselves all but crawling along a low tunnel hewn from the hard clay. It stank of foul water, which lay in yellow pools along its length.

In a few minutes they emerged into another beech wood, equally deserted and neglected, and the guide began to talk rapidly to Kershaw in German. Then he bowed briefly to the four men, and plunged back into the hidden tunnel.

'Gentlemen,' said Colonel Kershaw, 'we are now standing on the Polish territory of the Russian Empire. Soon, God willing, we shall be in Polanska Gory.'

Although they had ventured no more than a few hundred yards east, they realized immediately that they had entered another country. Tilled fields seemed to stretch to the horizon across a flat, open plain. Lines of picturesque single-storey houses ran along the edges of some of the fields, forming what could be called linear villages. Here and there a church tower rose from a clump of trees, though near the centre of the plain they could see a typical Russian church, its gilded onion domes catching the rays of the declining sun. The Polish guide, Kolinsky, had seen it, too, and remarked that it was a symbol of Catholic Poland's subjugation to Russia, and its Orthodox religion.

Groups of peasants were labouring in the fields, their backs bent to the earth. The men wore long, white smocks reaching to their ankles, and tied at the waist with a cord. Their heads were protected from the sun by round fur hats. The women were clad in drab black dresses, and their heads were covered by scarves. One or two of the peasants looked up at the travellers without curiosity, soon bending their heads once more to their toil.

'Those folk look very poor to me,' said Box to Kolinsky.

'They're tied to the land, Mr Box, because they come from families who have never been able to adjust to freedom. One day, perhaps, things will be different here.'

They had walked for nearly an hour along a rutted track when the landscape changed abruptly, and they found that they were walking along a defile between low, wooded hills. They could no longer see the wide fields and the toiling peasants, as the woods seemed to draw closer.

Was it fancy, or were there fleeting figures running silently beside them among those trees? There! thought Box. Surely that was a man, wearing a bandoleer, and carrying what appeared to be a musket? He glanced at Kershaw, and saw that the colonel, too, had seen the silent runners. He half opened the flap of his jacket, and Box saw the butt of an Army revolver nestling in a concealed holster.

The path began to climb upward, and soon they found themselves entering a kind of natural arena surrounded entirely on three sides by birch plantations. The fourth side of the clearing was occupied by one of the most fantastic buildings that Box had ever seen. At first sight, it seemed to be a fort, a crenellated tower with a narrow gate fronted by a drawbridge spanning a rushing stream. But merging into the tower was an ancient and massive Romanesque church, from the roof of which rose a great image in stone of an angel holding a shield, upon which a carved eagle could just be discerned. Was it a church, or a fortress? Or was it both?

By now, they were standing in a vast open space from which rose tall gravestones, some made of stone, and others of rusting iron. An enormous iron crucifix rose up among the tombs, leaning drunkenly towards the visitors.

'St Mary of the Icon,' Kershaw muttered, as though to himself, and at the same time several shots rang out. They flung themselves to the ground as one man, taking refuge in the long grass beside the tombs.

'They're firing high, Morrison,' said Kershaw. 'They're warning shots.'

'I agree, sir,' the sergeant-armourer replied. 'What shall we do?'

'The best thing, I think, is for us to stand up, raise our hands in surrender, and back off. Kolinsky, if you tell them that we've simply lost our way, they may believe us. I don't know who these people are – or who they think *we* are – but they've clearly got the advantage.'

The four men rose to their feet, hands raised. By now, at least a dozen men had appeared in the clearing before the fortress-church. They wore peasant dress, but they all carried ancient muskets, which they pointed at the intruders. Each man's face seemed devoid of expression, as though their action had been orchestrated by an intelligence superior to their own.

Kolinsky addressed the men in Polish, but they angrily waved him away, and began to talk among themselves. A tall, fair-haired man, who seemed to be their leader, remained with his musket trained on Kershaw and his party.

Arnold Box suddenly had an idea so brilliant that it almost took his breath away. He cautiously felt in his waistcoat pocket, and his fingers closed round the Polish coin that Bobby Fitz had found among Grunwalski's effects. Stepping boldly forward in front of the others, he held the coin up, for the fair-haired man with the musket to see.

The man started in surprise, and immediately bowed low. '*Magnat,*' he muttered, then spoke rapidly to his companions before motioning to Box and the others to follow the band of defenders across the drawbridge.

'Mr Box,' said Kershaw in a voice that was tinged with awe, 'you never cease to amaze me! They think you're one of The Thirty.'

Together they crossed the drawbridge, and entered the strange edifice known as St Mary of the Icon. The man who had addressed Box preceded them along a short passage to the right of the entrance, treating the inspector to little deferential bows, whilst scarcely acknowledging the presence of the others. He pushed open a door, and they found themselves entering an ancient, fantastic church.

It was dark and decayed inside St Mary of the Icon, with festoons of cobwebs draped across dull brass chandeliers. The floor space seemed to be filled with half-collapsed box tombs, and the broken remains of pews. Fragments of medieval stained glass glowed in the windows, though many of the panes had been replaced by squares of wood. At the far end of the church they could just glimpse a carved stone reredos rising above an altar, where a dim red light burned. In a side chapel stood an ancient, smoke-blackened icon of the Virgin and Child, before which a number of candles burned. Although partly ruinous, the place evidently still functioned as a church.

Their guide motioned to them to follow him through another door, which gave direct access to what was evidently the great hall of the fortress. It was a lofty room, with tall windows through which the late afternoon was pouring. Box glanced up at the high-pitched ceiling of elaborate carved beams, while noting the great coloured coats of arms, and images of the white eagle of Poland, arrayed along the walls. A long refectory table occupied the centre of the hall. The four men stood for a while to accustom their eyes to the brightness of the hall after the gloom of the adjacent church, and then they saw the figure of a man standing at one of the far windows, which overlooked a tangled garden. The man turned round, and greeted them in perfect English.

It was Baron Augustyniak.

13

Baron Augustyniak Talks

DRESSED IN A WELL-CUT morning coat, worn with fashionable pinstripe trousers, Baron Augustyniak looked as though he was standing in the drawing-room of his house in St John's Wood. His mane of blond hair was swept back from his brow, and his fine beard jutted forward as he confronted the four men with an understandable air of triumph. There was a mocking expression on his face that was not entirely unpleasant. Enemy or not, thought Box, he was a fine figure of a man.

'So, gentlemen,' he said, carefully fixing his rimmed monocle in his right eye, 'you have obligingly walked into my parlour! Well, it is the safest place for you to be at present, as this particular corner of Poland can be a trifle wild, as you've already found out.'

'I take it,' said Colonel Kershaw coolly, 'that I am addressing Baron Augustyniak? I thought you'd come to settle in England; evidently, I was mistaken.'

'Colonel Kershaw,' the baron replied courteously, 'I am indeed Augustyniak. You and I have not been formally introduced, but your fame has preceded you. And you were not mistaken about my taking up residence in England, but for the moment I have been summoned here by urgent business.'

It was the turn of Arnold Box and his companions to be the subject of Baron Augustyniak's wry humour. As he spoke, it became clear to all four men that all their movements since setting foot in Germany had been an open book to him.

'Inspector Box,' he said, 'I believe I once glimpsed you through my little telescope while I was watching the stirring events on Tower Bridge last month. You were standing on top of some kind of warehouse. Mr Morrison – I hope that rifle you're carrying has its safety catch on? Accidents can happen, you know. And finally, Mr Kolinsky – a fellow Pole.'

The baron switched effortlessly from English to Polish, and spoke a few words to the Polish interpreter.

'I'm very well, thank you, Baron,' said Kolinsky in reply. 'But while I'm here I prefer to speak in English, if it's all the same to you.'

'Of course. I appreciate that you Englishmen will want to stick together. And now, gentlemen, as you have wished yourselves upon us, I suppose we shall have to accommodate and feed you. There are many rooms in this fortress, and if you will give me your parole not to make any silly attempts to escape, I will have my servants conduct you to your quarters. They will also bring you hot water, so that you can wash away the stains of your long trek through so many dusty lanes.'

It all sounds very fine, thought Box, but somehow none of it rings true. There's something very odd about Baron Augustyniak. He was acting a part, but it was impossible to divine what that part was.

Colonel Kershaw said, 'You are very kind, Baron, and I can speak for all of us when I say that there will be no foolish heroics. I take it that you knew we would come this way?'

'You may indeed, Colonel. You were positively identified by one of my folk who's a ticket collector at Posen Station. After that, there was always someone keeping a benevolent eye upon you. But I knew, before ever you left London, that you were on our trail.'

The baron laughed heartily, and moved away from the window. The movement seemed to draw some of the tension from the air.

'It was very clever of you, Colonel Kershaw,' he said, 'to send your little girl spy to watch my every move – I refer to Miss Susan Moore, my yellow-haired housemaid. Dear me, what a nice child! At first, I thought that Sir Charles Napier had sent her, but on reflection I realized that his agents aren't normally assigned long-term tasks like infiltrating a gentleman's household. A pretty maiden with a courageous heart was more in your line.'

'I can assure you, Baron—'

'I'm sure you can. Well, we'll speak about Susan Moore later, after you've refreshed yourselves. I'll give you half an hour, and then my men will come to summon you here for a meal. It won't be quite like the Savoy, but it'll be wholesome fare.'

Baron Augustyniak clapped his hands, and two of the surly retainers appeared at the door. He spoke to them in Polish, and they motioned to the prisoners to precede them from the great hall. Kershaw made to lead his party into the corridor, but one of the retainers pushed him curtly aside. The man turned to Arnold Box, bowed low, and muttered the single word, '*Magnat*'. Box bowed in return, and led the others out of the room.

'Sir,' said Box, 'I can't believe that this is happening. I don't think we should relax our guard for a single moment. Baron Augustyniak is obviously a gentleman, but some of his colleagues in The Thirty are vicious thugs. Doctor Franz Kessler is a killer, and I've no doubt he's about here, somewhere.'

It was half an hour after their dramatic confrontation with the baron. They had been led to a row of cell-like rooms on the ground floor, each containing an iron bedstead with a straw mattress. Servants had appeared with cans of hot water and basins, and they had all been able to make themselves presentable. The very act of washing had banished much of their weariness. Box had been able to walk into Kershaw's room without anyone trying to prevent him.

'I don't quite understand the situation myself, Box,' said Kershaw. 'In fact, I'm completely bewildered. I think we must continue to be polite and accommodating, as our apparent acceptance that we are prisoners here could possibly make the Baron talk. I've a shrewd feeling, from his performance back there, that he's very fond of his own voice, and if we treat him in the right way, he'll probably tell us all we want to know. It also helps a little that his servants are convinced that you are a baron. It was providential that you still had the magic talisman in your waistcoat pocket.'

'If they think I'm a baron, sir,' Box replied, 'then they must be even dimmer than they look. Have you devised a secret plan to get us out of here, sir?'

Colonel Kershaw laughed, and regarded Box with something akin to affection.

'No, I have not!' he replied. 'You always think I can pull rabbits out of my hat. Well, I can't. We'll just have to live by our wits, Box. Meanwhile, let's contain ourselves in patience until we return to share the hospitality of the baron's table.'

Soon afterwards, one of the servants came into the corridor and spoke to Box in halting English. 'The food – it is prepared,' he said, and motioned the four to follow him back into the great hall.

The long table had been covered in an embroidered cloth, and someone had set out cutlery, tankards, and pewter flagons of what looked like dark beer. The baron was sitting at the head of the table. His earlier gloating skittishness seemed to have disappeared, to be replace by a quiet, collected seriousness. He told his guests to sit down along one side of the table to his right, where chairs had been placed. They noticed that two other places had been set at the table to the baron's left.

Two of the retainers appeared with plates of what appeared to be a kind of stew, which they placed in front of each of the diners, bowing low to Baron Augustyniak and Mr Arnold Box. They returned in a moment with a wooden platter piled high with pieces of black bread, and a bowl of coarse salt. Bowing a second time, they withdrew from the hall, and quietly closed its door.

'This is pork stew with spices, gentlemen,' said the Baron, 'a local dish. In the tankards you will find a strong Polish beer. Let us eat, and then we can talk.'

The stew was hot and appetizing, if rather over-spiced. The beer was excellent, though Box estimated that it was probably three times as strong as anything served in The King Lud. It was quiet in the hall, and the last rays of the declining sun crept in through the remaining stained-glass panes of the tall windows. All that Box could hear was the occasional sound of spoons and forks delving around inside the deep pewter basins in which the stew had been served.

'Baron Augustyniak,' asked Kershaw, when he had finished his meal, 'you will pardon me if I ask whether this fortified house is your property? You seem very much at home here.'

'My property? No, Colonel. This place – St Mary of the Icon – belongs to an old but impoverished Polish-German family, the Hardenbergs. They live not far away. The Hardenbergs make this place available for the likes of me, when business brings me back to this part of Poland. I, too, come from this remote and rather dangerous area.'

'And what business brings you here on this occasion, Baron?' asked Kershaw boldly.

Baron Augustyniak smiled, and shook his head. He was clearly more amused than angry.

'Let me remind you, Colonel Kershaw,' he replied, 'that I am a Polish nobleman, and, as such, a subject of the Russian Empire. I have every right to be here, and have made no secret of that fact. You and your companions, unfortunately, are here without papers, trespassers in our country....

'But let me give you one reason for my presence here. On the twenty-first of this month, the Tsar comes to Polanska Gory to open the new bridge. It will be a festive occasion, at which many of the local Russian and Polish nobility have been invited out of courtesy. So I shall be there when the Tsar sets foot on the stones of the Catherine Bridge.'

I bet you will, thought Box, and so will your friends Kessler and his mates, and the half-crazed Grunwalski. Well, we'll see what fate sends in the next few days.

'There are other things that I must tell you, gentlemen,' the baron continued, 'but I cannot do so until two of my friends have appeared. They will be here within minutes, if I'm not mistaken, and they will join us here at the table.'

He glanced at the two empty places on his left. Who would his two friends be? thought Box. One would certainly be Doctor Franz Kessler. Perhaps the other would be Gerdler, quartermaster of The Aquila Project, or Eidenschenk, whom Colonel Kershaw had described as a second Kessler. Germans.... And when they came, all hell would be let loose.

The door of the hall opened, and the two remaining guests were ushered in to the hall. It was Colonel Kershaw's gasp of surprise that caused Box to look up sharply. The guests were Count von und zu Thalberg, and his faithful tactician, Sergeant-Major Schmidt.

In a single dramatic moment, Box's whole world seemed to revolve dizzily, and then settle into an entirely new and unexpected pattern. He knew from personal experience that these two men were staunch allies of Colonel Kershaw, and devotees of the Balance of Power concept. Therefore, Baron Augustyniak could only be another ally, another devoted worker in the cause of peace and stability in Europe. He looked at the baron, and saw from the broad smile on his face, that his assumptions were true.

'How nice to see you again, Kershaw,' said Count von und zu Thalberg, sitting down at the table. 'And you, Mr Box. You remember *Oberfeldwebel* Schmidt, of course? Now, Baron,' he continued, leaving the four Englishmen temporarily speechless, 'our friends are completely in the dark about what's going on. Will you enlighten them, or shall I?'

'I think it's a task for you, Thalberg,' the baron replied. 'Tell them everything, including Morrison and Kolinsky. Where this matter is concerned, the more they know, the more effective they will be as allies. I'll only interrupt if I think it's advisable to do so.'

'Gentlemen,' Thalberg began, 'you must know at once that Baron Augustyniak is a senior officer of the Okhrana, the secret intelligence department of the Russian Imperial Police. For some years he was based at the Foreign Bureau of the organization in Paris, where he was able to monitor the activities of various dissidents who had escaped from Russia in order to continue their nefarious activities from France—'

'The Okhrana?' cried Colonel Kershaw. 'Good God, you might have told me, Thalberg! I'd not the slightest idea.... But there, I must stay quiet until you've done. I'm completely confused: in a moment, I'll doubt my sanity. The *Okhrana*?'

Baron Augustyniak threw back his head and laughed.

'An unlooked-for complication, hey, Kershaw? Yes, my chief vocation is to protect the life of the Tsar and his family from terrorists – what we call "bombists" – socialists, anarchists, and other malignants. But I digress. Please continue your narrative, Thalberg.'

'Baron Augustyniak and I have worked closely together for many years, giving our joint attention to matters effecting the security and stability of Central and Eastern Europe. We have had many successes, and a number of reversals, but between us we have forged an organization that is highly regarded both in Russia and Germany.

'And then, about three years ago, we began to detect the presence of a new dissident group, a group which gradually developed into what is now called The Thirty. Its aims were to assassinate the Tsar, Alexander III, and to see that the blame would be laid at the door of the Tsar's Polish subjects. Do I need to elaborate, Kershaw, or do you know all this?'

'I know it well enough. Russia would launch a punitive military invasion of its Polish lands, bringing its troops so perilously near to the Prussian border that military engagement between the two empires would be inevitable. It was the fear of that happening, Thalberg, that brought the four of us here today.'

'Yes, I know it was. I do wish you'd leave these Central European matters to us! Now, Baron Augustyniak there, and the Okhrana in general, are skilled and subtle opponents, and it was the baron who proposed getting himself accepted into The Thirty by a combination of bribery and principle—'

'I am a Polish patriot, gentlemen,' Augustyniak interrupted, 'but I believe that a viable Polish nation can only be achieved by the political expediency of creating it as a wholesome buffer state between the German and Russian empires. That's why I can work for both countries at once. But I have no time for dissident groups of murderers and anarchists. The Thirty are the same kind of people as the Eidgenossenschaft, that nest of German vipers that almost succeeded in plunging all Europe into the dark night of war. The destruction of that gang, Colonel, was one of your signal victories: the annihilation of The Thirty will be one of ours.'

Count von und zu Thalberg resumed his narrative.

'The Thirty, like many other dissidents before them, decided to operate from England, where many sympathizers were ready and waiting for someone to lead them. Some of these people were ideologues, others were opportunists, who saw a united Poland as a possible source of wealth.

'I learnt from various contacts in Berlin that Doctor Franz Kessler was about to be appointed Second Secretary at Prussia House, in London. He was a founder member of The Thirty, and it was clear that someone in Berlin – you know who I mean – had arranged for him to galvanize The Thirty into action. That was when Baron Augustyniak decided to settle in England, and establish his Polish cultural institute there.'

'You see, gentlemen,' observed Baron Augustyniak, 'I had myself been a member of The Thirty for nearly a year – the Okhrana had furnished me with all the necessary documents, incriminating letters, and so forth. Once I had arrived in England, it was easy enough for me to assume a kind of patronage of the group, who had no hesitation in confiding all their plans to me.'

'I see,' said Colonel Kershaw. 'A very clever piece of organization on your part, Baron. And so the time was ripe, I suppose, for The Thirty to look around for an assassin?'

'Indeed yes,' said Augustyniak. 'And so we recruited the man Anders Grunwalski, a terrorist who had already acquired a sinister reputation in Europe, and had just surfaced in England. He was a man of Polish extraction, easily persuaded as to the justice of the cause.'

'And then, sir,' said Box, truculently, suddenly breaking into the baron's narrative, 'you and your doubtful friends decided to stage that rehearsal on Tower Bridge?'

'We did, Mr Box, and I can understand your anger at what happened. For reasons that Kessler was unwilling to divulge, The Thirty determined to stage a rehearsal of their assassination attempt at Polanska Gory. It was to take place at the opening of Tower Bridge, and Grunwalski was to plant a bomb of his own devising in the boiler room. He was also to test the possibility of sprinting up on to the bridge brandishing a revolver. He did both things successfully, but then, as you know, a zealous young soldier contrived to knock him unconscious. I was present, as you know, watching the proceedings through my telescope, and saw the whole incident. It was vital, of course, that Grunwalski was rescued, and a plan was concocted by Gerdler, who had access to stores of explosive. We blew our man out of that police station and spirited him away.'

Box opened his mouth to make a comment, and then thought better of it. He glanced at Kershaw, and saw that the colonel, too, had realized something of great import. Neither Count von und zu Thalberg nor Baron Augustyniak knew that Grunwalski was, in fact, one of Colonel Kershaw's agents.

'Where are Kessler and his associates now?' asked Kershaw.

'Surely they're not here with you, in this fortress? I gather that they left England on the ninth.'

'They have not yet arrived in Poland,' said Augustyniak. 'Kessler thought it prudent that they should lie low for a while near the Russian border, and cross over this coming Wednesday, the eighteenth. When they do, they will all be surprised and arrested before ever they reach the Catherine Bridge. Polanska Gory is thick with Okhrana gendarmerie. Nothing can prevent their total destruction.'

The baron treated the company to one of his uninhibited laughs. He laughed so much, that the gold-rimmed monocle fell from is eye.

'Oh, Colonel Kershaw,' he cried, 'I still have fond memories of your little girl spy! It was impossible not to like her, and when she spilt mint sauce down the front of Kessler's coat, I felt that you'd done me a personal favour by sending her to my house. She was very brave, you know. She hid in my silver cupboard, and over-heard all the secrets of The Thirty. I'm quite certain that Kessler would have killed her, given the opportunity. When we all heard a noise in that cupboard, I flung open the door, dragged Susan out, and immediately accused her of being a thief. I knew, you see, that the safest place for her that night would be a police station. I rang the bell, and by good fortune my coachman entered the room immediately. He summoned the police, who came very quickly, and identified her as a common burglar. I'd been right about her, you see. So you employ criminals as well as law-abiding folk, Colonel Kershaw? Well, so do we, I must admit. The Okhrana, you know.'

'It was very kind of you to save this girl from the tender minis-trations of Kessler,' said Kershaw, 'but I can assure you, Baron, that I never employed this person in any capacity. It sounds to me that she was what the police said she was – a common thief.'

The baron smiled, but made no reply. So, my noble sir, thought Box, you evidently don't know everything. I wouldn't expect you to believe the colonel's fibs, but I did think you'd realize that both your coachman, and the two policemen, were all Colonel Kershaw's agents. We British are not as stupid as you evidently think we are.

'What will happen to us now?' asked Kershaw. The two noblemen exchanged a glance, which betrayed their air of puzzlement. Thalberg drew Augustyniak aside, and spoke rapidly to him in low tones. They saw the baron nod his assent to some whispered proposal.

'The truth is, gentlemen,' said Count von und zu Thalberg, 'that your coming here has proved to be a grave embarrassment. The business of rounding up this gang of dreamers was something that Baron Augustyniak and I had already addressed. Kessler, Balonek, Haremza, Gerdler, Eidenschenk – all those men will be here on the eighteenth, together with Grunwalski and his hired keepers. They will all be immediately arrested as soon as they set foot in Polanska Gory. They are all known, and they are never without an Okhrana shadow. They are doomed, and so are the other members of The Thirty. But if it becomes known that *you* are here—'

'If it becomes known that you are here, Colonel Kershaw,' the baron interrupted, 'there are people in St Petersburg who will immediately suspect that you have come here for some subtle and secret purpose connected with the British Government. There are people in Fontanka 16 who will want to believe that your Foreign Office is secretly in league with these fanatics.'

'So what do you propose we do, Baron?' Kershaw asked.

'I propose that tomorrow I take you with me to survey Polanska Gory, and see the Catherine Bridge, where the attempt upon the Tsar's life was to be made. You will be relieved to hear that the town is only a short walk away through the woods. Polanska Gory is full of my gendarmes, as well as units of the Russian Army, and if you are seen with me, all suspicion will be allayed. After that – well, I suggest that you make your way back discreetly into Germany, and take the swiftest means possible to return to England.'

'Sir,' said Box, when he and Kershaw were alone for a few minutes in the colonel's room, 'I don't like this business one little bit. When I agreed to accompany you on this mission, I didn't think I'd become involved with the Okhrana. It's hardly my cup of tea.'

'Nor mine, Box,' Kershaw replied. 'I've not exactly covered myself with glory over this escapade. Baron Augustyniak's right: the best thing we can do is to leave Russia as soon as possible. Have you had dealings with the Okhrana?'

'No, sir, but I've heard of it, and what I've heard hasn't been very pleasant.'

'Its roots stretch back to the late sixties,' said Kershaw, 'so that it has had decades to establish its power base. It operates from 16 Fontanka Street in St Petersburg, with secret offices in Moscow and Warsaw. The Okhrana uses covert operations and undercover agents, who often employ what is called "perlustration" – the reading of private correspondence – to gain the means to apply blackmail and extortion to achieve its ends. Its agents are every-where, and its methods are merciless. So it's not my cup of tea either, Mr Box.'

'What will happen to Kessler and the rest?'

'They will all be handed over to the civil power, which is the custom in Russia. They will be sentenced to death, and executed soon afterwards. The lesser fry will be sent to forced labour camps in Siberia.'

'And what about Grunwalski, sir? He's your own agent.'

The colonel's mouth set in a grim line, and not for the first time Box sensed the streak of ruthlessness that underlay the man's outwardly quiet and unassuming exterior.

'Grunwalski knows what to do if he finds escape impossible,' said Kershaw. 'Every day I remain in this place poses a danger for Baron Augustyniak and his agents. I have done what I could for

Grunwalski, and I can do no more. His future, if he has one, now lies in the lap of the gods.'

A further meal was served to the four Englishmen in the great hall that evening, but neither Augustyniak, Thalberg nor Schmidt was present. Kershaw was coldly silent, as though fearing criticism from his colleagues, and the conversation was stilted and banal. By unspoken consent, the party retired to their cell-like rooms just after eleven o'clock.

Box lay awake for over an hour. The room had become stiflingly hot, as though the heat of the summer's day had built up in the stone walls, and was now radiating back into the little room. But it was not only the heat that kept him awake. His mind constantly recalled his meeting with Colonel Kershaw at Burlington House a fortnight earlier, when they had examined together a great map of Europe spread out across a table.

He'd said to Kershaw that Germany seemed to be rubbing shoulders with all its foreign neighbours, and looked as though it might explode at any moment. He could see the borders now: France, Austria-Hungary, Russia, Switzerland.... Why should he remember that map now? Was there something about it that had escaped his notice?

Sleep came to him at last in the early hours of Tuesday morning, but it was an uneasy sleep, disturbed by fragments of memory distilled into fleeting dreams. Here was a great eagle, white and gold, flapping its wings lazily against a silver sunrise. And now a shadow, a great black eagle, its wings outspread, and with a crown on its head. *Aquila* was the Latin word for eagle. Project Aquila. So many eagles in Europe, some black, some white and gold.

Here was the map again, but it was a live map now, like the land viewed from a high-flying balloon; he could see the rivers flowing rapidly, and roads alive with people. France, a nice pale buff, the German Reich, tinted a bluish grey, and then the border with Russia. Stoop low, enter the tunnel. You're in Russia now, a land tinted a sober greenish grey. A black eagle soars above, menacing him from a clear summer sky.

Look at the names on the great map – a German map, the colonel had said, with all the names of the towns in German. Danzig, Posen, Stettin, Warschau. Look at those men, all crammed into one little corner of the map: he was one of them, and the little corner was St Mary of the Icon. All huddled together just inside the border of Russian Poland. Kershaw, Thalberg, Augustyniak, representing three secret services, all crammed in a corner!

The black eagle and the white eagle circled overhead.

What are you doing here? We are waiting for the 21st. All three? Yes, we are waiting for the 21st. Ah, yes! The attempt on the life of the Tsar. But wasn't there something else to do with the 21st? What was it? Of course! It—

No time for thought. You slept in the night. Sleep.... Augustyniak, sleek and catlike, was over-confident. Eagles, bridges, Tower Bridge, Catherine Bridge. A few Poles, but more Germans. Kessler, Balonek, Haremza, Gerdler, Eidenschenk, Grunwalski. A few Poles, but more Germans. Too many Germans.

The effort to make sense of these thoughts and images proved too much for Box's tired mind and body. He fell into a deep sleep, and when he eventually opened his eyes the little room was cheerful with the light of morning.

14

A Confusion of Eagles

OVER A BREAKFAST of black bread and salt butter, washed down by strong, milkless coffee, Kershaw told his companions that they would leave Poland early the next day, before Kessler and his fellow assassins arrived from Germany. Baron Augustyniak would furnish them with papers that would take them by railway from Brest Litovsk to Warsaw, from where they could return to Germany by catching one of the regular express trains to Posen.

'Meanwhile, gentlemen,' Kershaw concluded, 'Baron Augustyniak has invited us to inspect the security arrangements at Polanska Gory, so that we can leave the area secure in the knowledge that nothing untoward is going to happen on the twenty-first.'

The baron seemed to be very affable that morning: all the tension of the previous day had disappeared. Here, thought Box, is a man who is very sure of himself, a man who is enjoying the continuing discomfiture of his guests. Well, perhaps he was entitled to gloat, but over-confidence could lead to dangerous vulnerability.

'You may be surprised to hear, my friends,' said the baron, 'that Polanska Gory is no more than four hundred yards from here. We shall be there in less than twenty minutes, and then you will see how ably the Okhrana protects its Sovereign.'

They followed Baron Augustyniak along a maze of passages

that gave access to the tangled rear gardens of St Mary of the Icon. An overgrown path led them to a wicket gate, beyond which a silver-birch plantation glowed in the strong morning sun. They walked along a well-defined path, and then, with dramatic suddenness, emerged on to a wide road lined with luxurious villas. Box gasped in surprise.

They were standing on an elegant promenade, where men in straw boaters and women in fashionable summer dresses and carrying parasols, were taking the air. All around them rose white-painted town houses standing in colourful gardens and, as they progressed further into the town, they crossed a charming eighteenth-century square, in the centre of which a grand fountain was playing. Polanska Gory was a dramatic contrast to the wild and desperate land surrounding St Mary of the Icon.

Kershaw, who was walking soberly beside Box, whispered, 'They built this place in what had been a remote wilderness, Box, and I think that one day the trees and the wild plants will swallow up Empress Catherine's gracious resort. This eighteenth-century spa town, built in such a wild and lawless place, was conceived without any concern for a viable hinterland. It's the kind of dream-creation typical of the House of Romanoff. It puts me in mind of the elegant follies of Versailles.'

It was certainly a remarkable sight, thought Box, after they had admired a mellow stone pump room and its adjacent spa baths. On a hillside rising above the spa, a fine residence stood in magnificent gardens. Baron Augustyniak told them that it was the summer residence of the Tsar's kinsman, the Grand Duke George Constantine.

'The Tsar will stay with the Grand Duke for a week, venturing into the town first to open the Catherine Bridge, and then to take the waters, as his ancestors did. I doubt if it will do him any good, but it looks well if he is occasionally seen in an informal light. Court protocol at St Petersburg can be very stifling. When the Tsar's holiday is over, in just over a week's time, he will be journeying to Moscow, to take up residence in the Kremlin there until August.'

As the baron finished speaking, they came to the town's end, and there they saw the new Catherine Bridge, built to span the River Gor. As he looked at it, Box vividly recalled the photographs that Sir Charles Napier had showed to Colonel Kershaw and himself, when they had visited him at the Foreign Office. The bridge looked exactly as those images had shown: a modest, elegant construction, with stone balustrades bearing cast-iron lamp standards.

Yes, thought Box, there are the half-hidden store rooms built under the bridge at the bottom of the stone incline. The rooms were still obscured by vegetation, as the area had not yet been laid out as a garden. Across this bridge, on the 21st, would come the carriage of Tsar Alexander III and Empress Dagmar. What would the assassin have done then? Throw a bomb? Rush up the incline and discharge a pistol? And what would he have done afterwards? There was little cover around this bridge, no twisting alleys down which Grunwalski could escape. Was he prepared to stand his ground and either be shot dead on the spot, or be seized, and subjected to the tender mercies of the Okhrana?

Box shivered. There was something decidedly odd about the whole business. Why had Colonel Kershaw and Count von und zu Thalberg not realized that Polanska Gory would be heavily guarded by the Tsar's own Imperial Police? The colonel regarded Polanska Gory as a doomed enterprise, which one day would be reclaimed by nature. He felt the same about this assassination attempt, which had, apparently, been doomed from the beginning. It would not now take place, but even had Kessler and his gang eluded the Okhrana, they could never have succeeded in their attempt at the Catherine Bridge.

To start with, the terrain was all wrong, and the curve in the stone incline would have meant that Grunwalski would have been spotted long before the carriage had mounted the bridge. He would have been shot dead in an instant by any one of the armed civil police of the town. The Russian authorities would not have given any man behaving suspiciously the benefit of the doubt.

Did Kessler and his fellow conspirators not know this? Did they not realize the dangers into which they were leading Grunwalski? Or was Anders Grunwalski to be offered as a sacrifice to their misguided cause? A sacrifice.... Where was Grunwalski now? Where were Kessler and his fellow conspirators? Would such cunning men be foolish enough to walk into Augustyniak's trap?

The town seemed alive with civil police, all armed, and augmented by little detachments of Okhrana gendarmerie, conspicuous in their dark-green military uniforms. The Catherine Bridge was fully guarded, and when Box cautiously attempted a descent into the grassy space below the parapet, an Okhrana gendarme, rifle slung across his shoulder, appeared as if from nowhere, and motioned him away.

'They are everywhere, you see, Kershaw,' said the baron. 'You can appreciate now that your well-meaning interference in this matter was entirely unnecessary. The Okhrana can manage very nicely on its own!'

It was nearing eleven o'clock when the party returned through the beech wood to what seemed by contrast the rough and dangerous world of St Mary of the Icon. Baron Augustyniak paused at the rear entrance to the fortress, and addressed the four Englishmen.

'Colonel Kershaw,' he said, 'this would be a good moment for you and me to confer with Count von und zu Thalberg over some of the ramifications of this venture. I was teasing you just now, in the town, but there are ways that the co-operation of the three of us could be of great value in the future. I'm sure that there's information that we can share to our common advantage. Let us all meet again at noon in the great hall, when a meal will be served.'

Colonel Kershaw said nothing, He seemed understandably

subdued, and Box had a suspicion that he was now anxious to drop the whole matter, and return to England where, no doubt, other matters were awaiting him. Morrison and Kolinsky followed Kershaw and the baron into the fortress, but Box lingered behind in the overgrown garden. What was it about the business of Polanska Gory that eluded him? The clue to it had invaded his dreams, but the true picture was still obscured. He would walk around the quiet summer garden and try to collect his thoughts.

A faint sound came to his ears, the sound of someone humming a tune half to himself. Shouldering his way through a clump of bushes, he emerged on to a small, roughly scythed lawn, where he found Sergeant-Major Schmidt sitting at a little table, humming a song, and poring over a number of maps. A few rickety chairs were scattered around, as though the place was a favourite resort for folk with half an hour to spare.

Box vividly remembered the last occasion on which he had encountered Schmidt, sitting like that at a table in the garden of Count von und zu Thalberg's country house, Petershalle, on his remote Prussian estate. Somehow, Sergeant-Major Schmidt represented a fixed point in a turning world.

'Herr Box!' cried Schmidt. 'Quite like old times, isn't it? Come and sit down, and let us talk while the great ones are away.' He had been wearing little round gold-framed spectacles, which he removed and folded carefully into a tin case.

'You look distracted, my friend,' he said. 'What's amiss?'

'We've wasted our time, Mr Schmidt, coming all this way for nothing. It's not like the colonel to make this kind of blunder.'

'It's not wasted time, Herr Box, it's all experience – what's that English saying? All grist to the mill. As for the *Herr Oberst*, well, remember that he has his little ways! So, cheer up, and let you and me smoke a cigar together.'

'It's my turn, as I remember, Sergeant-Major,' said Box. He delved into an inside pocket, and pulled out his cigar case, at the same time dislodging a folded paper which fell on to the grass. He picked it up, and placed it tidily on Schmidt's little table.

He offered his open cigar-case to his old Prussian ally, and in returned Schmidt produced a box of wax vestas. Soon, the two men puffed away at their cigars, enjoying a few moments of silent companionship. Box picked up the folded paper that had dropped from his pocket, and saw written on it the words, 'Supt S. Lucas, at Brixton Road Police Station.'

Of course! That had been scribbled by his old guvnor Superintendent Radcliffe, when they'd met together at the Foreign Office in an attempt to seek some mercy for Bobby Fitz. And from Major Blythe's cryptic remarks on the train from Danzig to Posen, their attempt seemed to have been successful. Bobby Fitz was off the hook.

'What are you studying so carefully, my friend?' asked Schmidt.

'This?' Box turned over the sheet of paper. 'Oh! It's an invitation to a royal wedding in Berlin. My old boss had a stack of them in his office. He's part of the Royal Protection unit of the English Home Office. Do you want to see it? It's in German.'

Schmidt stretched out his hand, and took the sheet from Box. He gave vent to some indeterminate chuckles.

'Ah, yes! The royal wedding. Here you can see the engraved pictures of the happy couple, Prince Adalbert Victor of Savoy, and our own Princess Gretchen of Hesse-Darmstadt, a kinswoman of the Kaiser. Between you and me, the bride's papa has been trying to marry her off for years. In the end, he was successful in luring one of the Savoy princes into his matrimonial trap. Part of the bait was to promise that the Kaiser would be there.'

'What does it say, Mr Schmidt – all that German, I mean?'

'Let me translate it for you,' Schmidt replied good-naturedly.

' "The marriage of His Royal Highness Prince Adalbert Victor of Savoy, and Her Highness Princess Gretchen of Hesse-Darmstadt, will take place on Saturday, 21 July 1894, at Die Kapelle an der Brücke in Berlin, in the gracious presence of the

Kaiser, accompanied by the Empress Augusta Victoria. The public will already be aware of the romantic nature of the Royal couple's first encounter"—'

Sergeant-Major Schmidt broke off his translation to give one of his throaty chuckles.

'Romantic nature, indeed! It was all arranged, Herr Box, and no doubt an appropriate dowry was written into the marital agreement. And so, in the presence of His Imperial Majesty, the happy couple will be married in the ancient Hohenzollern chapel in Berlin – Die Kapelle an der Brücke: The Chapel on the Bridge, as you'd say in English— Why, what's the matter, my friend? You've turned as pale as a ghost!'

The Chapel on the Bridge.... The eagles.... The Aquila Project....

'We must see them at once,' Box stammered, 'the Heads of Intelligence, I mean. I can't tell you straight away what I've just realized, Mr Schmidt, because then I'll have to repeat it all to *them*. Come with me, now, so that I can tell you all at once.'

'Gentlemen,' said Arnold Box, 'I want you to listen carefully to what I have to say. This is not a time for any of us to stand on ceremony.'

He and Schmidt had found Colonel Kershaw, Baron Augustyniak and Count von und zu Thalberg conferring together in an inner chamber of the fortress. Their entrance had been so sudden and informal that the three Heads of Intelligence realized immediately that something of the gravest importance was afoot.

'This conspiracy, The Aquila Project,' said Box, 'has the theme of a bridge running through it, and I firmly believe that its whole purpose centres around a bridge. But it's not Tower Bridge, gentlemen, and it's not the Catherine Bridge. What was the point of Grunwalski's escapade at Tower Bridge? Was it a rehearsal, to test the viability of planting a bomb, later, under the bridge at Polanska Gory? Or was it a test of the possibility of discharging a pistol at some royal personage crossing a bridge – the Catherine

Bridge, for instance? No, it was neither of these things. It was an attempt to confuse and mislead.'

Box saw Colonel Kershaw shift uneasily in his chair. Was he about to silence him? It was more urgent than ever that he should speak out. If only he could find the right words!

'If a bomb had exploded under Tower Bridge, it would have caused minimal damage. A man brandishing a pistol would never have reached the carriageway, as the approaches to the bridge were thronging with police and soldiers. And what about the Catherine Bridge at Polanska Gory? No one could effectively conceal himself under that bridge, and all the approaches to it are open gardens. Don't you see, gentlemen, that these two bridges, and all this talk of bombs and pistols, were designed to mislead?'

'What do you mean?' asked Augustyniak truculently. 'What can you know of these matters? I tell you, I was fully privy to the conspiracy.'

'I know, sir,' Box replied, 'that our adversaries have very effectively contrived to lure the three Heads of Intelligence – the Okhrana, the Prussian Military Intelligence, and the British Secret Intelligence, to this little outpost of civilization in what strikes me as being a lawless, half-forgotten wilderness. Consider for a moment where you are – where Doctor Franz Kessler has lured you. You are camped out in this fortress beside a town bustling with special Russian police, a town which no experienced anarchist would even consider as a likely place to carry out an assassination. You have been got out of the way—'

'Are you denying that any attempt on the Tsar's life is to be made here on the twenty-first?' Baron Augustyniak's voice still held its assumption of arrogant certainty.

'Yes, sir, I am. Let me ask you a very pertinent question: *where are the conspirators*? If I were detailed to stake out a criminal's hideaway prior to a police swoop, I'd have my undercover men in position days before the event. You tell us that Kessler, Grunwalski and the rest are lying low in Germany, ready to cross the border on Wednesday. What evidence have you to make that assumption? Do you actually know where they are?'

'So you're saying—'

'I'm saying, Baron, that Kessler, Grunwalski, and the other members of the gang are in *Berlin*. It's there, gentlemen, that Project Aquila will be put into practice, because on the 21 July, the Kaiser and the Empress will ride in an open carriage across the Bridge of the Hohenzollern Chapel. That, gentlemen, is the bridge in question!'

'But this is a fantasy!' cried Baron Augustyniak, flushing angrily. 'I keep telling you that I myself infiltrated the organization long ago. I was present at its meetings, I orchestrated its actions – I am convinced that Kessler had no idea that I was an Okhrana agent.'

'I believe you, sir,' Box replied. 'They thought you were a well-meaning and influential Polish patriot – which you are – an ideal cover for their activities. So they led you to believe that the Tsar was to be their target, knowing that you would be watched as a matter of course by the British Secret Service, and that you would end up here, on the borders of the Russian Empire.'

Box saw that Baron Augustyniak had turned pale. It was an encouraging sign that his message was getting across to the three intelligence experts.

'It was an added bonus, Baron,' Box continued, 'that your activities drew Colonel Kershaw after you, while the conspirators assembled with impunity in Berlin. Aquila, I'm told, means an eagle, but there is more than one eagle in Europe. You will find them displayed on the arms of Poland and Russia, and very prominently on the arms of the German Empire. Kessler and his gang have assembled in Berlin *to take the life of the Kaiser*.'

For a moment it seemed that all pandemonium had been let loose. Augustyniak and Thalberg sprang to their feet, white-faced. They began talking rapidly to each other in German. Colonel Kershaw sat motionless at the table, looking at Box with what seemed like fascination. The clamour of voices suddenly stopped and, in the brief interval, Kershaw said, 'Is there anything else you want to tell us, Mr Box?'

'There is, sir. I beg you, gentlemen, listen to me. I believe this whole conspiracy to be an attempt to assassinate the Kaiser. You will know better than I do what the consequences of such an act would be. These men have used the old techniques of conjuring to mislead you all. They've made you accept images of bombs in boiler rooms, men brandishing pistols running openly up ramps to commit their atrocities. Conjuring! You will find that they will use some quite different method of assassination, and it will not be from an open venue like Tower Bridge, or the bridge at Polanska Gory. Perhaps it will be a high-powered rifle from a well-hidden position—'

'Have you forgotten Grunwalski, the trained assassin?' asked Kershaw.

'Oh, sir,' said Box, 'don't you see? Grunwalski is only another decoy. He will be sacrificed to their cause, as I've no doubt they intended all along. Perhaps Kessler will do the deed himself – didn't you once tell me, sir, that he was a crack shot with a rifle? But I wonder whether Doctor Franz Kessler is the brains behind the project? Wouldn't there have to be someone in the higher echelons of German society to make all this possible?'

Box saw Kershaw glanced at Count von und zu Thalberg, and mouth the words, 'Count von Donath.' He saw Thalberg nod in agreement.

'Perhaps I've spoken out of turn, gentlemen,' Box continued, 'if so, I ask your pardon. But there's one more aspect of this business that I want you to consider. To all outward appearances, this is a *Polish* plot to assassinate the Kaiser. Baron Augustyniak is a Pole, and so is Grunwalski. What were the names of those other men? Balonek and Haremza. They are Poles, too. The whole conspiracy has been engineered to allow the Poles to be blamed for the Kaiser's death. Do you understand what I am trying to say?'

'We understand you well enough, Inspector Box,' said Thalberg. 'It would be no exaggeration to say that, if these people succeeded in assassinating the Kaiser, then Germany would unleash a devastating invasion of Poland. No counsels of caution would prevail.'

'And that German invasion of Russian territory,' said Augustyniak, 'would bring the mighty Russian army pouring over its borders to repulse that attack. That army would not scruple to cross the German border if that became necessary. And all this nightmare would have been unleashed not by a few Polish dreamers, but by a cunning and ruthless nest of German traitors. And we must not forget the so-called secret treaty made last year between France and Russia. A German invasion of Russia would bring over a million French troops pouring into Germany—'

Colonel Kershaw suddenly sprang to his feet.

'Gentlemen,' he said, 'we have talked enough. We can't afford the luxury of disbelieving or debating Mr Box's thesis. It rings all too grimly true. Baron Augustyniak, you don't need our help in controlling your own forces in Polanska Gory. Let Thalberg and I, together with our party, set out with all speed to Berlin. There are only three full days left before the twenty-first, and I don't trust the telegraphs with a matter of this kind. They may have been already compromised. Our object now must be to protect the Kaiser, before all Europe is plunged into a conflict from which it may never recover.'

15

Cleansing the Eagle's Nest

THE MILITARY TRAIN thundered through the night of the 18 July on the second stage of a journey that would take it 150 winding German miles from Brest-Litovsk to Berlin. They had travelled by civilian railway to Posen, where they had boarded one of the drab, green trains of the Prussian Military Railway, hauled by a grimy but rugged black engine, which could reach a speed of fifty miles an hour.

At Posen, they had been joined in the single long compartment of the military train by a detachment of young soldiers in field grey, who wore the orange and gold collar tabs of the 4th Brandenburg Lancers. There were twenty of them, sitting in the forward seats of the carriage, where they were being addressed by Sergeant-Major Schmidt. It was four o'clock in the morning, and the carriage was lit by dim oil lamps.

'What's he saying, sir?' whispered Box, who knew that Kershaw was fluent in German.

'He's telling them that they have been detailed to assist in the overthrow of a desperate gang of traitors who have designs on the life of the Kaiser. They are to obey all orders given by him, and by the English *Oberst* Kershaw. I don't know what those orders are going to be, Box, and neither does Schmidt. We must play this piece by ear.'

'Couldn't you just inform the authorities in Berlin?'

'No, Box, because some of those "authorities" will be in the plot. There could be very sinister obstacles placed in our way if Berlin knew that we are coming. In a matter of this kind, an element of surprise is always crucial. The fewer who know about us, the better it will be.'

Sergeant-Major Schmidt finished his address to the soldiers seconded from the 4th Brandenburg Lancers, and resumed his seat. It was typical of the man that he immediately opened a map, and began to examine it closely. To Box, it looked like the map of a large city. Maybe it was a map of Berlin.

Schmidt looked up from his map for a moment, and spoke quietly to Kershaw, who sat opposite him across the gangway.

'This train, *Herr Oberst*, will eventually come into a military siding south of the Landwehr Canal in Berlin, where there is a barracks of the Prussian Civil District Militia. That's where we'll stay, discreetly hidden beyond the southern suburbs of Berlin, until this business is brought to a conclusion – one way or the other.'

The train rattled over a long bridge, and then on to an embankment. The carriage swayed slightly as the engine negotiated a rather dramatic curve. Sergeant-Major Schmidt looked up from his map, and Box heard him mutter what sounded like the name of a town or village.

'How long now, Sergeant-Major?' asked Kershaw.

'Another hour, *Herr Oberst*. We should be snug inside the Landwehr Barracks by five thirty.' He picked up a sheet of paper, on which, for the last few minutes, he had been drawing in pencil, and handed it to Kershaw across the gangway.

'I know Berlin very well, sir,' he said, 'and I've tried to draw from memory a plan of Die Kapelle an der Brücke – The Chapel on the Bridge. You can see from that drawing that the bridge crosses a tributary of the River Weser running across König Friedrich Strasse, which is only a few hundred yards from the Imperial Palace, between the Old Town Hall and St Nicholas's

Church. It's a section of the old town, where the streets can be narrow and winding. The stream runs across the street and under the bridge. I've shown the stream in blue crayon, and the bridge in red.'

'Are there any store rooms or hidden chambers beneath the bridge?' asked Box.

'No, Herr Box. The stream is about six feet wide, and flows rapidly under the bridge, which is supported by three solid piers. It was built in 1438. From the roadway, you wouldn't realize that it *was* a bridge. And there' – he pointed to another part of his careful drawing – 'you can see the archway at the end of the bridge that leads into the courtyard of the Hohenzollern Chapel. The Kaiser and the Empress will come along here in an open carriage from the Imperial Palace, cross the bridge, and go under the arch. From that point, they'll be lost to the sight of the public.'

'*Oberfeldwebel*,' said Kershaw, 'this is an excellent piece of work. Whenever I see you, you're poring over some map or diagram! Count von und zu Thalberg is very lucky to have you in his service. Now, let you and me look at this situation as a couple of soldiers. If we wanted to shoot the Kaiser, where would we place ourselves?'

Sergeant-Major Schmidt looked primly shocked at Kershaw's blunt language, but forbore to make any comment. Instead, he pointed with a pencil first to a kind of guardroom built above the entrance arch to the chapel, and then to a square building facing it across the narrow street. Reaching into a canvas bag, he rummaged around until he found a red crayon, which he used to draw a bold circle around the chapel entrance arch and the square building facing it.

'There, gentlemen,' he said, 'are the two obvious points of vantage – the only viable ones for a serious assassin. You could fire a shot at any carriage crossing the bridge from the window of that chamber above the arch; or you could do the same thing from that building across the street. So from a military point of view it would be expedient to occupy both those buildings on Saturday, when the Kaiser and Kaiserin come to the Hohenzollern Chapel.'

'A marvellous exposition, Sergeant-Major,' murmured Kershaw. 'Do you know, I'm feeling more optimistic of success after seeing your splendid drawing. But there are other aspects of the matter to consider apart from the military solution – which is a good one, and which would make good use of those Brandenburg Lancers of ours. But if we occupied both buildings, the enemy would be warned off. They would withdraw, and resume their planning for another day. I should like us both to inspect this site personally, and then we can concoct an emergency plan for Saturday. I already have something viable in mind. This building facing the chapel across the street – is it occupied?'

'It contains the offices of a number of commercial companies, *Herr Oberst*. Such places are usually closed on Saturdays, but in any case we could ensure that they were left vacant on the twenty-first. The Führer of the District Militia could present them with a decree of requisition. His Excellency Count von und zu Thalberg can easily attend to the matter.'

As dawn broke quite suddenly over the Brandenburg Plain, the military train entered Berlin. It reduced speed, travelling slowly along a curved track that passed through an area of factories and warehouses on the southern fringe of the great city.

Colonel Kershaw beckoned to Morrison, who was sitting in front of Schmidt.

'Yes, sir?'

'Morrison, make quite sure that the rifle is in tiptop condition at all times until we leave Berlin. On Saturday morning, you'd better give it the M.O.S.'

The train lurched on to a branch line, and soon they could see a covered platform, and some military buildings. A number of soldiers came out on to the platform to watch their arrival.

'Here we are at Landwehr Barracks, gentlemen,' said Sergeant-Major Schmidt.

As Arnold Box moved along the aisle carrying his valise, he asked the sergeant armourer a question.

'Mr Morrison, what did Colonel Kershaw mean by "give it the M.O.S."? When he was talking about that rifle that you're still carrying?'

'Oh, that's army talk, Mr Box,' Morrison replied. 'It stands for "magazine on, one in the breech, safety-catch off".'

'One in the breech?'

'Yes, that's to ensure that a shot's fired as soon as the trigger's pulled. I reckon the colonel's anticipating some serious action on Saturday.'

Looking back upon the events of those few days before the fatal twenty-first of July, Box found that he could remember very little with clarity. Apart from a hurried visit to the bridge, during which Kershaw and Schmidt had conferred together at length, nothing dramatic occurred. Count von und zu Thalberg had mysteriously disappeared, and when Box asked Kershaw where he was, he just smiled and shook his head. For most of those three days they idled away their time in the militia barracks beyond the Landwehr Canal.

The twenty-first dawned a hot and sunny day. The royal wedding was to take place at eleven o'clock in the morning, and Thalberg had sent an orderly to Kershaw with a detailed plan of the procession. Die Kapelle an der Brücke had a rear entrance in a side road beyond the bridge, and when the party approached it, just after half past ten, they were saluted by one of Thalberg's detachment of Brandenburg Lancers, posted at the door.

A winding stair led up to the room over the arch. It contained two windows, one overlooking the building on the opposite side of the road, and another, little more than a decorative slit, from which it was possible to see down the bridge to the road beyond. The room was evidently used for storing chairs and old bundles of music from the chapel below.

'Now, gentlemen,' said Kershaw, 'there is little time left. Box, and you, Kolinsky, please sit against the back wall on those chairs. Sergeant-Major Schmidt, take up your position at the side-window, and identify each carriage as it begins to cross the bridge. Here is the printed programme. Morrison, prepare the rifle, and hold yourself in readiness. Pray God that our mission today be successful. If we fail, and The Thirty triumph, then I think we shall all die.'

He's right, thought Box, and all our lives will depend on how good a shot the colonel is when the moment arrives. He sat back on his rickety chair, and thought fondly of King James's Rents. The cheerful conversations of the waiting crowds came up to them from the street below.

At half past ten, Colonel Kershaw moved into action. He took up a position in the centre of the room, his left foot slightly advanced, to provide the necessary counter to the anticipated weight of the Lee-Metford. He stared out of the open window for what seemed an age, while the others listened to the excited babble of voices rising up to them from the festive crowd.

'He's there now,' said Kershaw quietly, still staring straight ahead. 'He's facing the open window of a room on the second floor of that building. He seems to be alone.'

A sudden cheer went up from the street, and Sergeant-Major Schmidt, who had been posted as observer at the narrow side window, said, 'The first carriage, holding six foreign guests.' They could all hear it clattering over the bridge, and then a moment later the cheering was renewed, this time more prolonged, and accompanied by wild clapping.

'Second carriage: the bride and groom with their attendants.'

'He's raising a rifle to his shoulder,' said Kershaw. 'Morrison, give me the Lee-Metford.'

Morrison placed the rifle carefully in Kershaw's hands, at the same time saying crisply, 'Magazine on, one in the breech, safety-catch off.' Kershaw raised the weapon swiftly to his right shoulder, fixing his eye on the brass telescopic sight. The cheering continued; it had taken upon itself the character of a continuous approving commentary on the day's events.

'Third carriage: the Chancellor and his wife, with Colonel-General von Lowenstein and the Grand Steward.'

Colonel Kershaw seemed to have been transmuted from a man to a statue. He stood quite motionless, and scarcely breathing, or so it seemed to Box. This was not the quiet, diffident gentleman whom Box usually encountered in some odd corner of London. The figure now standing in the centre of this little room was an instrument of Nemesis, in which all the powers of intellect and emotion had been refined to one single, overriding purpose.

Outside, the cheering suddenly rose to a deafening crescendo, and at the same time a military band launched into the solemn melody of the Imperial Anthem, *Deutschland über Alles*. It was hardly necessary for Schmidt to tell them that the Kaiser's carriage was about to cross the bridge.

Box, sitting transfixed on his chair near the door, saw Kershaw's finger tighten on the trigger of his rifle. The sound of the shot, when it came, was deafening, but effectively masked by the frantic cheering down in the street, and at the same time a triumphant ringing of bells from the chapel bell tower conspired with the adulation of the frantic crowd to hide the sound of Kershaw's single shot.

'Got him,' said Kershaw, quietly, and they all saw the expression of quiet pride that transformed his face, even though he had gone as white as a sheet. He handed the rifle back to Morrison, and turned to face Arnold Box.

'Sir,' whispered Box, 'have you killed your own man, Grunwalski? Was that the only way?'

'It wasn't Grunwalski, Mr Box. It was Doctor Kessler, and he was alone in that room. I waited until I saw his finger moving from beyond the guard to fire his cursed assassin's bullet, and then

I shot him through the heart. He should have left his finger on the trigger, as I did; his over-cautiousness cost him his life.'

When Kershaw and his party emerged cautiously into the side-road behind the chapel, they found the Lancer still on duty. In the main road, the crowds showed no sign of dispersing, and it was impossible not to catch something of the festive atmosphere. Excited children were waving little German and Italian flags, while their parents chattered and laughed as they waited for the newlyweds to emerge from the chapel. They were also waiting to cheer their popular 35-year-old sovereign, who, unknown to them, had just escaped death by a hair's breadth.

Box could see the orange and gold collar tabs of the Brandenburg Lancers gleaming as they stood on guard in front of the gaunt office building facing the bridge. Those men would have ensured that no one entered or left the building without prior authorization. It had been Thalberg's responsibility to arrange this, and other matters. Box could see the still open window on the second floor.

The guard on the main entrance stood aside, and Kershaw led his men up a narrow wooden staircase. The first-floor landing gave entrance to a number of offices, all locked for the weekend. They ran up to the second floor, where a door stood wide open. They rushed into the room that had been used by the would-be assassin.

Count von und zu Thalberg, who was kneeling beside Doctor Franz Kessler's body, looked up as they entered. He was holding two folded sheets of paper in his hand.

'Well done, Kershaw,' he said. 'You got him straight through the heart. Look at him! Look at the surprise in his dead eyes. He never saw you, of course.'

'Like all these fanatics, he was an over-reacher,' said Kershaw. 'I'll go now, and look in some of these other rooms. I expect you know what I'll be looking for.'

When Kershaw left the room, Box watched as Thalberg carefully placed the two folded documents into the inside pocket of Kessler's jacket. When he withdrew his hand, it was covered in blood. Count von und zu Thalberg saw Box's sudden movement of revulsion, and got to his feet.

'Inspector Box,' he said, in his faultless unaccented English, 'you and I have been allies in the past, and I think you know what desperate fanatics myself and Colonel Kershaw have to deal with. To us, and to Baron Augustyniak, the peace of Europe, and the security of its peoples, are of paramount interest. You look with distaste at this dead fanatic lying at our feet; think of the millions – yes, *millions* – of innocent people whose lives we have saved by preventing that man from plunging all Europe into eternal night.'

'Sir—'

'It's all right, Mr Box. No apology is necessary. But I just want to say a few words more to you before we bring this business at the bridge to a close. I'm speaking to you now as a German. Your brilliant deductions at Polanska Gory have led directly to the preservation today of our Kaiser and Fatherland. I think you'll find that your deeds of this fateful week will not go unnoticed or unrewarded by the Imperial Family.'

Count von und zu Thalberg retrieved a black overcoat and a silk hat from a chair where he had thrown them. He looked angry and determined, like a man bent on a mission of vengeance.

'I'm going now, Mr Box,' he said. 'There's a great deal to be done in Berlin today, as this fellow was only the agent of another. This gang – The Thirty – will be rounded up and rendered impotent by nightfall. Once we have ensured that the Prussian State Telegraph system is uncompromised, Colonel Kershaw will use his own special powers to see that the remnants of this criminal gang in England are removed permanently from the political scene. Baron Augustyniak will do likewise, once we have communicated this afternoon to his adjutant in Warsaw. Goodbye, Mr Box. Perhaps we will meet again, some time.'

When Thalberg had gone, Box looked down at the dead body lying at his feet. He noted that a powerful rifle lay on the floor nearby, where it had dropped from Kessler's nerveless fingers. He had first seen this cruel and crazed man at the gunsmith's near Covent Garden, and now he had come to this, his mad dreams of power smashed by Colonel Kershaw's unerring bullet. Count von und zu Thalberg had hinted at further bloodletting to take place in Berlin that day. Well, that was his affair.

Box walked out on to the deserted landing. Strong sunlight was pouring through a window on to the polished boards of the corridor. What were those scratches running parallel across the floor? They disappeared into a room further along the passage. Box the detective knew what those marks were: the scraping left by the heels of boots when their owner was being dragged, unconscious or dead, across a floor. Box entered the room.

Colonel Kershaw was standing motionless, with arms folded, over the body of Anton Grunwalski. He lay on his back in a pool of blood, and it did not take an expert to see that his throat had been cut.

'You were right, Box,' said Kershaw, glancing at the inspector. 'You said that Grunwalski was merely a detail of the grand deception. Kessler would have brought him up here, continuing the pretence that Grunwalski was to be the assassin. God knows what the poor man would have done if that had really been the case. I am convinced that he would never have betrayed my trust.'

'Perhaps he would have shot Kessler instead, sir.'

'He might well have done. Perhaps Kessler feared that. So he stunned Grunwalski, dragged him in here, and cut his throat. It's quieter than a gun, you know.'

Colonel Kershaw looked down at the body once more, and then walked to the door.

'I'm very angry at what has happened to Grunwalski,' he said. 'Kessler was merely the agent of someone else, and I intend to destroy that "someone" for this. But not just yet. Come on, Box, let's get out of this slaughterhouse. By next Tuesday, God willing, you and I will be back in good old England.'

As the two men descended the stairs to the street below, the bells of the Chapel on the Bridge rang out again, and the crowds set up a mighty cheer to greet the reappearance on the bridge of William II, Emperor of Germany and King of Prussia.

As the sun set over Berlin in a splendour of red and gold, Arnold Box and his old ally Sergeant-Major Schmidt stood on the roof of the barracks of the 32nd Imperial Field Regiment, savouring the peace and stillness of the scene spread out before them. It was the evening of Sunday, 22 July.

'You can see the whole city from up here,' Schmidt was saying. 'There's the new cathedral, rising up above the Kaiser Wilhelm Bridge. There's the Column of Victory.... That's the Reichstag over there: magnificent, don't you think, Herr Box? There's the Brandenburg Gate.... There's....'

The old sergeant-major's voice faltered, and he gave vent to a deep sigh.

'What's the matter, Mr Schmidt?' asked Box.

'I don't know, Herr Box, it's just a feeling. That sunset – I some-times think that there's more to this twilight than just the time of day. There's a raging spirit abroad, a spirit of greed and violence, of self-interest, and a growing love of the kind of nightmare that that madman Nietzsche exalts as the coming world. Will our great city of Berlin endure? Or is it just waiting in readiness for its own sun to set? One day, people like Kessler might triumph, and then all this will fall to ruin.'

The sun disappeared from sight beyond the Tiergarten, and a sudden breeze made the two men shiver. Sergeant-Major Schmidt seemed to awake from his gloomy reverie. He gave vent to one of his throaty chuckles.

'There, Mr Box! I'm dreaming! This weekend has been a glorious victory, and next week you will be back in England. The great ones have conferred together, and the eagle's nest is cleansed. So come, my friend, let us go downstairs and drink each other's health. All will be well.'

16

A Time for Rewards

Vanessa Drake looked critically at her reflection in the bedroom mirror. She saw a young lady of twenty-one, very fair and slim, clad in a long dark-blue coat with a high collar. She was wearing a designedly frivolous matching hat, adorned with dyed feathers, and a decorative half veil. Yes, she would do.

On the Wednesday morning following her night at Lipton's Hotel she had been taken by Arnold Box to his old father's Cigar Divan and Hair-Cutting Rooms in Oxford Street, and there she had stayed very comfortably in a suite of upstairs rooms recently vacated by old Mr Box. She had lived there for a fortnight, enjoying the company of Toby Box and his faithful staff, and listening to stirring tales of life on the beat in the 1860s.

Yesterday, the 26 July, Inspector Box and Jack Knollys had called upon her in Oxford Street, to tell her that she was no longer in danger, and that they had come to escort her home to Westminster. They had travelled by cab, and Mr Box had taken the opportunity to tell her that Doctor Franz Kessler was dead. So much for old Mr Minty, she'd thought. He'd been a rude, silly, bad-tempered man, who had no idea how to treat a young woman. How dare he call her a clumsy clodhopper!

And now, Colonel Kershaw had invited her to accompany him to Baron Augustyniak's house in St John's Wood, so that she could hear some facts about the mission in which she'd been involved.

He would be here within minutes. Did she look all right? There was the bell jangling downstairs. She picked up her reticule from the table, and hurried out on to the landing. The colonel's carriage had arrived.

The white villa in Cavendish Gardens glowed in the strong morning sun as Colonel Kershaw rang the bell. Evidently, Quiller the butler was busy elsewhere, because it was sixteen-year-old Ellen Saunders who opened the front door.

'Colonel Kershaw and Miss Drake, to see Baron Augustyniak.'

Ellen gave them both a neutral glance, dropped her eyes, and curtsied. It came as a shock to Vanessa to realize that her fellow-housemaid of a fortnight ago had failed to recognize her.

'Come this way, please,' said Ellen, and preceded them to the baron's study. 'Colonel Kershaw and Miss Drake,' she said, and closed the door quietly behind them.

Baron Augustyniak sprang up from his desk, and shook hands with Kershaw. He looked in the best of spirits, his mane of blond hair swept back from his high forehead, his beard newly trimmed, and his monocle in his right eye.

'Colonel!' he cried. 'And Miss, er—'

'Drake. Miss Drake is my confidential secretary. She knows as much as I do about The Thirty.'

'Indeed? Well, then, we can speak openly of our business in Poland. It would seem that The so-called Thirty have been rendered harmless. None of them escaped us in Poland, and Thalberg has been very busy indeed in Germany these last few days. He did well, and so did your associate, Inspector Box. A remarkable young man, that.'

Baron Augustyniak was almost unconsciously admiring the elegant Miss Drake as he spoke. Vanessa noted the little puzzled frown that marred his brow, and smiled to herself.

'All's well here, too, Baron,' said Kershaw. 'A number of people in high places have been rendered neutral, and others have taken warning at what happened to them. The fangs of The Thirty have been well and truly drawn. And so you have decided to settle permanently in England?'

Baron Augustyniak sighed, and shook his head.

'I will not beat about the bush, Kershaw. I've been dismissed. The Okhrana was not very pleased with my role in the affair. They said, in fact, that I had allowed myself to be used as a dupe, and that it would be agreeable to all if I retired. I agreed, of course.

'So here I am, domiciled in England, where I can devote my time to building up my Polish Institute. I have a lovely home, a lovely wife, and a new vocation!'

Vanessa saw Colonel Kershaw smile, but he made no reply.

'And now— Ah!' cried Augustyniak, springing up once again from his chair. 'Of course! Miss Drake – or Susan Moore, isn't it? My dear girl, I wondered....'

'Yes, sir,' said Vanessa. She found herself blushing in spite of herself. For a fleeting moment she was the housemaid, and he was the master of the house.

'Well, I think you did very well, my dear, though I knew all along that you were actually Colonel Kershaw's little girl spy. Your real name, I seem to remember, is Gertie Miller, and you were already known to the police. Still, if you were working for Colonel Kershaw all the time, that puts a different complexion on things.'

The baron's words told Vanessa and Kershaw that he still did not know that both the police constable and the sergeant who had 'arrested' Gertie Miller were also Kershaw's agents.

The baron went over to his desk, and picked up the framed Polish coin.

'I'd like you to have this, Miss Drake,' he said, 'as a token of my personal esteem. It will remind you of the desperate adventure in which you participated, a venture which ultimately saved the whole of Europe, and Britain too, from a devastating war. And I'd like to take this opportunity to apologize for treating you so roughly when I discovered you in the silver-cupboard. I had to convince the others, you see, that I was really angry, so that I could deliver you safely into the hands of the police.'

Baron Augustyniak placed the Polish coin into Vanessa's hand.

'Goodbye, Miss Drake,' he said. 'Kershaw, I think we are all agreed that this business in Berlin should remain a secret, at least for the near future. Europe is calm again. Let sleeping dogs lie.'

Some minutes later, they took their leave of Baron Augustyniak. Ellen passed them in the corridor as they made their way to the front door, and automatically dropped them a little curtsy.

'Sir,' whispered Vanessa, 'will you wait for me in the carriage? I shan't be a few minutes.'

Vanessa hurried after the little housemaid, who was on her way to the flower-room.

'Ellen!' she cried. 'Don't you recognize me? It's Susan!'

The girl turned round sharply, and her face broke out into a brilliant smile.

'Coo! Is it really you, Susan? They said you were a thief, and known to the police. I cried myself to sleep that night, thinking of you. So you're really called Miss Drake? Are you a spy, like the Master?'

Vanessa started in surprise. How on earth did Ellen know that? Somebody had once told her that servants knew everything. Perhaps it was true.

'Yes,' Vanessa replied, 'I'm a spy, but it's a big secret, and you're not to tell anyone. As for the baron – well, he's doing special secret work for England, and when I was caught by the gang in the silver closet, he pretended that I was a thief, so that the police would come and rescue me. And they did. But don't tell anyone.'

'I won't, Susan, I promise. And what about your young man? The one who turned out to be a brute? Did he ever come back to you?'

'Yes, he did. He went down on his knees on the cobbles and asked me to forgive him, which I did. He's a spy, too. But you're not to tell anyone.'

'Oh, no. It's like a story, isn't it? I'm ever so glad to know you're all right.'

Vanessa opened her reticule, and withdrew a beautifully wrapped one-pound box of Fortnum and Mason's chocolates.

'These are for you, my dear,' she said. 'You were very kind to me when I worked with you here, and I'll never forget you.'

Vanessa gave Ellen a quick hug, and hurried away to join Colonel Kershaw. No one was about, so she pulled the front door shut after her.

'Coo!' said Ellen Saunders in ecstasy.

As the carriage turned into Regent's Park, Colonel Kershaw asked Vanessa a question.

'When is Sergeant Knollys going to marry you, missy? Or, to put it another way, when are you going to marry *him*?'

Should she blush? No, the question was a serious one, and, coming from Colonel Kershaw, it would have an ulterior motive.

'If he would name the day, sir, I'd marry him in a flash.'

'Hm.... And I suppose that after you were married, you'd want to give up being one of my nobodies. Or perhaps Sergeant Knollys would expect you to do so.'

'No, sir!' Vanessa was surprised at the vehemence of her tone. 'I want to work for you until I'm no longer of use. And Jack thinks the same as I do. We've discussed all this before.'

'Good, I'm glad. Now, during the last year, you've carried out two missions for me in which you've infiltrated a private house, and set yourself the task of finding things out. When I sent you to Baroness Felssen's mansion, you almost lost your life – your fault, I hasten to add, not mine. And you lasted just long enough at Baron Augustyniak's to find out things of prime importance. You're no longer a "nobody", Miss Drake, and I should like to offer you promotion in my organization to the rank of *agent surveillant*. That is a person who trains to assume a number of different roles – a servant, perhaps, or a clerk, or even a nursemaid, and the work involves penetration of a suspect household. It can be dangerous work, but as you know, you would never be more than a breath away from help. There's a stipend that goes with being an *agent surveillant* – twenty-five pounds a year. It makes you a fully-fledged agent in the Secret Intelligence. Do you accept?'

'Oh, yes, sir!' There seemed no more to say, but perhaps it would be as well to show that she was not entirely consumed by emotion.

'Poor Baron Augustyniak,' she sighed. 'It was kind of him to give me his coin as a keepsake. It seems so unfair that he should be dismissed, after all that he did to lure The Thirty into his net.'

Colonel Kershaw laughed. What a splendid girl she was! He rather hoped that she would never lose that endearing quality of naïvety.

'Dismissed? Nonsense! The good baron's firmly fixed in the higher echelons of the Imperial Russian Police. They've decided to station him permanently here in England, and "dismissal" is as good an excuse as any other. He knows I don't believe him. Well, I rather like the idea of having him here. Like speaks to like, you know. Whenever the Russian Question rears its head, I'll talk directly to him, and leave Sir Charles Napier to engage in subtle talk with the diplomats.'

When they finally reached Tufton Street in Westminster, Kershaw handed Vanessa down from the carriage, and stood watching her as she entered the gaunt former convent building where she had her home.

On the 30 July, which was a Wednesday, Colonel Kershaw broke one of his unwritten rules by calling for Arnold Box at King James's Rents. He waited patiently in the vestibule until Box came hurrying out of his office to join him. The inspector was wearing a sober black suit, relieved at the throat by one of the new wing collars and a dark blue tie. He was wearing black gloves, and was rather self-consciously carrying a tall silk hat.

'Hello, Mr Box,' said Kershaw, 'you're looking very distinguished this morning, if I may say so. Now, we've plenty of time, so I suggest we take a leisurely walk to 9 Carlton House Gardens, and on the way I'll tell you a few things about our adventure that haven't yet come to the public notice.'

The two men were going to visit the German Embassy at Prussia House, at the express invitation of the Ambassador, Count Paul von Hatzfeldt-Wildenburg, where they were both to receive the official thanks of the German Emperor for their part in the destruction of his would-be assassins.

'There's nothing to be nervous about, Box,' said Kershaw, as they walked from Great Scotland Yard into Whitehall. 'The ambassador will greet us by name, and then say whatever he's going to say. After that, we'll be free to go about our business.'

'There's something that I've been wanting to ask you, sir,' said Box. 'When we came upon the dead body of Kessler, Count Thalberg seemed to be stuffing the dead man's pockets with papers or letters—'

'Let me tell you the story of those papers,' Kershaw interrupted. 'You recall Major Blythe? Well, I commissioned him to save your colleague Detective-Inspector Fitzgerald from disgrace and dismissal, and then I promptly got him and his light fantastic boys to burgle Kessler's safe in Prussia House. A very valuable addition to my people, is Bobby Fitz. Oh, yes, he's working full time for me, now.

'Those papers included a list of English professional men who were willing to assist Kessler and his master in the event of their being successful in Berlin. I have already acted on the contents of that paper, Box. But there were also copies of letters from Kessler to his master, a man called Count von Donath, President of the Prussian Court of Requests, which revealed both men's treachery to the Kaiser and the German Empire. I entrusted Count von und zu Thalberg with the task of "planting" those papers on Kessler's corpse. By doing so, we ensured that both Kessler and the slippery von Donath would be brought to book. Clever, don't you think?'

'And this man von Donath—'

'That man von Donath, Mr Box, was the evil genius behind the whole enterprise. Sir Charles Napier had severe doubts about him, and alerted me to his existence last May. He was a man who connived at secret murders. It was his hand, as much as that of Kessler, that was on the hilt of the dagger that killed Grunwalski.'

Colonel Kershaw stopped speaking, and his mouth set in a grim line. Box knew that he was thinking of his failure to save the life of his own agent.

'What will happen to this Count von Donath?' asked Box, as they turned into Cockspur Street.

'Happen? He's dead, Box. A few days after we foiled the attempt on the Kaiser's life, he drank cyanide mixed in a glass of wine, and perished immediately. Beside him was a freshly-opened letter, which hinted at blackmail, and revealed that the writer knew all about his secret plans for the Germany of the future.'

'So he committed suicide?' said Box, half to himself.

'Yes. Or maybe – maybe someone set out to avenge the death of one of von Donath's victims. That is not at all beyond the bounds of possibility.'

Box glanced at the stern face of the man walking beside him, and knew what his veiled words had signified. What was it that Sergeant-Major Schmidt had said? 'The colonel has his little ways.'

'Strewth!' said Box, under his breath, and then asked the colonel another question.

'What were those plans, sir? Do we know what von Donath had in mind?'

'It's the opinion of Sir Charles Napier that von Donath aimed at ruling the German Empire through the Kaiser's heir, Crown Prince William, who's only twelve years of age. He knew that, after the cataclysm of total war in Europe, the old order of things would lie in ruins, and he would be able to mould a whole continent to his will. It's a fearful picture, Box, but I think Napier has not gone far enough.'

'You mean—'

'I mean that von Donath probably envisioned a German Republic, with himself at its head, and with Franz Kessler as Chancellor. The new order would be born from the ruins of the old, the Balance of Power concept would be abrogated, and Germany would have established hegemony over the whole of Western Europe. More wars, Box, and more mass slaughter on countless battlefields. Well, it didn't happen – but it might one day. As President Andrew Jackson said, "You must remember, my fellow-citizens, that eternal vigilance by the people is the price of liberty".'

The German Ambassador received Kershaw and Box in the grand reception room of Prussia House. He motioned to them to sit down on two gilt chairs, while he himself stood rather stiffly behind an ornate table. After a few preliminary pleasantries, he picked up a square leather box, which he held in his hand while addressing Kershaw.

'Colonel Sir Adrian Kershaw,' he said, 'The Kaiser conveys through me his grateful thanks to you for preserving his life and, as a signal mark of his gratitude, he has conferred upon you the Prussian Military Order *"Pour le Mérite"*, with Gilt Oak Leaves.'

Count von Hatzfeldt-Wildenburg opened the leather case, and removed a blue-enamelled Maltese Cross with eagles between the arms, the Prussian Royal cipher, and the French legend *Pour le Mérite* arranged on the arms of the cross. He showed it briefly to Kershaw, and then returned it to its case. He bowed to Kershaw, who returned the courtesy.

'This order,' the ambassador continued, 'is normally bestowed upon its recipients for outstanding valour in battle. In your case,

Colonel, it is a personal gift of the Kaiser. In my view, it has never been more fittingly bestowed.'

The Ambassador picked up another leather case from the table, and opened its clasp.

'Detective Inspector Arnold Box,' he said, 'it was your brilliant deductions that helped to preserve the Kaiser's life, and it is His Majesty's wish that you should be awarded the Gold Medal of the Hohenzollern Family Order, which is in the Kaiser's personal gift. Possession of this medal brings with it a life pension of twenty pounds a year.'

The ambassador solemnly shook hands with both men. He looked both pleased and moved by the unusual presentation to two foreigners who had served his master so well.

'As well as these awards, gentlemen,' he concluded, handing the leather cases to Kershaw and Box, 'you take away with you today the thanks of the whole German people. May God grant that the abiding friendship between our two nations continues to flourish.'

'Well, there it is, Box,' said Kershaw when they had left Prussia House, 'that neatly rounds the whole thing off. I'm delighted to see that, for once, you have been very nicely rewarded for your work, and I must confess that I'm very honoured to receive such a very high distinction from the Emperor.'

Colonel Kershaw raised his hat to Box, and turned his face towards Whitehall.

'Goodbye, Box,' he said, 'you and I have had a good run for our money this month. I hope that we shall work together again, some time.'

'I hope so too, sir,' Box replied. 'Goodbye.'

He watched Kershaw until he was lost to sight among the crowd of people thronging the pavement, and then made his way back to King James's Rents.